As someone said of *Just Say Cheese*:

"A stylish, hilarious romp. Bring your foie gras, fedora and figleaf to the party."

Just Say Cheese

A novel by

Luke Hudson Fox

Altamesa Press

ISBN 978-0-6151-4340-8

JUST SAY CHEESE

PROLOG

Christmas Morning, two months later, the year of our big Halloween adventure.

Nestled between my legs... like a log roasting on an open fire, the most amazing, entertaining, intelligent, butch, industrious, mechanically inclined six-pack of man muscle...

"This tastes great." said Parker. "The combination of spices is very interesting."

I sat behind him, propped up against the arm chair in my living room with my legs by his sides. I'm Luke, he's Parker, and he fits like a new pair of gloves. He's certainly my favorite Christmas package. Across the room, our tree was a joint effort, hung with pretty balls, big icicles and a twinkling cosmos of lights. Get the picture?

Jingle Bells faded into a writhing downtempo from the Troublemakers and then into the latest harmonies from Betty. That was Parker's influence too, in his quest to expand my musical horizons.

"And what about this one?" chimed in Liz, sleekly coiled into the sofa. "The, uh, spikey icing right here looks rather fiendish!" And then suddenly, "It's not a gay thing, is it?"

"Oh geez, you straight people," exclaimed Jack, "does everything have to be gay, gay, gay? We aren't the only ones with deviant imaginations." Jack never ceases to surprise me. More than just a talented friend, sometimes he's an ingenious nightmare. You'll see.

Everyone sat around fondling their devious holiday confections. "We're calling them Holesome Desserts!" said Jack with glee, falling into Jerry's kneading hands, much as he had during Halloween.

"And wait till you see our website I'm working on! Jack keeps me up all night with his ideas—and that, eh, imagination of his," added Jerry with a devilish smirk.

As we all—Parker and I, Liz, Jack and Jerry—fondled our erotic dessert creations, it was clear we enjoyed working out the 'kinks' together. That seems to be the case in all our projects and pleasures. Read on and you'll find out.

ONE

"Where'd you get this tie, Toys'R'Us?" Sue Barrymore wrestled the knot at the man's throat with the tips of her fingers, careful of her manicure. The noose was tightened and left hanging off center.

Gregory Thicke swallowed. "It was a gift from my aunt."

"Oh, your ahh-nt. Do tell." Her body turned following the roll of her eyes.

"Ms. Barrymore, two minutes to air. Please take your seats for sound check." The voice echoed from above.

She stood fast, surveying the traditional walnut bookcases lined with classic volumes all crafted of faux painted styrofoam. They were surmounted by an arch full of paned plastic windows looking toward the Lincoln Memorial photo mural. She flicked the wad of dust collected from her stroke of the shelf.

Dr. Sue Barrymore cased her domain. Wide high heels plodded the long way around on her approach to the desk and a pair of stuffed swivel chairs. Harnessed with straps, buckles, tufts, studs and leather the color of dried blood, she sat in the smart wool tweed seat and crossed a full calf.

With a frosted apricot nail, she wiped the corner of her matching colored lip. "Tell your aunt to buy you striped ties. Those polka dots will distract the TV viewers with moiré patterns." She patted the microphone at her cleavage, "Testing, testing."

Her guest today, local political candidate Thicke, fumbled with the knot at his throat, struggled to take a breath and find words. He was tripped up by "moiré" and replied by clearing his throat with part of a laugh.

"Mr. Thicke? Test your mike," the speaker boomed.

Greg cleared his throat and hesitantly peeked under his bushy black eyebrows toward the sound booth beyond. "One, two, um, five, six, s-"

The theme music to Town Hall, LIVE! began. Sue swiveled to face the Lincoln Memorial. After the first signature opening chords, the music picked up tempo. The stage lighting was raised to full, and the tune changed key, racing into the fever pitch of the daily cable nooner that was

Town Hall, LIVE! Sally, Jesse, Jerry, Ricki and Dr. Sue—fodder for the masses.

Sue slowly swiveled her ample self toward camera. She cocked her head, wrinkled her nose for the close-up and delivered her infamous smile. It warmed the screen like sunrise on December seventh. As the music died down, she opened with an alarmingly bright *"HI! I'm Dr. Sue Barrymore and welcome to today's edition of Town Hall, LIVE!"* Three descending notes tied up the coda. Sue flung out her right hand. *"We welcome Gregory Thicke, candidate for Ward 4 Council Chairman here to discuss today's topic—the upcoming Halloween festivities and the notorious Transvestite Triathlon. So stay tuned. We'll be right back with the start of today's show!"*

During the break, Sue lost the smile. She was half a size too large and a decade too old for the leather outfit. As she wrestled it like Houdini in a straightjacket, gritting her teeth, the good doctor handed Greg his prescription. "Thicke, back me up on this triathlon story, maybe you'll get yourself a few more votes."

Before he had a chance to think of a reply, the theme music returned and his thoughts bubbled up to lodge in his throat. Sue's smile returned with a look that cut him off. She re-introduced, and spun out her diatribe.

"...SCURRILOUS! Grown men running through these streets like vermin, mud wrestling for prize money. I think it's PAGAN!"

Greg was the handsome-enough hopeful, making his rounds in the spotlights about town. He looked the part, and spoke the part, but sometimes his brain went on vacation. He sat smirking like Howdy Doody while watching the leather clad dummy rant next to him. Finally, and uneasily, he butted in to Dr. Sue's monologue. *"—and, AND you know they spend weeks TRYING to look like streetwalkers and Saddam masochists. Flashy dresses, high heel boots, piles of hair... The price of leather chaps can feed a family of four! They should donate all these trappings to needy families. That's what they SHOULD be doing."*

Dr. Sue Barrymore sat on the edge of her seat through the interruption; her breath held, and eyes bugged behind perched rim glasses. She let go with undue force. "Itjustmakesmesicktotears... Sick—to—tears." Her expression changed from vein-popping to forlorn puppy. On cue, a phlegmy whelp inched past her frosted apricot lips. Her delivery slowed, and her voice dropped two full octaves. "I can see the busloads of families and thousands of innocent school children traveling hundreds of miles from sheltered farm towns across America to visit the splendors of our great capital *city.*" She paused to audibly inhale after her run-on sentence and continued with a noticeable key change. *"Imagine them strolling down the street hand-in-hand, in search of a decent supper. LAST SUPPER,"* she screamed. Dr. Sue pounded on her Chippendale desk possessed by an evangelical personality. *"See the horror on their faces as they are mowed down by the Bulls of Pamplona! Hundreds of banshee screaming man-whores driven by thirsty greed."* With a toss of hair she calmly decreed, *"It's a travesty that mocks all womanhood."*

Across town, Jack spun away from the stove, and walked toward the TV. When he was inches from the screen his hands sprang to either side of his mouth. He didn't need the megaphone effect, because he shouted loud enough to be heard for several blocks. "SHUT YOUR HOLE Barrymore! And where'd you get that outfit? Steal it off a Lazy Boy recliner?"

Is this soap opera? A cheesy gay novel? The dream scene, in Community Theater?

Jack Betz and I, Luke Hudson, started our restaurant three months ago to escape the daily grind. We opened the Hudson Grille and wished that our former backstabbing colleagues would SIT on all those knives they had yet to throw. Jack dreamed we'd be rich enough for diamonds, have time enough for the clubs, and somewhere along the way he'd pick up a neighborhood heart-throb or two. Seven-day work weeks dampened his dream but at least we worked for ourselves.

The TV din went on. *"Stay tuned for more of Town Hall, LIVE! with Dr. Sue Barrymore as we break for this announcement from our sponsor."* The camera zoomed in for her smile. The camera zoomed out on the set. Dr. Sue's stillness would have made Madame Tussaud proud. Greg's politically correct facade crinkled and broke the frozen tableau. All of a sudden, Dr. Sue's wax arm lurched out to slug Greg Thicke. The short silent movie continued as Greg mouthed a slow "ow-chh". A few techies ran on stage, arms up in the air in shock.

The screen quickly switched to a commercial, a video of a well-preserved blonde broad, bustily promoting recliners from a warehouse showroom. She was mute, however. Suddenly the studio audio broke in.

"Don't you ever, EVER, interrupt me again, you little snot." Dr. Sue's words did not sync with the broad reciting the recliner spiel. Then, with a click, the audio portion of the commercial resumed, chirping its own dialog and silly jingle. Such was the sloppiness of cable TV programming.

I'll use the commercial break for more background on Jack. I've known him since our days in parochial elementary school. He's now our chef and my energetic foil. Jack has always been fiendishly clever with wit, household tools, appliances and whatnots. At school, with glue gun in hand, he offered to make new drapes for a nun as he tugged at her habit while testing for fabric quality. These days he whips up costumes to die for, and wild roller-coaster events or fun house antics to show them off in. Honestly. Some of the costumes would kill you! All of this is fueled by Extra-Strength Co-Dependent Tylenol. Jack spins out of control and Luke gets caught up in the tailwind.

"Welcome back to Town Hall, LIVE! Today's Topic? Transvestite Triathlon: What is happening to our community? This Thursday night is Halloween and the East Dupont Restaurant Association is sponsoring its fourth annual race for charities down U Street. The race attracts hundreds of revelers, transvestites and anyone in high heels. Contestants run to participating stores, buying things to add to their costume, then to bars where they gulp down Candy Corn Shooters. They continue from shop to bar until the designated circuit is completed. The first two contestants to cross the finish line vie for final victory and the grand prize of one thousand dollars by wrestling in a mud pit. It is an increasingly popular event drawing thousands of spectators and raises money for local charities. However, the race also brings great anxiety to the more conservative neighbors. No one has championed the conservatives' cause more, than our very own, Dr. Sue Barrymore and Ward Councilman candidate, Greg Thicke. Friends?"

The TV audience had the pleasure of viewing Dr. Sue on screen in one of her rare moments of silence. But the picture of her was eloquent enough. During the announcer's intro, she swayed forward anticipating an opportunity to speak. Her hair swung front, then paused midpendulum as the announcer continued to describe the impending evening of doom. She recomposed herself with a hair swing Almay left, followed by compulsory finger fidgets. Finally, cueing up to her introduction, she executed a rump roll left, and a right, full-kick, leg cross. What a waste of talent.

"Thank you Bob. I'm Dr. Sue Barrymore, and we're back with more of Town Hall, LIVE! with my dear friend, Gregory Thicke. Blah Blah. Ladies and gentlemen, I'm pleased to inform you, during our commercial break I had the pleasure of speaking directly with the mayor of our city. He has agreed to meet with me immediately following today's show to discuss shutting DOWN this Thursday's tawdry Transvestite Triathlon. I hope that he will be able to join me on tomorrow's show and give us the benefit of his wisdom and judgment."

The cozy bubbles of my fond musings popped as Jack woke the dead. "CUNT!" he shrieked.

I started for Jack, but stopped in my tracks. The Grille's dining room audience stared, waiting for a reaction. Two crew-cut women perked with interest. A pair of leather-clad men froze in horror at the vaginal word. In the corner of the room with a cold cup of coffee, Gilbert the vagrant stirred his way out of sleep to lift an eyelid. Then, self-esteem gripped my throat. It jerked me back a step and a half. I found my eyes laser-locked with the tall, silver and strapping Parker Fox.

Eleven eyes (Gilbert had only one) burned holes in my new poly-something Kenneth Cole. Black, short-sleeved, of course. I bore down, stood fast, and summoned every fiber (poly or otherwise) to hold my stare with Mr. Fox. We hadn't formally met, but I knew who he was. I had imagined our honeymoon more than once, serving him my bagels and BLT's, ever since he became a regular at the Grille.

Blood rose and colored my cheeks. He stared. I managed another inch of stretch out of Kenneth Cole. We stared. And then, all in the course of six seconds, our lifeline snapped, and my lower lip buckled, and I grimaced. My shoulders hunched forward, and I turned, pretending to watch Jack watch TV. Maybe Fox hadn't noticed my efforts.

Jack stood shaking. There seemed to be more steam pouring out of his collar than from his blindly stirred pot. "She'll never get away with this. Everyone will show up, dressed to kill, and run anyway. If she wasn't such a caricature, I would never watch that whore. We should ALL dress up and try the Tri tomorrow. Let's see, Luke. I'll wrap you up in this colander thing, two funnels, we have these trash can liners, black AND white, tuck here, and then I could hot glue some—"

"JACK! What is this WE?" I snapped.

Jack bent his chin down, and raised his big brown eyes up to his master. He bit his bottom lip, and held his tongue for the moment. You could see the cartoon cloud "just thinking" appear above his head. "Luke, look around honey," he pointed, "Six customers, five paying, and a pile of bills. There's the grim landlord right outside beckoning us from the gutter. We NEED that thousand bucks prize."

My cartoon bubble looked more like a scrolling stock ticker. "Run, Luke, RUN! He's already planning your outfit!" I could see the Hudson Grille and myself sinking into the mud wrestling pit with a dizzy spin of wigs and heels. Dilemma gripped as I tried to swallow. A fateful black cloud was heading toward me.

Breathily, Jack let out a slow "L u k e" in an effort to calm me. "You know I'll be right there behind you e v e r y step of the way. I'll fix your hair. I'll make sure you look your best for the big money shot…"

"No, Jack, no," I said. "I'll be arrested for lewd conduct, we'll lose our beverage license, and we'll be living in a dumpster. Make that—you'll be living in a dumpster because I'll be moving to Mykonos."

Jack kept at it slowly, petting down my feathers. "Luke, there is no need to worry, worry, worry. I'll make sure you can't even be recognized. Of course, the outfit will be UN-forgettable, but no one, trust me sweetness, no one will even know it's you. Think of the fresh air, the aerobic exercise, showing off your fabulous legs to a crowd of horny, cheering men."

I glared and continued, "I'm thinking I can feel you shoving me down a laundry chute to HELL. Nothing short of reconstructive surgery is going to make me un-recognizable."

Jack nursed a slow smile. "Oh, I don't know about that. We know how clever I am, don't we? I'm thinking, maybe, you could be the first, trans-racial transvestite triathlete. Something very Whitney, Beyoncé, you know…"

I turned white, but managed to say, "Black??"

TWO

"Good afternoon, thank you for calling OZ, Bethany speaking, how can we make your day more beautiful?"

Liz Osbourne's vision of OZ, hair salon to the stars, went a long way beyond the likes of dial-a-Bethany. New York, London, Paris maybe, someday. Right now she was trying to conquer Chevy Chase, Maryland.

To some degree, she had. There seemed to be no end to the network of her bread and butter clientele. They came by the score with clouds of frosted hair, dressed in yards of Sante Fe art-dyed gauze and yards of diamond tennis bracelet. Bags and shoes to match. American craft style, of course.

This steady stream of women lived in the salon's back yard, in high-rise luxury condos. Their phone chain reached out to many surrounding neighborhoods, where semi-estates were larger and husbands lived more at the office. There was lots of money and tales of woe. With a little extra pampering or listening, the money flowed freely, as did the recommendations. Liz Osbourne was starting to sit pretty.

Most of her bread and butter clients were weaned on Alsatian bread and Plugra butter. But things were not always so nouveau-riche charming in OZ. Sometimes the heartbreak of psoriasis and comb-over paid a visit.

"Oh, why me," Liz thought. "Why Merritt Smears, and why in my chair? What was God thinking? Well, thank God we didn't have to service the whole combed-over Smears family."

Liz first met Merritt (the ferret, she later called him) at some community function. Merritt, as director of the Ward 4 Business District Bureau of Development, had grudgingly helped her navigate the permitting process in setting up OZ. In turn, she had been unable to refuse him as a client. He certainly needed help with his ratty red hair. It started with one hand doing a comb-over, but it could not avoid smelling like rodent droppings. To add to the foul mix, she was sure he just blasted a fart. She wondered if those things were dangerous around peroxide.

On the right was a bank of hair dryers. A chorus line of ladies sat like identical alien septuplets. All bonnet-topped, with the same slack-jaw expression, replete with manicure assistant and cotton between the toes.

Two months ago, in a brainstorm, Liz had had TV audio headsets installed in the hair dryer bonnets. She had even considered mikes, so that one notable patron could communicate with another. At least that might cut down on the shouting. Most of these babes were hard of hearing as it was. For now they were mesmerized. It was the noon hour and everyone faced east to watch Town Hall, LIVE! Dr. Sue Barrymore was break dancing on her soap box as usual.

"Gee," Liz thought, "the news affiliate is only two blocks away and I could just slip over there, ram my thinning shears into her neck and be back to finish another wet-set."

The alien septuplets started chirping like a nest full of baby robins. Dr. Sue must have come up with a good one, because the drying-out ladies were in a frenzy, fighting for a worm in edgewise. Merritt Smears interrupted his flaky comb-over.

He said, "She deserves a medal."

Liz said, "She deserves bad plastic surgery." She still had a sharp object in her hand, but Merritt rashly dared to continue.

"I am certainly glad someone has the balls to speak up about the degenerating fate of this city."

Liz had to restrain herself. Her shears were hovering dangerously close to his scrawny neck when Bethany's greeting squeaked. "Dr. Barrymore! How can we make your day more beautiful?"

The robins' heads turned right in a wave. Jaws slid open wider. Wasn't Town Hall, LIVE! live? There, not twenty feet away, sure enough was Dr. Sue.

With all that bluster, oddly enough, Dr. Sue looked a full foot shorter and ten years older in person. It certainly couldn't be the lighting. Liz had paid a small fortune in full spectrum light bulbs to subconsciously pamper her bevy of broads. From non-glare fixtures, Liz had conceived that the light would bounce off equally expensive surfaces, all on the pink side of bisque. Fawn sueded walls, diaphanous malt ceiling drapes, and café-au-lait marble floor tiles for her cadre of couture clad clients to click their heels upon.

Bethany was hovering around Dr. Sue like a humming bird. Bethany was frantically waving Liz to come over. Bethany might become history tomorrow.

Merritt had spun around in his chair, gripping the arms on the second time around, then planted his feet on the floor, dumbstruck.

Thinking ahead, Liz laid down her shears and hauled herself, best foot forward, across the floor. The closer Liz got, the worse Dr. Sue looked. Liz caught the gist of the prima donna's dilemma. "Quick comb-out... Meeting with The Mayor in twenty minutes."

As Bethany tried to bleat a response, Liz Osbourne swept her aside, gushing. "Doctor Barrymore, let me introduce you to our finest stylist, Enrique Ramorez." To keep things rolling right along, Liz grabbed Dr. Sue's remarkably flabby arm, and spun her into Enrique's chair.

Liz kept Enrique displayed right up front. He was healthy, humpable, and just the ticket to tickle the parade of posh gals. At least until he opened his mouth. His lyrical Latino mezzo hysteria always took a moment to fade its way back into the charm of his well built package.

Enrique, on tip-toe, stood back in mock annoyance at the intervention. "Meez OzBOURNeh! ¡Que susto!" His limps wrists were held prone at shoulder height as if he just discovered a dead field mouse on the floor.

Liz thanked her heavenly ceiling she hadn't studied Spanish in high school. She was sure Enrique would deliver her one of his staccato tongue-lashings when this was all over. Liz imagined herself being peppered in deaf silence, then to take it all out on a shell-shocked Bethany. She turned back to finish off Merritt Smears. Back at her station, Merritt had turned back around and was primping his unfinished do in the mirror. They short-smiled each other, and Liz tried to recover.

"Now, there's a bit of excitement for our day, isn't there."

Merritt heard the comment, but it didn't register. Vanity had taken over. In the presence of such voluptuous power as Dr. Sue, he was gripped by a manic necessity to look his best. His forearms expressed the jitter in his brain, resulting in a finger-shakey thing at his graying temples. "Merritt, get a hold of yourself," he thought. "If I could just scooch down and lean to the left—attaboy—there she is, my mirror can see her in her mirror. Think of the things that woman could do for my career. Better yet, think of the things she could do in bed!"

Liz could hardly believe her eyes. What in the world was this man doing, slumping in his chair like, uh, a dead ferret? What was this arm flailing about? Does he need a doctor? I'm sure there is a doctor's wife somewhere in this place. Oh my God, please make this stop!

"PAGING Ms. Osbourne, Liz Osbourne, telephone call on line two..." Bethany chimed in, reviving Liz back to reality. Liz reminded herself to be kind to Bethany when she gave her the ax.

Merritt saw Dr. Sue glancing in her mirror this way and that. He saw the muscle-bound Hispanic doing flamenco around her chair. Somewhere during 'that', Dr. Sue caught Ward 4 Business District Bureau of Development director, Merritt Smears, smiling goofily at her through a fun house maze of mirrors.

She giggled to herself. "Isn't this fun," she thought. "Isn't that Merrill Shears or somebody from City Hall? Might be easy pickings for the show."

She leaned forward toward the mirror and wiped her ring finger along the lower edge of her lipstick. All the while, she held her gaze with Merritt. She winked once and barely nodded her head. Dr. Sue had masterfully baited another hook and Merritt Smears almost choked on it. Without looking away, she reached down and reclaimed her purse. Dr. Sue stood, then clop, clop, clop, walked proudly to the reception desk.

The audience of seven robins watched her every move. Enrique, hardly finished with his masterpiece, just stood there with his hands on hips, thumbs forward. Liz Osbourne, with her panic attack on temporary hold, found herself face-to-face with a standing Merritt Smears. She was still somewhat bemused but heard him say, "Thanks, nice cut, see you in three weeks." Then squeak, squeak, squeak went his cheap shoes as he trotted off purposefully. "Ew, I'm glad that's over," thought Liz, as the errant comb-over bounced in time with his gait.

Dr. Sue Barrymore's 36Ds approached an anxious Bethany more amply than the rest of her. And Bingo! Merritt Smears sidled up to them on the Fiesta Deck. Bethany tried to look professional, tallying up bills while in the midst of quasi-celebrities. Unfortunately, she sniggered so hard she had to pat up dots of spittle. Ink ran.

Merritt and Dr. Sue were equally nervous, but with age came wisdom, and actions spoke louder than words. His baritone matched her contralto and their dialog was delivered in unison.

"Dr. Sue Barrymore?" he oozed.

"Merrill Spears?" she ventured, her consonants luckily masked by his.

Hands, shake.

"Please call me Merritt / Suzette."

They paused to giggle like little schoolgirls.

Both of them sang, "I'm so glad we've finally met!"

She came off like a little schoolgirl. He came off, well, like a little schoolgirl.

Suzette (yuck) pressed her business card into Merritt's hand and delivered a signature smile that could peel sueded paint. Merritt grinned ineptly and, as the Doctor turned towards the door, almost threw his jacket on the floor before lunging to open it for her. Dr. Suzette sashayed past his extended arm and trailed her frosted apricot nails under his chin.

It was satisfying to think that her boss, Big Al Siegel, might appreciate the small coup of getting Merritt Smears, and/or her next target the Mayor, on the show. "That cigar-chomping little chauvinist thinks he has all the power," she thought. "Well he doesn't, especially in bed. I'll show him."

Behind their exit, Salon OZ flushed a miasma of peroxide air and eau de Sue onto a sidewalk of pedestrians. Inside, Enrique plopped down in his chair. He muttered a barrage of Spanish under his breath. The robins were chirping, their wings fluttering back and forth. Bethany wiped a forehead of shiny glow back through her frosted tangled mane. She summoned the last of her strength to reach the intercom button for a breathless, "Liz Osbourne, line two is on hold."

Irritated at forgetting about the earlier page, and frayed by all the previous mayhem, Liz hoisted the phone receiver and barked, "Liz Osbourne." Her tense face relaxed with a smile. "Hi Luke, you'll never guess who just flew in and out of OZ."

THREE

Luke stood behind the bar and surveyed the empty dining room, trying to untangle the phone cord as he waited. He hated having to go through the bimbo Bethany to speak to his best girl friend. She'd probably forgotten he was on hold. He desperately needed to fish out Liz's pity for his latest predicament, the prospect of being transmogrified into "black by Jack". Not just black, but a bad black witch in high heels. The "maybe we'll be able to afford the cell phone next month" argument was his only consolation. That and the hope there might be a good dinner crowd tonight. Then again, it was a Monday.

The afternoon sun poured past the stained wood storefront of the narrow townhouse, casting warm shadows across the bronzed tin ceiling. The glow brought out the sheen on the eggshell finish of the pale walls. Reflections sparkled from a set of modestly framed mirrors hanging like artwork. Luke admired the assortment of mismatched chairs they had nurtured back to life from second hand stores, and recalled with dread all the hours of stripping, refinishing and upholstering. He had picked the lightest cherry stain. Jack had found the favorably masculine car seat fabric 'on the cheap' from a last gasp shop down the street. The chairs faced matching banquettes that flanked the walls, and tall plants in terra cotta pots broke up the effect of the corridor. The charcoal stained concrete floor matched the tabletops, and their waxed surfaces picked up hints of sunlight. Luke reflected with pride.

Jack was out gathering grubs or something. Then, jarring Luke out of his reverie, Liz Osbourne returned shrilly to the line. Before Luke could gather his wits to launch into his sympathy pitch, Liz was uttering the profanity of "Dr. Sue Barrymore!"

He inhaled a slow "eeech" down his throat, and realized her story had him beat. Stretching and pulling at the knotty phone cord, he listened to the abbreviated blow-by-blow-dry that had just transpired in the land of OZ. The evil ways of Dr. Sue created a kinship between Luke and Liz, one of profound distaste.

Luke let Liz pour out her tale of humor and disbelief. He offered a palliative: "I'd call out the flying monkey, but Jack's out shopping at the market right now." They both shared some relief laughing at the imagery of 'Suzette' in nothing more that a short white apron wielding cat-o-nines. And flailing it at the ferret, no less.

Biding his time, Luke could finally plead, "Look Liz, I'm gonna need your help. Jack is cooking up another stew, and I'm in the pot. Yeah, another one of his dress-to-the-death extravaganzas…"

But just then, he was drowned out by an entire off-key chorus:

"…'till we're bringing in the sheeves,

Look to the day, when He will wipe away all of our tears…"

From next door there was stomping, clapping, tambourine rattles, a pounding piano and a glissando soprano key change. Luke tried to shout above the noise. "Liz! Class has started. At the Mission next door." He was sure she couldn't make out what he said, so he hung up the phone with resigned futility. He figured she knew the drill and would understand.

Mercy Mission was next door to the Hudson Grille. In this once burned-out, far east Dupont neighborhood, The Reverend (as she styled herself) Blanche Pickens played grandmother, den mother and mother superior to all those with little hope. There were kids, the elderly, and the sort of half crazy, half homeless. Some were all four at the same time, others just sought some company. But they all had a good enough time, especially when The Reverend Pickens was cooking or playing the piano. Both came with a lot of heart, soul and volume.

At four-thirty, right on schedule, it was time for "Bible-robics." Luke walked down the dining aisle, past Jack's cooking pulpit, and back into the kitchen. From the walk-in refrigerator, he would take out a pan or a tub of food to take over to the Mission. He wasn't sure if the less fortunate were truly appreciative of Jack's culinary inspirations, but Luke enjoyed the look in the eye of the Reverend Pickens when he dropped by with a not-so-burnt offering.

The cool air blew by his face as the fridge door opened and he explored its contents. Reaching for today's pan, he moved Jack's blue gel eye compress to yet another location.

Luke came back into the dining room. An early customer was waiting near the front door. Luke put the pan in the small oven at Jack's sauté station, and proceeded to meet and greet.

"Mmn," he thought. "Kinda cute too. Not quite as grungy as most residents around here. Run him through the dishwasher and he might be ready to marry." On approach, Luke recognized his face from around town, and shouted above the noise, "Hi, welcome to Hudson

Grille. I'm Luke." He decided in this case to make the guy feel at home with the introduction. He extended his hand.

To complete the exchange, 'kinda cute' shook Luke's hand, and returned the greeting, "Jerry Callahan."

The space between them held the passing, almost cruisy smiles that acknowledged the surrounding din. "Nice firm handshake," thought Luke. As he fixed Jerry's drink request, he loudly apologized that they wouldn't be serving food till six.

Where was Jack? He welcomed Jerry to stay for the concert as it was, and they hung around the bar. Conversation was kept to a minimum between infrequent stops of rhythm.

Next door, things were reaching a fever pitch. Reverend Pickens was breaking out in a big smile and a healthy glow. About fifteen elderly men and women and a few little kids were reaching toward the rafters. The oldsters reached mostly from the elbow. A rainbow of 60's plaid, floral prints and polka dots swayed to the left, and creaked on their way back. Most of them moved half time to the music. A few, as well as the kids, went full tilt. "May He Be Our Witness" never looked or felt so good. The older guys and gals seemed to have shed ten years from their average age. It didn't go a long way at eighty or ninety, but their amazing grace and happy faces made up for limited mobility.

Crazy Gilbert was in another corner, head swinging back and forth to the beat of a beat-up tambourine. For all his vacant appearance, he was surprisingly coordinated. To his side, he was accompanied by a singing youth. The kid was shorter than Gilbert when seated, and about a quarter the width. Gilbert, a rail himself, barely pushed all of one-seventy.

Reverend Pickens called out to the boy to "bring it home, Slim!" The singing swayers clapped then double clapped, and the Reverend crooned out, "Oooh yeah Slim, let the Lord hear you up in heaven!"

Slim rolled his eyes, and let loose with an amazing boy-soprano riff, "My heart is open to the Lord, His arms..." Slim hated being called Slim. His whole forty pound body flushed with embarrassment every time he heard the name. He really wanted to be called "Ice," but Reverend Pickens would have "none of that drug dealin' rappin' nonsense" spoken in her house.

He knew he was pretty darn lucky to be in the care of Reverend Pickens. It seemed far better, compared to those people who visited that day from something called Human Services. He would never forget that dark week a month ago. The Reverend had fought back the tears but he knew she was crying privately.

Slim's mom had been put in jail. He didn't really understand everything that Human Services had told him, though he nodded his head as though he did. It was all so confusing. He had cried so much, his head ached, and just thinking about it brought back the pain in his stomach. He knew his mom couldn't do anything that bad, but Human Services made it sound that way. They said his mom would be home before Christmas, and meanwhile there was Reverend Pickens. Just to make sure she made it home, Slim clapped harder, and sang out twice as loud as a prayer.

The room rocked in a thin mist of dust that puffed around the floor. If you looked beyond the joy escaping from the flowered dresses and sweat-stained baseball caps, you would notice the half dried pool of rust to one side of the refrigerator in the corner. Bare light bulbs hung below the tall ceiling. Some light peered through the filmy barred windows up front, but did not make its way back through the dingy room.

But the light of laughter lit up the space. A mad vagrant on a tambourine grinned at a small boy with a big voice.

"Rock Him to the left and rock Him to the right." Gilbert bellowed the bass line.

Slim looked up at Gilbert, inspired. With a smile, he exulted, "Reach up to the sky, He'll guide you through the night." The roomful added the final crescendo chords to a sigh of relief and a small round of applause. The front door opened with the first note in a chime. The down note didn't follow.

At the incongruous sight of the fit new guest, silver-haired Blanche Pickens in her teal pinstripe suit rose from the piano, hastily clutching her plumey-feathered Sunday pulpit hat. Smile met smile, and the visitor declared in his own rich baritone, "Reverend Pickens, I could hear all those hymns down the street, four blocks away!"

The Reverend hugged back, gushing, "Oh my, Mr. Parker Fox sir, where you been all day? I was startin' to get a bit worried." She called out, "Slim, and you Gilbert, keep these folks movin' a bit, so they can cool down and not catch a death of somethin' now."

The two went arm in arm over to an old lawn chair, a peach crate and a plaid waiting-room sofa. There was duct tape holding on to the frayed edges of the arms, and the legs didn't all match. Nothing collapsed as they sat down.

Blanche leaned forward conspiratorially. "Mr. Parker Fox sir, I'm telling you, we have got to do something about these bathrooms here. The plumbing just ain't right, like I been sayin', and sometimes it just about talks back to you when you're trying to finish your business. Mrs. Oates over there come out in a crying spell just this morning, telling us all about the devil speakin' to her out of the commode! It's a fright, that's what it is."

Parker Fox sat shaking his head and holding her hand. He straightened up on the peach crate. "Now Reverend Pickens, I know. I've been trying to figure out how to take care of all that. I promise you everything will be all fixed in a couple of days. I'm meeting my boss, Mr. Jon Miller, tonight for dinner. He owns the building, and he let me know earlier that he'd foot the bill to make sure things were done right for Mercy Mission. Tomorrow morning, first thing, I'll be down at the Ward Business office picking up the permits, allowing us to get the work done. We're going to take care of you, Blanche. I know it's been real inconvenient and we're very concerned."

The pastor sat listening to everything Parker Fox had to say. Her jaw was slowly munching, though it was clear she wasn't eating anything. She added, "And Mr. Atkins is so scared to go into the men's room, he nearly had to pee his self. Thank Jesus Mr. Luke next door is so nice to us. I finally had to ask him to get over there to help take care of things. I don't like having to wear out our welcome at Mr. Luke's. It's such a nice eatin' place."

Parker Fox smiled in relief. He continued, "Blanche my dear, you don't have to pester the neighbors or call up every bureaucrat in the city to get this fixed. Since we found out about it, which is only just now," he lied, "Mr. Miller and I have been doing everything we can."

Reverend Pickens seemed a bit calmer. Things seemed like they were gonna be put back together. "All right children," she said. She moved to get up from the sofa and Parker was quick to lend a hand. They were standing when The Reverend shouted across the room.

"Okay Slim, time to strike up another hymn!" And then, turning to her guest, "Thank you Mr. Parker for stoppin' by. I'm feelin' a bit less worried now."

They walked toward the door and paused for another round of hugs. They were almost to the door when the solo note chimed again. Luke Hudson swung the door open with his hip. He was holding a foil-wrapped pan with oven mitts that looked like Guernsey cows. A quarter turn later, he was face-to-face with no less than his silver-haired heart-throb, reaching to help with the door. Luke saw him staring at the mitts with a smile. Parker looked up, "Smells good."

Luke, stuck between the door and a hard place, mumbled his thanks.

The action sped up as Reverend Pickens exclaimed, "Oh Mr. Luke! One sniff of that and I'll be puttin' on fifteen pounds. Go on now, get over there and make the people's day. You have a good evenin', now, Mr. Parker." And he was out the door, to Luke's dismay.

Across the room, Luke saw the inmates looking at him in mid-stretch. Gilbert had switched back to his vacant gaze. Reverend Pickens was standing there, her improbable hat in hand, beaming from earring to, well, her other earlobe. Slim was racing across the floor, jumping over the peach crate yelling, "Mr. Luke, Mr. Luke!"

FOUR

Back at the Grille, Jerry Callahan found himself holding down the fort. He sat tentatively, wondering what to do if anyone arrived. He smiled, thinking back to Luke trying to explain all the reverie, resorting to crude sign language. He had gone off to the kitchen, and returned cradling a pan with cow mitts. Luke mouthed an apology and 'moo-ed' that he'd be back in a moment, smiling awkwardly as he backed into the door on his way out. It seemed to make an otherwise crazy situation somewhat normal. Any other queen would have served attitude instead of Shepherd's Pie.

The door opened behind Jerry, which prompted him to turn around. "Shit," he said to himself. Here he had thought to drop by Hudson Grille some night after work. It took him nearly two weeks to talk himself over here. There had been a review in the *Blade*, the local gay paper that featured Hudson Grille and its two partners, Luke Hudson and Jack Betz braving the frontier of East Dupont. They intended to run a reasonably serious restaurant, featuring good home cooking, using inspired ingredients. It wasn't entirely original, but the local guys, making a stretch of it in a neighborhood before its prime, somehow appealed to him.

He wasn't one to go out alone. He forced himself to discover new places and venture around in the company of new faces and personalities. He had moved to Washington, as so many people did in this transient city, on a whim to escape his small town. Back there, he had been in PR, but it had been so unfulfilling in such a small pond. Now he had his new job, better stability (he hoped), a few acquaintances, but no one to fill the 'someone special' void in his life.

The *Blade* article had said "casual and comfortable." The re-viewer didn't think much of the music they played, but seemed to bless the food with high marks, and Jerry felt drawn to a seek-and-explore mission. The picture of Jack Betz, flashing a smile next to his partner, added to the allure. He knew it was a frozen moment, that could easily be a bust, but he let his imagination run wild. He had thoughts of a live-in-husband who could melt him with a smile as well as create sensational meals. Jerry loved to eat, and was glad none of it showed on his fit but average frame.

Jerry made sure that morning to wear something understated and interesting—something that could fit in at work, but meet an approving eye by dinner. He figured he should go early, but not too early to the Grille. He preferred a few people about for comfort, but not too crowded. Then, of course, the door had opened and he was five feet away from Jack Betz. Alone.

The rumble next door had subsided. Ella's jazzy torch lyrics purred from the restaurant's speakers. Jerry vowed never again to do so much planning with his head. Best laid schemes always go awry.

Jack muscled his way through the door, carrying a cardboard crate of vegetables and a brown bag containing his "epicurean playthings" for tonight's menu. He was surprised to see someone sitting at the bar this early. His laden arms flashed the "early, single, nice hair" message to his brain. His brain then signaled his shoulders to broaden (under all that strain), and flashed him a reminder to watch/lower his voice.

"Quick now Jack," the brain said, "think of something pleasant, smart but not too colorful to engage. I can't see the ring finger. Is he straight? Can't possibly be." The man turned and was facing Jack. Jack's mind went on analyzing with the speed of Evelyn Wood. "Mn. No expression on face, minus two. Uhp. There's a bit of a smile, better. Clean cut, average face, but that's okay. Nice shirt though. It would look better on me. Look at those strong thighs stretching the fabric on his pants! I think I could make this do..."

Finally aloud Jack began, "Early bird gets the Jack. I'm Jack. I'm also running a little late. Have you seen Luke? Sorry, grocery shopping down at the wholesaler. I know, I know, I'm supposed to get this done first thing in the morning, but I got an idea in my head this afternoon to make some blackened lamb, then the butcher had to show me nearly every piece of fresh prime meat, not that there was much left at this hour, (Jack, stop), I really think he was coming on to me, (bad move Jack, recover), NOT that I was interested, (Jack, wrap it up darling) WAIT! Just let me put these things down. I can be so rude. Rushing, rushing to get back and just couldn't stop my self. So I'm Jack, and..."

"I'm Jerry Callahan, that's okay." (My, how people go on around here.)

Jerry had sat stunned. He felt his stomach drop, and forced himself through a slow, deep breath back to normal. He had watched Jack pile through the door, chatter about in front of the bar, stop to reverse direction, then move around to the back of the bar. Jerry couldn't even recall much of what Jack said. He did recall liking the rear view as much of the front. With all the awkward rambling, he felt more at ease. He fathomed that there might be a real person behind all the non-stop audio-visual. Score nine, okay, eight and a half.

Luke left Mercy Mission for the Grille feeling a wide smile in his heart. The Reverend Pickens radiated. She was as happy to see him as she was to receive today's evening meal.

Through the Hudson Grille storefront he saw Jack doing a full twirl in front of a captive Jerry Callahan. Jack was beaming, and Luke surmised he was consciously or unconsciously trying to make an impression if not a full touch-down. He smiled at himself for even thinking in football terms, and steered into the restaurant. Perhaps he should take off the oven mitts. They didn't make much sense with yesterday's cleaned-out pan.

As he walked through the door, he was thinking how cute Jack could be sometimes. He found himself staring at four doe eyes, caught in backwood headlights, paused in mid-sentence. Yup. Jack was on the make alright.

Jack's eyes, nose, throat and hips telegraphed back to Luke the "I saw him first, sorry I was late at the market, but I just wanted to play with him" pout. He interceded with a quarterback sneak. "Hey man, how are mom and the kids? Have you met Jerry Callahan yet? He's gonna be our first victim tonight."

Luke looked at Jack, "I was wondering where you were. I can SEE what you've been up to! Yes, Jerry and I met before I took Blanche her victuals."

Jack clucked his tongue and retorted, "Jerry, Mr. Hudson is being mean, AGAIN. Go on over there and give him a smack for me."

Jerry was feeling a whole lot more comfortable. He slid off the barstool to smack a little play dust off Luke's deltoid with the back of his hand. Jerry added, "I say we should cube him up and eat him for dinner."

Luke laughed it off, and went behind the bar to check out Jack's stack of goodies.

Jerry asked the two, "So how's business over here? I saw the write-up in the *Blade*."

Jack replied, arms folded to lean on the bar, with a slight thrust of his chest toward Jerry. "Well Jerry, as long as you order a few family bonanza meals tonight we may be able to re-open tomorrow."

Luke blended in, "Jack's a great chef. With a little more press, and some great word of mouth, Jerry, I'm sure things will be just fine. It's a bit slow getting started though."

Luke came back around and sat next to Jerry. "Did you stop by for a drink, or are you going to have some dinner tonight? Feel free to eat here at the bar. I'm sure Jack would love to take care of you, till he has to go slave in the galley. After that, you'll have to put up with me."

Luke tossed the end of the invitation back toward Jack instead of directly to Jerry. Jack, drying and arranging the bar glasses, began to squeak out a shrill note by sliding a stiff middle finger around the top of the wet wine glass. He shyly held it toward Luke's direction.

Luke got up from the barstool to take the cardboard carton back to Jack's sauté station when the phone rang. Luke picked up before Jack could do his Olympic-style, back three-and-a-half Lutz for Jerry. "Good Evening, Hudson Grille, this is Luke. Hey Liz! Yes, Bible-robics, yeah, another happy customer. She's sweet. Wanna do some old people hair? Yeah, He's standing right here." Luke turned to Jack and spoke face-tiously over the top of the receiver, "Liz said to give you a big kiss..."

Jack returned the barb with a short raspberry, and with much drama stared into the back bar mirror mimicking feminine hair fluffing, lipstick checking, and the horror of discovering under-eye bags. Jack didn't dislike Liz, he just thought she was a little vain, and envious that she was getting rich before he did. He had no room to chastise vanity, so he treated her with childish jealousy.

Luke continued, "You got it Liz, he's up to something very big this time. I'm sure it involves a big costume, and like it or not I'm sure at some point it's going to involve you." After a brief spell of listening, Luke's voice rose. "NO! Of course I don't want anything to do with it. But you know Jack. Listen, I can't give you all the details, we have company." Luke glanced at Jerry, who mock-toasted.

"When can you get down here to help me reason with Jack, or maybe you could take my role this time?" Luke held the receiver away from his ear, "Didn't think so, so when? Tomorrow after dinner! Not tonight? I may be in jail by then. Yes, jail! I said it was serious. Okay, tomorrow for dinner. Well I hope we'll be busy, but we'll figure it out. Thanks. Love you too. Don't be late!" He hung up the phone.

Luke turned back to Jerry. Jack stood behind the bar chomping on his gum, double time, arms folded across his chest, and right foot tapping like periods on an old electric typewriter.

Jack began, "MISS Hudson, could you lay on the drama any thicker?" He then whispered to Jerry, "Didn't I tell you he was mean to me?" Jack tromped toward the crate, and hoisted it to his shoulder (really now, Jack). He picked up the shopping bag, and continued tromping back to serve his time slaving in the galley.

Jack boomed back over his shoulder, "You haven't heard the last from me. I'm goin' to work. Keep your hands off the customer."

Luke turned to Jerry and asked, "Would you rather watch Jack or the evening news?"

Jerry replied, "Yup, *Entertainment Tonight*." Jerry was smitten.

Later, Luke and Jack were back up front. "This evening is going pretty well," Luke said.

Jack was tending bar while Luke counted the latest totals. The front door opened. Jack turned to face the back bar and whispered to Luke with a nudge. "Tall, silver and strapping at six o'clock. Okay, eight-fifteen but turn around slow." Luke turned to see the black leather jacket from the doorway, standing near the bar with another man. (Drat!)

Parker spoke toward Luke, "Miller for two." (Does this man ever speak in full sentences?)

Luke looked right at Parker's face and very professionally declared, "Mr. Miller, it's very nice to see you joining us for dinner tonight."

Parker Fox just stood there, looking a bit perplexed, and then got the misunderstanding, "I'm not Miller." He then turned to Jon, "This is," pausing past the mister, "Jon Miller." Then added, "I'm Parker Fox."

Luke had come around the bar, picked up two menus, crossed the name off the (short) list, and was so pleased with his timing he could have skipped. Instead he continued the charade professionally and calmly. "Well, Parker Fox," extending his hand to shake, "I'm certainly glad we have finally met." He shook the big strong hand, and didn't bother to formally offer his name. Parker Fox would just have to formally wait, even though it was probably well enough known who the Hudson was in Hudson Grille. He sat the two at a good table farther back, and managed not to bow. One could be a little too formal.

At the bar, Jack nearly hemorrhaged. He kept playing with the bar ware until a restrained Luke marched back up front. Jack hugged

Luke's shoulder from the side. "You finally did it! After all these weeks, I'm so proud of you! It was perfect! Not too femme, not too butch. I don't know what the hell you have been waiting for, he's really not all that. Too Chris Meloni for me, but who's the Bruce Wayne he's with? I smell money."

Luke finally got a chance to speak. "To each his own, and you know what I've been going through. He's so much more than 'that.' I was hardly able to stand there, let alone talk to him. I just needed my moment. Thank God, I didn't let you match-make."

At the Miller-Fox table, dinner arrived and was followed by more serious conversation. Parker briefed Jon Miller on the situation at Mercy Mission. "The bathrooms are just the ticking on the time bomb, Jon. The water lines, waste lines and mains going out to the street are looking pretty rough. They were inspected and approved when you and Al bought the building, but that was years ago. Problem now is, the street outside was not built to handle all the additional bus and truck traffic round here these days. And they built the new government building and the new subway station. All the constant vibration is affecting utility piping, and buildings all over now have foundation cracks. On top of that, during winter and in heavy rain, they have leaks in the basement."

Jon Miller nodded gravely, and Parker continued. "We can get the trade permit to handle the restroom work, but if anyone goes downstairs and inspects things too closely—I hate to say it, but they might close down the Mission till it's fixed."

Jon's reply was balanced. "The whole area is being developed, but I agree we can't displace these people who have made this their home for decades. For now, I think we should be supporting the work Mercy Mission is trying to accomplish in the neighborhood. Is it dangerous at this point? I'm all for their cause, but I have to be concerned about our liability. "

Parker went on appraising the situation with Jon, but noticed the animated chef across the aisle. With all the motion, it looked like he was juggling, even though he was only tending to flank steak. Parker Fox didn't think much of flamboyant, but all the extra activity amused him. He passed a friendly nod to the chef, and brought his attention back to Jon. "I'm going to pick up the signed permit tomorrow down at the Ward Business Office. They are so annoying and inept though, it seems like they are trying to create obstacles."

Jon replied, "Well, let's hope for the best. I haven't made any friends down there either. And, those guys, not that I ever would, but they aren't the kind I would want to start paying off. Something isn't quite kosher down there. I think we should swing by Al Siegel's after we finish here. After all, he owns the building with me, and he lives just down the street. We can see if he has any ideas. Just don't let on about the real problems downstairs. I know he would just love to kick out the Mercy Mission, though he'd be the last one to let anyone know. Bad press. It's been all I could do over the past year or two to keep his paws off doing anything with the building. Good thing he's so tied up with the TV station, and all the fun and games from that Barrymore woman."

The dinner 'rush' died down. "Twenty-three covers on a Monday night, not bad," thought Luke. "Only about 500 more this month and we can afford two more frying pans."

Jack dragged himself up front, feigning a variety of hypochondria.

"Poor Jack," Luke rewarded. "And the Emmy in the category of 'Tired Old Queen' goes to Jack Betz for his performance with Charred Lamb in Apricot Glaze."

Luke turned toward Jack, "By the way, Jerry had to leave without giving you a big hug and kiss..." Luke pulled a rabbit out of the hat, and swung the little surprise in the air, baiting toward Jack. "But, not before asking me to give you his business card!"

Jack grabbed the card, "Well, isn't that flattering, and I wasn't even trying. You know he's not my type though."

Luke laughed out loud, "Jack! This wet bar rag is your type."

Jack looked at the card and squeaked, "Ew, government bureaucrat! Definitely not my type." He tossed the card on the bar with mock disgust, and turned to Luke, "By the way, Hudson, why are you feeding our dear friend, Liz, all that fear-for-your-life garbage with the Transvestite Triathlon? You know she is just going to come over here tomorrow and start acting like a beaver, gnawing at me AND our gorgeous dining room chairs. You made it sound like I am going to tar and feather you!"

Luke leaned on the bar toward him, "Jack, you said I had to have a BLACK FACE! Knowing you, tar and feathers wouldn't surprise me."

Jack pulled out his pout, "You know I'm doing this for the financial benefit of the Grille, and I'll be sure your precious reputation is kept out of the papers." He snatched the business card off the bar, slid it into his chest pocket, and added, "Somehow."

FIVE

Luke was wiping up the bar. Jack minced back up front. "By the way, Hudson, I don't think you have to worry about Parker's date tonight. Business, strictly business, and my gaydar definitely didn't ping. A friend of the 'family', but he's not family. They were talking for-EV-er about Mercy Mission though. It sounded serious. Something about pipes and infra-red structure or something. My brain went on 'dull, dull, dull', then my reduction interrupted so I didn't get all the details. I think I caught him looking at me though."

Luke bit back, "You stay away from him Jack. Don't even think about thinking about it. For Christ's sake, you look like a fire baton twirler back there. Who wouldn't be looking at you?"

Jack tsk-ed and answered, "He's all yours if you ever get up your nerve to make another move. Just remember, man cannot live by his baguette ALONE! Jack stood there, wiggling his pelvis, thrust toward Luke.

Not far away, Parker and Jon Miller were walking down the street, heading toward Al Siegel's house. It was time to discuss what tactics to take with Al. Parker found Jon an intelligent but very private person, and there was no doubting his business savvy. Parker tried to draw him out. "So, I knew you owned the Mission building with Al, but how did you ever get involved with him? He seems kind of low rent from all I've heard."

Jon replied, "Oh, trust me. I keep my distance without being distant. He can be a shrewd one. Actually we went to Georgetown together. He was a few years ahead of me though. MBA grad student. We crossed paths a couple of times. When he got out, he went to work at his dad's radio station. Dad dropped dead, Al bought a box of cigars and a TV station, and became a small media mogul. Some people call him 'Big' Al, but he's still working on buying his way up into the 'Big' part.

One day, a few years back, Al calls me up with the Mission building deal. I had been puttering around with those P Street condos, so this was a commercial break for me. He needed the write-off. It just seemed to work. I did most of the work though. In a year or two, the neighborhood will be a lot more solid, and we'll do a bit more with the building. But from the way you make it sound, we better give Al some clues to cough up some more bucks, or sell out."

Al Siegel sat in his big TV chair, cigar in hand, gazing up to the ceiling with his eyes closed. He inhaled slowly, and exhaled through un-whistling lips. Before he resumed with another breath, he hacked on his phlegm, then moaned a guttural sigh. He dreamed of an ever expanding Siegel empire. Like a mantra he spoke the words 'dark fiber'. Exhaling he declared, "That's where my next fortune will be made, dark fiber." He breathed in through his nose. On exhale he chortled. His palms slowly ran down across the dark carpet of curls through his open shirt. Up, up they went over his rounded abdomen. Then slid down to his exposed waist and further down to the thatch at his groin. To the ceiling he uttered, "You're gonna be a star."

He felt the scrape of fingernails under the heft of his nuts hanging off the chair's edge and between the fur of his dark, hairy thighs. They dragged against the mohair plush as the hand slid tightly up his club. Thousands of fiber tines picked at him below and a halo of warmth surrounded him above. The hand twisted when it reached the lip of its summit. An electric jolt shot back down his spine, past his butt and then out through his hamstrings. He clenched an orgasm back into his prostate and breathed deep as the sensations began once again.

"Igga Ahl, ache ih IG-ga," mumbled the impaired diction.

He felt the tongue lap at his balls. Teeth pulled at hairs here and there. The voice continued to talk to his straining, clenched penis. "Big Al," it cooed. The nails began again. He felt them tingling then tickling as his balls rose and fell with his breathing. Delicious fear poured over him as he imagined the thin sack of skin perilously close to the length of sharp, frosted apricot knives.

Sue Barrymore sublimated the fact she was on her knees. While she drew 'Big Al' in to explore the back of her throat, the back of her mind reasoned that she was just making a small down payment to the Fates, as she serviced her way to the top.

He was BIG, she'd give him that. While she had been here many times before, tonight was a little more fun. Every time she purred "Al," she was thinking of Merritt Smears. In her fantasy Merritt was Mr. Clean, with a full head of hair and a decade younger. Without his suit she imagined him in much better shape than the lump before her. She also imagined herself in the chair chomping on the cigar while Merritt chomped elsewhere. As she flicked ash on Merritt's bare back, the fervor of her present mission doubled. She sniffed for the smell of burning flesh and allowed the thick pole to inch down her throat. She bided her time and continued working on her investment. She gagged.

She continued to work in spite of jaw fatigue and back strain. She wondered if this was that "carpet tunnel syndrome" business. Al continued to breathe, blab on and hack every now and then. Snippets of Al's monologue peppered her daze.

"Dark fiber, big star, great tits, faster, harder, slower."

"What a prick," she thought.

By now, Al was breathing and speaking faster. "...assholes down in Development and that hobo neighborhood..." His thighs were swinging open and shut on her ears. Earrings prodded into her and her vision was blurred through crooked, steamed up glasses. She crossed her eyes, and a few syllables drifted across her consciousness: "asshole... Development... hood." At that moment, she thought herself quite smart to add the three and come up with Merritt Smears on the other side of the equation. She made a mental note to call him in the morning for further calculations, and faster on she went.

At least until the doorbell played its tune, and Big Al popped out of her mouth.

"JEE.........SUS CHRIST!' yelled Al. The door tuned again. (Ride of the Valkyries, it was a media mogul thing.)   From the TV chair Al pounded the intercom buzzer. "Who the hell is it?"

Outside Jon and Parker were swaying and staring into the security camera as if they could see inside. Jon spoke, "Al, it's Jon Miller. If it's a bad time, I can call you in the morning—"

"Naahrgh-oww!" Al turned his head to the left and coughed as Dr. Sue examined his now swinging dick. "I'll be right down." He leaned forward to grope Sue's boobs, but backed up at the look of her pouty, frost smeared lips, teary mascara and Wolfman hair. "Stay here and don't turn on the TV. I'll be right back." He patted her mane and began to tug his clothes back together.

Big Al bounced around as Siegel came down the stairs buttoning up. He hop-scotched through the foyer trying to put on his left shoe then his right. He nearly fell into the door but grabbed it just in time to turn the knob. As he opened the dark stained door, Jon stood in front with Parker peeking over his shoulder through a wrought iron gate.

Behind bars, Al gasped, "Sorry Miller. You caught me dozed off at the news. Isn't it a little late for business?"

Jon glanced at his watch and volunteered, "Sorry, Al. Parker and I were having dinner down the street, and thought we'd swing by."

Dr. Sue looked down at the bubbles in her puddle of spit on the carpet. She sat on the floor with her head swathed in the cloud of cigar smoke that hung in the room. She began to gag again, struggled up, and fell toward the powder room door in the corner of the den. She made it in time to heave.

Sue hung over the bowl having a flashback to her days in Georgetown when she was an exotic dancer, sometimes hooking to pay expenses. Al had "hooked up" with her one day, and she soon got used to his money as much as he got to use her. Not long after he bought the station, she took her career from one stage to another. Now as she clung to the cold porcelain she realized things hadn't changed all that much.

At the sink, her eyes did not look in the mirror as she doused her face with water, and wiped away the black streaks. Cool air blew in from an open window. She went to the source of relief, and parted the drapes. Outside, she saw the stars above and the railing of the fire escape below.

"If you can't go up, might as well go down," she thought.

With new resolve, Sue Barrymore surveyed the situation. As she hiked up her skirt, she angrily muttered, "What the fuck are you doing here woman? Go home, and get some beauty sleep." She remembered today's meeting with the Mayor. She remembered its success, and the earlier one with Merritt Smears. She was dying to tell Al Siegel, to further her need to display her powers. But she never got to boast. He shoved her to his zipper before the front door had closed. "He'll just have to hear it all on tomorrow's show. Prick. I can already see the look on his face. I hope it gives him a heart attack." One could imagine her fangs as she looked at the moon.

Evil in her eyes turned fearful as she considered Al coming back upstairs to find her gone. "Screw him," she thought. "I'll have him wrapped back around my finger in no time."

She straddled the sill, and grunted as she swung her other leg outside. Gingerly, she walked across the grate on the balls of her high heel shoes. Cold air blew up her skirt as she reached for the ladder and rode down with a clatter. Her neck jarred when iron hit dirt with a thud.

She felt determined and boldly marched down the dark alley. The far streetlight guided her past a minefield of rain-filled potholes. The shadowy trees were whipped by a crisp fall wind. She could smell fall leaves, city dirt, and a hint of garbage.

The sound of a little 'clank' above the traffic noise surprised her quick steps. She looked back over her shoulder and wondered what part of the old fire escape had slid into place. Not seeing a tambourine slip from a tense hand, she turned and skittered into the street ahead.

Al Siegel bounded back up the stairs while unbuckling his belt. He reached the doorway to an empty den, and marched to the powder room door in the corner. He flipped the light switch and saw his face in the mirror.

It was slashed with lines of frosted apricot lipstick that said, "It sucks to be a STAR."

SIX

The morning sun felt warm through the crisp fall air as Luke walked to the Grille. He was in good spirits and looking forward to another day of challenges at his restaurant. "His restaurant"—the sound of it warmed him like the sun on his face. Then, he felt a curdle in the pit of his stomach as he recalled the impending mayhem, Jack's scheming and the Triathlon. All the details had yet to surface, but his experience of Jack's 'creativity' made him wary. Luke tried to relax, fast forwarding through his thoughts. Jack would be down at the wholesaler, cruising the meat stalls. Luke had an hour or so of 'safe' time handling breakfast customers before he had to deal with the whirling dervish.

He mused at yesterday's encounters with Parker Fox. It had been a collection of awkwardness and quiet delight. He wasn't sure what to make of it all. Luke wondered where all the events would lead. He wondered if his cards would fall into place, and if he'd ever get to know the guy. He considered how foolish all this 'crush' nonsense could be, but tossed that thought aside so he could enjoy the rush of excitement. It was like opening up a present maybe a bit too carefully, to savor the potential of getting to play with a new toy.

Three blocks north, Parker Fox had finished his early morning run and a short workout. He was assessing the day ahead under the hot spray of the shower. He felt the dread of having to be polite with the goons down at City Hall, and hoped to get out of there without losing his temper. It shouldn't be any big deal, but then they might be in the mood to ask too many questions. Maybe life would be kind today, and Mercy Mission would get fixed without any interference from the meddling inspectors.

He tried to count his blessings once a day or week to keep his head going in the right direction. These days, it seemed the blessings were small, but steady. Life was much simpler now that he was working for Jon Miller, developing or keeping his properties in order.

He was glad that he had thrown out his ecstasy-popping live-in, the drummer, after two years. He did miss playing with their band, The Grease Monkeys; he reveled in the backbeat and of course the limelight. On the other hand there were the goddamn groupies. He couldn't continue working and living with a little tramp who constantly got it on there too.

Today's thanks boiled down to the job, a clean house and good health. He wanted something more, but wasn't sure how much he was willing to relinquish to get it.

Of course there was that twink down at the Hudson Grille. Well, he wasn't really a twink, and Parker thought he was trying to flatter himself to think a smart, young guy like Hudson had an eye on him. Yesterday was a little too coincidental for comfort though.

Parker got out of the shower and was drying off in front of the mirror. "Not bad for forty-five," he thought, "except do I have to go gray on my chest too? I'd certainly have to cross a generation gap to attract Hudson, though it might be amusing to push a few buttons over there."

His body was still damp. He climbed into a light gray t-shirt that stretched across well-muscled shoulders and flat abdomen. His short gray hair was done with a quick paw of his hand. He pulled on some jeans, tucked in the T, and zipped. Stretching his arms front, he cracked his back, and rocked his head from one side to the other for two more pops. In front of the mirror, he surveyed the image. He ran the butt of his left hand across the two mounds of his chest, and tugged at his crotch with the right. He played a bit down there, kneading until he swelled with pride. Satisfied, he turned for the kitchen, finished off a swig of coffee, and left for a new day.

Luke found the vagrant in front of the Grille like he had so many times before. Gilbert was asleep. Luke gently nudged his leg with the top of his foot until Gilbert stirred. "Okay bud, time for coffee. Come on in whenever you're ready." He unlocked the door, turned on the lights, and went back to heat up the griddle. He came back out front, and found Gilbert at his usual post, holding up the wall with an ostentatious snore. He came back with a cup of coffee after starting the breakfast basics, and Gilbert reached for the hot mug with an honest "Thanks."

A few customers dropped by for quick take-out, while others stayed on with their morning paper. Luke managed with the menus, the orders and scrambling before the natives got restless. Jack should be back soon, but Luke wasn't sure if that would be a blessing or the opening of Pandora's Box.

All of that didn't matter when Parker Fox entered the Grille.

Luke walked up front, trying very hard not to smile too loud, but it was all he could do to stifle the glee bubbling up from his stomach. "Morning," (pause), "Parker."

Parker sort of smiled back with a "Hi, Luke."

Luke told him to have a seat anywhere as his mind raced with the fact that Parker hadn't twitched when Luke addressed him by his first name, and Luke hadn't sunk through the floor when Parker used his. He slapped his brain back into reality, and took a deep breath along with Parker's order.

Luke was up front at the bar ringing up a check when he saw Blanche Pickens coming toward the door. Her eyes looked big, and she was moving like an economy-sized speed walker. Since The Reverend usually sashayed, it was likely to be urgent. "Maybe she's running from the Devil," he thought.

She opened the door halfway through her sentence, "—Luke, Mr. Luke, we sprung a leak downstairs, PLEASE can you help?"

Luke glanced back at the dining room. Parker Fox was already walking toward the front, and Gilbert was surprisingly right behind him. Luke held the door and followed in a hurry.

Reverend Pickens let them know that Slim was downstairs at the Mission holding a bucket, and the few patrons that had stayed overnight were scrounging around for other containers. Parker made it in first and went downstairs. Luke called back to Gilbert to find the flashlight, but he said he already had one, as Luke ran down behind Parker. In spite of the havoc at hand, Luke noticed the broad v-shape of Parker's back. He glanced up at the water-stained ceiling and mouthed a "thank you" to anyone looking down from above. Parker called out to Slim to hear where he might be in the dark cellar.

"Hurry Mr. Fox! It sounds like the water is coming at me faster."

Parker ran to the boy and felt around for the source of the water. Gilbert came hopping down the steps, and the beam of the flashlight slashed back and forth through the darkness. Parker started barking orders, "Gilbert! Bring that flashlight over here! Luke, give me a hand." Gilbert swung the beam of the flashlight over onto Slim. He was standing, wide-eyed and half-soaked holding a plastic bucket toward the stream of water squirting from the pipe.

Parker found the valve near the source of the leak. He grabbed it with both hands, grunted as he turned to the side and put all his might to the task. Luke eased his way closer to the straining hunk, not sure whether to reach and help with the valve, the squirting water, Parker's shoulders, waist or just dive in for his butt. He tried to hold back another giggle opting for an involuntary baritone cough. Satisfied that he had turned his girly moment into something close enough to butch, Luke barked his own order, "Tell me what to do!"

"Get me a TOWEL!" Parker's command slammed Luke back on the tender side of his ego.

He turned this way and that reaching for anything that might please his master and wipe away the sting that had accompanied his bark. When he caught the sight of a rag on the wood crate only ten steps ahead, it glowed like the Holy Grail and seemed miles away. Luke rushed as fast as he could to his quest, but felt like he was wading through jello compared to the urgency required of his mission. His mind raced. "Rag, rag, get the rag, gotta get the—"

Luke tripped and the top corner of the crate slammed into his gut as his outstretched arm whacked over the top of the rough wood slats. His finger tips felt the satisfying texture of terry cloth.

Parker shouted out toward the darkness. "Luke! Didya run into the wall over there?"

Luke clutched the rag and gasped for air, creating a loud rasping wheeze. "Shit, shit, I must get fit," he thought. Painfully he caught a slight puff of air and tried to answer Parker's question that hung amongst the trickling sound of water from the pipe. "No, no," Luke croaked giddily, "just trying to knock some sense into myself."

He stumbled back to Parker to hand him the towel. Parker had managed to turn the valve so that the water was down to a slight dribble and was facing Luke in the glow of the flashlight. Luke hoped that the dim lighting would conceal the fact that he was pale white with bugged-out eyes. He tried to regain normal breathing as well as his pride.

Gilbert pulled at a string cord that hung from the ceiling and turned on the dusty bare bulb that swung from the ceiling. Twenty-five watts of light bobbed around the scene to find Slim sitting on another crate shielding his squinted eyes, Gilbert surveying the room with wonder, and Parker blinking at a dumbfounded Luke. They stood amongst five good-sized crates, toe deep in a pool of shiny black water.

Slim was the first to speak as they all adjusted to the view. "What's Missals, Inc.?" Each of the five crates made of plywood and rough corner boards looked fairly new amidst the squalor of the basement and one was stenciled with small black letters.

"Must be religious stuff," Parker suggested, turning the crate away dismissively. He sloshed through the pool on the floor wiping his arms with the towel. "What a mess. The plumbing inspector is going to have a field day with this place." He paused to consider the situation and continued, "I hope I can talk my way through the permit and get this plumbing fixed. With our luck, they could really blow this out of proportion. Well, what they don't know can't hurt us."

Slim childishly taunted back, "He's gonna LIE, isn't he."

Luke smacked him lightly up the back of his head. "You better keep this a secret kid. Mr. Fox isn't going to lie, he just isn't gonna tell the whole story. And, your Grandma Pickens isn't about to crawl down here, so don't you be telling her either. You don't want to upset her with any more worrying."

Parker spoke to the crew. "Well, it looks like we've got this under control, for now anyway. Let's get out of here and clean up." He headed for the stairs while Gilbert continued to lumber around the crates. Gilbert paused and kicked at one of the crates, making a patter of hollow sounding thuds.

When Gilbert turned and began up the steps, Slim followed. His attention focused on Gilbert's soft and squishing shoes and the neat round hole in one that revealed a holey sock in turn. He was amazed with the sight, and felt a pang of guilt, knowing he was lucky to get new sneaks pretty regularly, care of the church donation stuff.

Luke looked around the basement wondering who was going to mop up the floor and bail out the excess water. Everyone was ahead of him heading up the steps. He certainly didn't want to be left down there alone in water teeming with critters with more legs and teeth. He clutched at his hurting gut and hurriedly pulled at the cord to switch off the light. He bounded upstairs and was behind Slim in less than a half dozen steps.

Luke whispered to Slim, "Getcher butt up these stairs and remember you don't have to lie, just don't tell the whole story. If the Reverend comes running to me all rattled, you're gonna be cleaning toilets at the Hudson Grille for six months. Tell her Mr. Parker has it all under control and will clean up after he gets back with the trade permit." As they reached the top of the steps, Luke poked the kid with a terse "Shh." He whispered his final directive through clenched teeth, "Just ACT scared."

Slim scampered across the floor to Blanche Pickens and to the huddled ladies in their flowered and plaid day dresses. Luke hung back hoping for the best from him.

Luke was caught off guard in his day dream when Parker barked at him again. "Luke, gimme your arm!" It took Luke half a half a nano-second to obey and recoil when he heard Parker continue. "Look at it. How did you get that scrape?"

Luke looked at it with horror, breathed in deep and it brought back the pain in his stomach. He wondered whether to play up the moment of dizziness and fall into the big damp sweaty arms; but he gamely reconsidered. He shuffled, carefully avoiding tiptoeing, behind his Florence Nightingale toward the sink in the corner of the room.

He tried to appear brave and nonchalant, especially when Parker off-handedly declared "I hope you're not always going to require this much maintenance."

Luke would cherish the word "always" at least for a couple of months, and didn't seem to mind that the whole room probably heard. He was sure he would have some explaining to do to the Reverend, whose frizzy mop of hair spun round at the exact moment the word was delivered.

Worse yet was the despairing look he got from Slim. The look asked, "How am I going to get the Reverend to believe it's all hunky-dory downstairs with you prancing around a bloody mess?" Then, Slim threw a different and knowing look over the rims of his glasses. The wise guy seemed to understand the notion of what was going on between Luke and Parker. Luke wondered how he got himself in the middle of so much good and bad in the same spoonful.

"There," Parker declared, "cleaned up almost like new. Why don't you get back to the Grille, and I'll catch up with you later after I've put Reverend Pickens at her ease."

Luke stammered, "I, really, uh, thank you. Hey! Breakfast's on me. Get back to the Grille as soon as you can, and it'll be ready waiting for you. Really, thanks."

"Why," Luke thought, "is he still holding my hand, and why am I pulling away trying to get back to the Grille, and why is his face so stoic, and why does it feel like he's pulling me back? Luke's hand slid from Parker's grasp and he turned to walk the long gauntlet in front of the circumspect plaid stares. He kept his eyes focused on the door ahead, daring to peek over his shoulder just once to see if Parker might be watching.

Parker was making a bee-line toward Blanche Pickens, and as he effused "My dear Blanche" Luke caught a glimpse of the Mission Mother responding with one of those looks out of the corner of her squint. Luke detoured past Blanche to reassure her, "I'll be by this afternoon with a big vat of lobster pasta. Your favorite!" Luke kept heading for the door assuring her that all this mess would be over soon.

If only that were true.

SEVEN

When Luke returned to the Grille, Jack gave him a look of utter amazement. "Where have you been, and LOOK at you, what on earth happened? It looks like you been gettin' some, out back in the dumpster! And your ARM, war wounds too?"

"Jack!" Luke interrupted. "The only thing squirting was the leaking pipe over at the Mission. I had to go help Park—Blanche, I had to go help Blanche. She came running over here, you should have seen her, like a twirling dervish!"

"Wait a minute mister." Jack had caught the bone and wasn't going to let go. "You were over there with Parker! Pulling on his pipe no doubt, you little hussy. Tell, tell, tell me now, how big, come on, details, I want details. You're filthy, absolutely filthy! I am loving this."

"Jack, calm down already. It was nothing really. The Mission has some serious problems downstairs, so don't go over there and try to get a story out Blanche. We're playing it down so she doesn't get frantic. Let's get back to the customers and I promise you I will fill you in on all the steamy details, LATER! Boy, you are nosy girl."

"Steamy! I'll bet. It looks like you worked up quite a sweat. Look at how damp you are, and what is that musty smell? Listen to me. This is not a good look for you. What are our customers going to think? Your shoes! They're ruined! Listen to that squishing sound you're making. Not pretty, not pretty at all. Get back there and put on my extra chef's jacket and make yourself presentable. Go. Get on now."

Luke went to the back and changed. He rushed to get back up front to help Jack with breakfast patrons, but also to preoccupy his mind with anything other than the swirl of his presumptions involving Parker. When he returned, Jack was leaning over the bar chatting up Parker who had returned to the Grille. Luke frowned and focused. "JACK! Go rustle up this man some breakfast. Go!"

Jack clucked his tongue loud enough to break the front window, turned on his heel and went back to do as he was told. As he passed Luke, they knocked shoulders and Jack mumbled sotto voce, "Work it tramp."

Luke marched forward asking Parker how the Reverend Pickens was holding up.

"She'll be okay. How's the arm?" Luke tipped his head left and Parker continued, "I only have time for a second cup, then I have to head down to meet with the City Engineer and get this permit thing out of the way. You better wish me luck. It's going to take a miracle. They really don't give out the paperwork without making some kind of inspection first. Hopefully they'll be too busy to get around to it until after I get things fixed."

Luke took note that it was unlike Parker to ramble nervously. "You'll be fine," Luke said earnestly. He turned to pour Parker fresh coffee and continued, "You just give them a good calm and serious act, and they'll let you slide through." He placed the cup of coffee in front of Parker, and reached below the counter. "Here, put this on." Luke tossed a fresh white folded T-shirt on the counter. "Your shirt is still wet."

Parker considered the white bundle, picked it up and snapped it open. "Good idea." In one quick motion, he pulled off his own shirt from the waist with crossed muscled arms without the slightest hesitation of self-consciousness.

As quick as it happened, Luke's mind ran the strip in slow motion. Orchestral music, twittering, chirping birds, orbits of twinkling stars, the works. Luke's eyes took in the belt buckle, navel nest, nicely rippled abs pulled taut in the stretch, a trail of fur up over broad pecs with nice cleft, primed nipples flanked by the delicious hollows of armpits that reached toward the ceiling. Parker's head popped out of the neck hole followed by the release of well rounded forearms. And the whole show reversed, as Parker climbed into the other T. Tug, stretch, pull, yum.

"Little tight?" Parker grinned as he was shoving his meaty paws in and out of his pants to tuck in the shirt.

"Nuh-uh," Luke said weakly. His locked knees broke, and his hands gripped at the inside edge of the bar, the only link to earth as he steadied himself. Parker stood erect and rocked his shoulders to settle into the clean, straining shirt. He smirked slyly at Luke for all it was worth, and Luke's gaze zoomed in for a close-up of the Hudson Grille logo and text arching perfectly over Parker's beckoning left breast.

Parker grabbed a swig from the mug of coffee. He leaned toward Luke and rested his forearms on the bar. "Gotta get going. I'll stop back later and let you know how it went with the permit."

Luke stood speechless as he watched Parker's locomotion as he headed out the door. His eyes burned with the image of the Grille's logo pulled across his quarry's chest followed by the tag line "Good Eats."

Jack came strolling back up front holding two plates of steaming breakfast looking around, up down, sideways and out under his elbow. "Whadidya do, eat him up already? Where'd he go?

Luke rolled his eyes looking around and asked, "Who?"

"Who, who? You're asking me who? You're standing there two feet off the floor with a shit-eating grin, halo, wings, a hard-on, and drool running down my new chef's coat!" Jack stood bouncing like a little boy begging for chocolate treats.

"Drool, there isn't any drool" Luke wiped fictional sweat from his brow and tried to look innocent in spite of an uncontrollable smile.

Jack stood there tapping his foot at Luke with a stare that demanded the whole story. It would only be a matter of time before Luke caved in unable to contain all the glee and glory, and Jack knew it would bubble up like any hot pot on his stove.

EIGHT

While things went bump in the plight of Mercy Mission, three stooges were having an early morning meeting of their own down at the Ward 4 Central Business District Bureau of Development office. There was the oleaginous Merritt Smears presiding, accompanied by Lou Thicke. Lou was the City Engineer and brother of Council Chairman candidate Greg Thicke. Lou, hard to imagine, was thicker than Greg in many respects. These included his neck, shoulders, waist and regrettably, his skull. He alone gave the constipated permit office its frustrating reputation and by all other accounts and events that crossed his path, the reputation of most engineers as well.

The last stooge was none other than the notorious media and property magnate "Big" Al Siegel. Al sat at the other head of the short table, dressed in a grubby suit, far too rumpled for so early in the morning. He was shoveling the whole of a blueberry crumb muffin into his mouth. There were more crumbs tumbling down the front of the suit, scurrying to escape.

The office was fairly prestigious in size and regularly appointed in that circa-60's city-salvage style. The walls, a predictable mold green, were thick with the mustard patina honed from several decades of second-hand tar and nicotine. Even the windows were coated with the opaque grime.

The crew was huddled around a small oblong table uncomfortably cramped close to one wall. It had obviously been moved there to make room for a lengthy, mechanized golf-putting astro-turf runway and the large chipping net, posed like a gauzy trampoline tilted on end. The room hung with a dense swirl of smoke from three power-chomped cigars.

In the middle of slobbering chomps from his fourth muffin, Al continued their conversation about his property now occupied by the Mercy Mission. "If we play our cards right, we can turn that old building into a goldmine. Beneath the street out front, are cable, power and telephone trunk line junctions that tie into to most of the northwest and east side of the town. If I move my operation over there, I'll save a bundle expanding my trunk line, have ten times more room to expand, and maybe even open up some production studio space. Now I know there might be a lot of opposition to this kind of business in that neighborhood, but given the tax income, discounted tax income it would generate, with your help it could turn out to be a win-win situation for all of us. And, if you give me the assistance I need, I won't mind letting you avail your-selves to some of our services as well as some, eh, reimbursement."

Thicke and Smears bobbed their heads with sickening glee. They weren't rubbing their hands together but you could see the dollar signs ringing up in their eye sockets and could sense they were sprouting little horns. Al waited for some verbal agreement or at least some response other than their moronic grins. The moment grew long and awkward.

Out front in the reception area Jerry Callahan was fervently spraying a can of air freshener toward the door to Merritt Smears' office, which billowed smoke from the edges of the jamb and overhead transom. The phone rang. Annoyed, he paused his fumigating. Normally, Jerry was assigned to clerical work and processing permits. As usual however, a colleague of his, who had worked an hour already, needed to take a nine a.m. lunch. He was grudgingly left alone to handle phones. Such was the life in bureaucracy.

He caught the phone on the fourth ring, and announced, "CBDBD Ward 4, Mr. Callahan speaking." He paused to listen and his face froze with utter surprise. "Uh huh. One moment please." He clicked that line on hold with professional precision, and clicked the intercom to Smears office. "Mr. Smears, pick up please."

He waited till he was sure Merritt picked up the handset. "You have a call. Don't think you want this one on speaker-phone. Dr. Sue Barrymore on line one." Jerry dropped his handset back into the cradle. He cast his glance toward the office door and sneered, "And you're welcome, asshole."

Inside the room, Merritt nearly tipped over backwards out of his red leatherette, brass-tacky high-back desk chair. He aimed for the blinking button on the console, and slowly jittered his extended index finger along a jagged path as though the flashing light might duck, dive and run away. When he connected, he spoke with boastful bravado for all to hear in spite of the schoolboy flutters ping-ponging his paunch. "Huh-lo beautiful! Are you trying to make my—"

On the other end of the line, chortling determination cut him off at the balls, so to speak, and got to the point. Merritt listened with a variety of exaggerated facial expressions and several loud misplaced coughing guffaws.

When he finally could add to the conversation, he shot his small load. "To-daay? I'd be de-LIGHTed." His nearly soprano reply caused the other two meatheads to wince as they orally gratified their smoking tobacco tools.

Jerry went back to spraying floral mist at the door; not only to keep the growing cloud at bay, but to try and forage for any overheard inklings from Line One. He was rewarded with mixed blessings. In between outbursts of insidious brewhah, the words Hudson and Mission that floated out on puffs of smoke flung themselves into the pit of his stomach like so many kamikaze poison darts. He gulped wondering how he would ever find his way out of the web weaving around him.

The other door, to the corridor, opened behind him with its burping grind, created by the built-up layers of paint on the jamb. Jerry whipped around startled. His heart skipped a beat at the interruption of his eavesdropping, then two more at the sight of the silver crew-cut topping off a nice collection of mounded muscles, weighty pouch and thighs filling out the pair of soft worn jeans. Jerry's voice cracked as he offered his cheeriest, "Good morning, help you?"

"Parker Fox, I'm here to meet with Lou Thicke at 9:15."

Jerry offered his hand across the low dividing wall that usually restrained the hoards of grumbling tradesmen and contractors. Parker met the match and Jerry introduced himself shaking the slab of hand that made him weak. The second Jerry's concentration broke from the handsome face, his eyes recognized the logo proudly presented on Parker's pec and he snapped his hand, arm and shoulder from the friendly grasp. It was if he got burned.

Parker acted surprised at the spontaneous reaction, then coughed as he caught wind of the smoke.

Jerry's head started to ache. Hudson Grille, Good Eats, Mercy Mission, Dr. Sue, handsome Fox, Luke, Jack, Merritt, Lou, Al, all up in smoke that crowded the room and made it hard to breathe. He started to hyper-ventilate. Then he hacked.

Parker reached across the wall and slapped Jerry on the back with few smart whacks. "Hey, hey, you okay?" Jerry patted his palms on the air in front of him to assure Parker that everything was fine.

Everything was obviously not fine, but Parker remembered Luke's advice of the 'calm and serious' and decided to stay quiet. After all he was in potentially hostile territory. No use fanning the flame or doing anything memorable. Just get in and get out.

Jerry stumbled back to his desk try to compose himself. He buzzed Merritt's office and declared efficiently, "Lou Thicke, your 9:15 appointment has arrived." He then went on with another bout of freshening spray that hung in the air as Lou stepped out from the office.

Lou flailed his arms through the cloud of freshened air like a gnat trapped in an insecticide mist. "Jeez Jerry, it smells like a friggin' women's room out here." He choked on his words as he saw Parker turn to meet him. Without a word, Thicke slipped back into the puffing room.

Lou rasped to his fellow conspirators, "You'd better stay put, I don't want any one to see us coming out of some m-e-e-t-i-n-g together." Lou swung back out to resume an introduction. As he reappeared through the door in another plume of gas, his upper teeth hung over his bottom lip while he tried to smile. The image of "Goofy Grape" of the Funny Face drink mix stirred Parker's memories and he stifled the urge to burst into laughter. Something was very wrong with this whole place today. He wanted to remark to Jerry, obviously family, with one of his favorite lines: "And they call ME queer?"

Lou approached Parker hastily. Parker took a step backward to brace his stance, his mouth curling with disgust. Lou's feet clop-clopped behind Jerry's desk and swerved through the opening in the low wall.

"Hi. I'm Lou Thicke. Have we met before?" He got close enough to shake Parker's hand, and therefore close enough to see the logo'd pec and perky nipple. Not that it was Thicke's thing, but the logo knocked him for a loop anyway. The Goofy Grape teeth gaped wider as their jaw dropped, and the caricature smile was replaced by a tense black hole below flared nostrils and mortified eyes.

"Parker Fox, I'm here to see if I can walk-through a trade permit for some minor work at a property over on U Street." Parker kept up the 'calm-serious' appearance with all the strength he could muster. He was on the verge of blurting out in spittle-spraying hysteria.

Lou paused to think for a moment. U Street and Hudson Grille seemed to mean Trouble in Dodge. It was really all too much for him to add, equate and total the parts so he decided to whisk through the whole thing so it would simply not exist anymore. He dealt with much of his life in the same manner. In hindsight, his wife, the kids, six of his former employers and even the mailman thanked God after they were vanished by Lou. Now that Lou had found his nepotistic niche here in the bureauc-

racy, he had found his true calling. He was also safe and soundly employed, thanks to the grace of his brother.

Lou's head had tried to spin around on his thick neck several
times. Then, without murmur or question, he snatched the paperwork
from Parker's paw, scribbled his signature, walked over to Jerry's desk,
picked up the official stamp, and pounded his pad then the paper back
and forth, five, count'em five times when one was quite enough. He
didn't say "Goodbye," "Have a nice day" or even "Fuck you." Lou Thicke
just turned and clopped back to the office and disappeared behind the
door.

Parker's disgust changed to disbelief and then utter relief. The
profound, ultimate, satisfying 'utter relief' familiar from a urinal experience after having held one's pee for several hours in stuck traffic. "Is he
always so, pneumatic?" Parker turned to Jerry, "What on earth was all
that about?"

Jerry sat and considered. He shook the scene out of his head, and
replied, "I gave up asking questions a long time ago. I'm the one that
usually pounds the pad around here, but if he wants to pound the pad, let
him. Just count your blessings, and get out of here before he changes his
mind."

Parker shrugged his shoulders, and turned to leave. He waved
over his shoulder, "See you around." He opened the grunting door and
escaped.

Jerry watched the choreography of muscle motion exit stage
right. The *pas de deux* of buns made him shiver. Then, his stomach had
that sinking feeling of being trapped in a Stephen King novel. He was
used to unusual behavior from Lou Thicke, but this time the guy seemed
truly possessed. The cast of characters, the call from Dr. Sue, catching
snippets about the Grille and then the Grille logo making an appearance
on Mr. Fox added up to trouble. Jerry knew that it was only a matter of
time before the other shoe dropped into his lap.

The door to Smears' office opened on a creaking hinge. Merritt's
head poked out at waist height and scanned the room for potential
guerrilla snipers. Gradually it appeared through the door attached to his
body. He announced the safe house with the code word, "Clear." His two
other cronies joined him in a mumbling huddle outside the door for a
round of humfing and hand-shaking. Lou went down the hall toward his
office. Al Siegel left through the front entrance, farting.

Jerry kept his gaze glued to shuffling paperwork on his desk, trying to appear unconscious of the meeting of meddling minds around him. He was the obedient civil servant, hoping everyone would go about their business. Jerry Callahan was so sensitive at that moment, he felt the chill in the air before him as a body eclipsed the warmth of fluorescent light in front his desk.

The shadow spoke and startled Jerry out of his feigned concentration. "Morning Callahan," Merritt bellowed. "Pull the utility plat plans for the blocks around 12th and U Streets. Hand-deliver them this afternoon to this address." He put a scribbled muffin-stained napkin on Jerry's desk with an assertive thump. I'll be out for a few hours attending a VERY important meeting so I won't be able to follow up. Make sure the plans are delivered." He went back to his office and shut the door.

Jerry inhaled slowly, and exhaled with relief. He used his arms to raise himself from the desk and began to count to ten. "Don't think, just do," he thought. He floated unconsciously to the plan room as if on a conveyor walkway, and began the task of unearthing the correct document from the flat file. He paged through the layers of drawings and pulled out the sheet, checking the streets to make sure it was the correct plan. His mind walked down the streets on paper of the familiar neighborhood. The overlay of veiny lines representing all the utility routing converged on the very block of Merritt Smears' request. Jerry's hands went numb cold, realizing he had walked down that street the night before.

Jack stood at the bar, spot-lit by sunrays pouring through the window of Hudson Grille. He inspected the card, flipping it over in one hand and holding the better portion of a lemon curd filled donut in the other. Lemon curd and donuts were so last season, but he loved them anyway.

"May be a cute lobbyist, but a city employee?" He weighed his considerations as critically as choosing between Prada and Lauren. These were decisions that could truly affect the course of life. "Fuck it," he said to himself with abandon. He dialed Jerry Callahan's office number. His mind dreamed about the warmth of those strong thighs warming his ears, a sack of nuggets hanging above his serpent tongue and waiting to strike while the iron was hot.

A dollop of lemon curd rolled off the edge of Jack's lip. He caught it with his finger and licked.

Jerry was running blueprints when the phone peppered him with its annoying bleep. He jerked, ground his teeth, yanked the handle off the wall set and managed the whole spiel in one breath. "CBDBDWard4 CallahanCanIhelpyou."

Jack rankled and pulled the phone away from his ear. "Mm, Miss Girl has a thorn up her butt, doesn't she," he thought. He continued speaking with the cheeriest stream he could garner. "My name is Jack Betz and I'm calling from the 'Let's Make a Betz Show' that I can bring some sunshine into the life of—let me see here, is a Mr. Jerry Callahan available?" He stood with the phone in his hand as he puckered his lips and threw his eyelashes up toward the glinting bronze ceiling. He waited to the sound of deaf silence on the other end of the line. When the pause lasted for more than an unbearable two seconds, he continued, this time a little louder. "I'm try-ing to reach a Mr. Jerr-ee Cal-laa-haaen? JERRY! Snap OUT of it!"

Jerry's crankshaft turned over and allowed a smile to waft across his face. He breathed a sigh of relief, hugged the receiver in his hand and spoke to his savior at the other end. "Good grief, you have ab-sol-utely no idea how great it is to hear your voice." But the relief of a friendly voice was short when his stomach flipped over the morning's string of coinci- dences, this being another. He considered what to say next.

Small girl-talk seemed like a good start. "It's been quite a morn- ing around here. If I knew it was you on the line, I certainly wouldn't have gabbled like that. I apologize. I see Luke did me the favor of passing on my card. I'm really glad you used it."

Jack replied, "You talk to me like THAT again, and I'll wash your mouth out and it won't be with soap, mister."

Jerry countered, "I can just imagine what you have in mind, but if it's as good as that lamb you dished up last night, I'll scream a little louder this time and be right over! It was terrific."

"Go on, go on...go on and on and on! How did you know? I LOVE being buttered up!" Jack also loved to banter. "And, if you keep it up, I'll be serving you my Puffed Daddy instead of my little ol'lamb chop"

"Stop it, STOP it. You're gonna make me SCREAM—" Jerry was laughing out loud.

"Hold the screaming," Merritt Smears snarled behind him, "and all that carrying on till after hours, Callahan. We're paying you to be of service, not chat people up on the City's phone." There was dead silence in the room and Jerry turned rhubarb red. Smears continued bossing, "AND they'd BETTER be those plans I asked you for or you're going to be laughing yourself right out the front door. I'm going to my meeting now. Whether I'm coming back or not, well—you'll just have to stay on your toes. Not that you don't flutter around on them as it is."

Jerry stood stunned and waited till the door burped and slammed shut. Then with vengeance, he growled through his teeth, "Lick my asshole, you prick."

Jack nearly dropped the receiver. "A little difficult through the phone, but if you insist..."

"No, not you. My boss, that gross hog. He just gave me a rash of shit. Thank God he's gone. Look, I gotta finish running these blueprints; then I have to deliver them somewhere over in your neighborhood. How 'bout I drop by the Grille after lunch sometime. I think there's a few things I need to tell you about."

Jack's brain started flashing the warning lights. "Oh shit," he thought. "Here it comes. I should have known better than to go foraging for dick in the city morgue. Okay, it isn't the morgue, but what's the difference?"

NINE

Merritt Smears took a cab up to Chevy Chase. The chill was gone from the morning air and the day was starting to heat up. Inside the cab it was even hotter. Merritt cringed as he slid into the back seat when he caught sight of the driver. Though it was hard to expect a jolly, white Irish hack in DC, it wasn't hard to imagine Merritt Smears never getting over such a simple everyday fact of life. It seemed to insult the very core of his being. The cabbie's beaded wood seat cover was distasteful to him. The stench of incense invading his every pore annoyed him. The Rasta-Peruvian-Samba music blaring from the ten dollar radio grated on him. He could have just enjoyed the sunny scenery on the drive uptown. Instead he got what he deserved.

The cab ground to a halt in traffic even though it was mid-morning. They were six blocks from Salon OZ. Merritt was working up to a nervous breakdown and in his frustration decided to walk the rest of the way. He didn't even inform the driver. He just opened the door and hopped out. The cabbie started shouting, but from the imagined safety of the curb, Merritt just started giving the foreigner a barrage of garbled syllables, rude arm gestures and the finger before he sped off into the crowd.

Sweat was pouring down his forehead and bleeding through the lining, interfacing and cheap fabric of his jacket. The wet spots under his arms, down his back and on the seat of his pants joined the white rings of previous perspiration episodes, most likely as far back as April and the last time he visited the dry cleaner.

By the time Merritt reached the salon, having knocked into several old ladies in his path as well as pissing-off the cab driver, his humor was improving. The warm anticipation of being pampered at OZ, the frisson of an assignation (isn't that what she intended?) with Dr. Suzette, and the flattery of an appearance on Town Hall, LIVE! added up to a potent stimulant. While he exuded bravado worthy of a trapped bull, inside he was hanging on to stretched nerves and oddly giddy about his manic prospects with the less fortunate peons left in his wake. He entered the salon giggle-coughing.

Liz was at home, sitting on her bed cross-legged surrounded by mounds of fluffy white duvet. Everything in the room was fluffy and white in one way or another. Eyelet here, lace there, from sculptured carpet to the gauzy canopy above her head, fluffy and white. Her head was wrapped in a white turban towel. She was swaddled in a plush white hotel robe. The sun streamed in to warm the pristine feminine retreat of softness. Her head leaned to hold the phone as she cautiously painted her nails red.

"Well, it's about time you found someone to go heels over head about. Ever since you got into the restaurant business, I thought you had completely given up trying to tie the knot. The only knots you have been tying are in your stomach." Liz gingerly took the phone in thumb and forefinger and gently blew at the nails on her other hand. "If you let this last for longer than twenty-four hours you're gonna have to let me meet this Fox."

"Oh, by the way," she sighed. "I'm having the OZ-blahs today. I always feel so guilty the morning after I ax a receptionist. Poor Bethany was in tears when I told her we couldn't make another day more beautiful with her manning the front desk." Liz accelerated. "Then, I get an earful from Enrique. He tells me he needs five days notice to prepare himself to handle celebrity hair. I almost choked him. When he said I owed him to hire his cousin from Recoleta or somewhere, I nearly choked him again! So, I didn't tell him I was up against the wall without a receptionist and I made him wait three hours while I supposedly thought about it. He asked me about it every twenty minutes until he was literally begging me to give that kid a job. When I finally mentioned a possible opening for a receptionist, I had him dancing around the salon using curlers for castanets. The things I've done for immigrants. I deserve a citation—"

"Liz, Liz? LIZ! My ear is numb!" Luke was happily straightening out the drawer at the maitre d' stand, but he loved to remind Liz when she tended to go on. Of course it didn't hurt that he was floating around on cloud nine and a half, or maybe ten. "So have you met this new receptionist?"

"Uh, no. But Enrique swears 'that I will love heeem.' I figure if I don't love 'heeem' then Enrique will owe ME and I can get him under control. Of course I love all the business his hip hugger pants bring to the salon. But there's room for only one reigning Queen at OZ, and that's me."

Merritt felt immediately refreshed with the rush of ice-cold hair spray air as he opened the door and entered OZ. He could get used to coming to this bastion of beauty knowing that only a guy completely sure of his manhood would dare be seen in such a place. He also got the opportunity to chat up some pretty decent looking rich snatch. He was actually doing Liz a favor with his patronage.

The new receptionist rolled his eyes at the sight of Merritt Smears and wondered if he should high-tail it back to Argentina. "Good morning, belcome to Oss. May we help jew?"

His cousin Enrique had coached him all morning with the subtle nuances of the English language and they had practiced the greeting dozens of times. It was the bottle blonde leading the bottle blonde. Alberto Culver (pronounced "Cool-bear" in Spanglish) and his mentor had been up late celebrating his first job, and he would long be indebted to cousin Enrique.

Four-foot-eleven Alberto barely cleared the top of the reception counter. His twenty-five inch waist and perky butt were swallowed up in the swivel chair as he swung his feet from the edge. He felt quite grown up at such a prestigious salon, and thought he looked very sexy in his sister's black stretch see-through lace shirt. It was a men's cut, except for the ruffle collar. He hoped Miss Osbourne would be pleased with his style.

Alberto was having much more fun in his mental reverie than dealing with the gross man before him. He had put him on hold as if he were the phone. "He thinks he can get my attention with all that finger-drumming on my reception desk, he's got another think coming," Alberto thought (in Spanish) and kept his long black eyelashes and his copper tone complexion fixed on the appointment book before him. He ran the end of his pen up one column, down the other, flipped the page and started again. He continued his search for possible boy-band star bookings.

Merritt Smears stood there beginning to work up a new head of steam. It didn't do much for his comb-over. "HEY! Sweetheart, you wanna get me hooked up with a haircut or not?"

Alberto twirled his finger to the intercom button and chirped, "En-rri-que, jew hab a cli-ent-eh..."

Enrique's head appeared from the portal of the backroom followed by his body. The muscles moved like Martha Graham and were painted with his shiny white T-shirt and black velvet bell bottoms. He ran manicured nails through his black streak and tipped mane then wrung his fingers before perching in front of Merritt. "Meester Smear, back so soon? Mees Osbourneh not-a here jet! Jew hab appointment?"

"NOT HERE? Waddyoumean not'here?" Merritt boomed, start-ling the looks of the few ladies in various stages of repair around the salon. Alberto cowered in his seat, the nail of his center finger hooked on a lower tooth.

"She not arrive yet! But I could feex you eef jew like, come, come, En-rrique take goood care of jew." Enrique pulled the stained elbow of Merritt's suit and dragged him across the floor. They both looked morti-fied for whole sets of distinct reasons.

Merritt muttered along with a patter of, "but, but, but."

Enrique told him not to worry. He swept the large biscuit-colored bib around Merritt, laid him down in the chair, shoved his head into the sink with insistent fingertips and turned on the spray nozzle for a vigor-ous de-lousing. "Mr. Smear, stop SHAKING! Ebrreeting gonna be alright. En-rrique make jew look wandaful." He twirled a steaming hot towel around Merritt's face, mostly to muffle the man's whimpering and got to the business of scrubbing scalp into a soapy wig. A squeak caught in Enrique's throat when his dangling charm bracelet snagged in the length of unraveled comb-over. Merritt snorted at the tug to his head and Enrique continued a slower massage with the snagged arm. He pushed his groin into Merritt's shoulder and laid his tight tummy across the damp towel muting Merritt's garble to stretch a reach for the scissors. His pelvis humped at Merritt. He grabbed the scissors, lifted the snare on his wrist, snipped with authority and released a full breath.

He resumed the soapy kneading with double-time fervor ripping dripping hair from his wrist on every third beat. Soapy water flew in torrents toward Merritt's bib and turned Enrique's tight white-T magi-cally translucent. " Meester Smear laaaub Enrique strrong massage? Meester Smear feel berry relax, no?" He theatrically worked the final spray rinse, slowly moving the armed spigot from hot to cold. He pulled the damp towel from Merritt's face, patted with a dry one, lifted Merritt up to sit, and wrapped his head in a tight turban. Jowly Merritt looked like the other jowly matrons being serviced around the room.

"Ok-ee doe-kee." Enrique prodded Merritt's shoulders to help him stand. Merritt obeyed as listlessly as a nursing home patient being led by the hand and paraded in front of the seated matrons who strained not to miss a beat of the dramatic choreography. Whether they were mesmerized by Enrique's damp nipples or Merritt's impersonation of a drag queen with out her make-up was hard to tell. Their heads leaned clockwise like feeding finches.

"Come, come," urged Enrique. Merritt sat down in the chair facing Enrique and spoke weakly, "Look sweetheart, I gotta be on TV in an hour. Could you just get through your business without all the bullshit? I can't understand a fucking word you're saying. And, if you give me some fag haircut, I'll have your nuts cut off. Do you under-standay?"

Enrique could sense the insolent tone. He shifted course. He cocked his head and, through slits for eyes, glared at the back of Merritt's wet hair in the mirror. He lunged for clippers, whip-lashed the cord and turned the power on high with a vengeance. Merritt braced his arms and planted his feet. He tried in vain to nudge the chair around so he could keep an eye on the buzzing madness. Enrique tucked his butt and clenched the seat of the chair between his knees to hold it in place. He hunched over his victim and worked with a frenzy. He ran the clippers up the sides and down the back, working the comb and machine like a Teppanyaki chef. Merritt continued to buck the chair. Enrique clenched his butt, knees and teeth tighter for the finish. A minute-thirty-four seconds later the drone of the clippers was silenced. Satisfied, he took a giant step out of the way allowing the chair to fend for itself under Merritt's building pressure. Merritt spun out of control.

Little Alberto popped from his chair clutching his necklace and fanning himself like an overheated sorority sister. He mewed little squeaks between bouts of hyperventilation. Enrique whipped his cell phone from his rhinestoned hip holster to speed dial Liz. Merritt's shoes squeaked their way cautiously over to the mirror. Was an uptown haircut usually so expeditious?

TEN

The frosted round incandescent bulbs framed Dr. Sue's face as she sat in front of the apricot lacquered counter and mirrors. Her face twisted and stretched, performing mute mouth and tongue enunciation exercises. Behind her, the smug male attendant clad in snug trendy black worked a curling iron in her hair. As he paused for hair to set, he reached for the spray can and caught her mastications. He was reminded of a fish sucking scum from its bowl and knew better than to mention it to his humorless assignee. As she added humming and guttural noise to her routine, his mind tried to fast forward through the dubbed porn-like soundtrack. What might have turned on the average white male reviled his gay sensibility. He focused on curling while his stomach recoiled.

When he paused to review his art, Sue over-articulated a deep alto "Thahn-quue Rahn-dee," as his dismissal.

As he gathered his implements, balms, brushes and spackling pots, a fist knocked on the shiny black doorframe. Dozens of eyes turned to look, the multiple faces of Randy and Sue echoing across walls lined with gilt framed mirrors hanging on volumes of velvet apricot swagger. With the black mirror ceiling it was reminiscent of Halloween in the not-so-fun house. Randy, attempting to vanish, squeezed by the man in the doorway, and wrinkled his nose at the smell of stale cigars, sweaty summer-weight wool and barber talc.

Sue seated, swiveled then squirmed in her chair, charmed at the sight before her. Her chin lowered and lashes lapped her batty blinking eyeballs. The signature smile, once again warming a well powdered face broke to deliver its lip-smacking venom. "Oh Merritt daahling, what HAVE you done?"

Merritt Smears stood sheepishly in the doorway like a sorry Samson wondering if he still had his powers. His eyes begged at the Delilah before him.

Dr. Sue lifted herself from the swivel chair in a flurry of apricot chiffon dressing robe and a sidekick from her peachy marabou mules. She gargled an 'R' in the back of her throat for the full four counts it took her to reach her prey. "General Smears, you look absolutely military!" She purred as she moved around him in the jamb. "It's amazing how a crew cut can make a man look so, uh, distinguished. In fact, just last night I imagined you hitting the beach like my little Schwarzkopf." She brushed her tines across his stubbly head. His little soldier was saluting for the both of them.

The intercom clicked. "Ten minutes Dr. Barrymore."

She pulled him into the room by his earlobe and shut the door. "We need to keep you a secret for the moment. Have a seat while I change into my TV personality and try not to drool on the carpet." She turned away from Merritt in the proper sense but worked every mirror in the room as she slipped off her gown and let it drop to the floor. "So, Merritt, what ever made you cut off your hair?" She reached for the navy blue skirt with all her puffiness trussed up like a pale, pebbled capon in lycra white lace underthings. Her sex appeal was a mix of wanton willingness and a smattering of actual glamour. "Tigers usually don't change their stripes, especially at your age..." It was like a big pot calling Pa Kettle black.

Merritt winced at the barb but sat behaved, jittering and playing with his fingers (or something) in his lap. He realized he was alone in the same room with Dr. Sue Barrymore while she gave him a private show. He ogled her ample cleavage as the tease unwound, his reverie compounded with visions of Enrique working him over with possessed clippers. It took a long moment for Dr. Sue's question to register in his consciousness, time enough for him to twist his tale. "They, uh, didn't finish my trim yesterday, so I had to go back before the show today. I told that fag to clean it up, figuring a dame like you would get a kick out of it. You do like it, don't you?"

Dr. Sue was paying scant heed to Merritt's pubescent insecurity as well as to his physical discomfort. She was absorbed in her own perverse delusions, plotting to manipulate this fragile figure before her into a thorn to prick the boundless ego of Big Al. A perfect double down! She put underarm shields in the pits of her jacket, thrust herself inside and her boobs toward Merritt, then buttoned up to the neck. The doctor was now 'on' and nervously hoped that everything would go as planned. To string him along her path, she spun out her leash. "Merritt sweetheart, if we didn't have to do this show, I'd have you use that sexy new brush cut to wake up my little Suzy."

By this time, Merritt's senses were raw like bundles of nerve endings trying to find a brain. Even his pants were panting. He shot up from his perch and flung his arms to embrace her just as she bent over the counter to inspect her lip liner in the mirror. As his arms missed and continued in motion to hug himself, his voice pleaded, "Suzette, whatever you say…" He wrung his hands and fell to his knees.

She snapped, leaving him without a leg to stand on, "Okay Merritt, pull your self together, it's show time. Time to make sure we shut down that obscene triathlon. Make sure you give me some good ammunition from the business angle. COME ON! What on earth are you doing down there on the floor?"

As he groaned to get back up, she grabbed the crook of his arm to hasten their exit. He barreled into her as she was opening the door. "MERRITT," she screeched, "Get OFF me!" Dr. Sue heaved him with an elbow, turned to peek out the door and survey the corridor. "Are you ready now? We can't have anyone see you coming out my dressing room. They'd have a field day with that one."

Merritt snorted behind her.

As they entered the gray, fluorescent hallway of the Siegel Studios, the black vinyl floor enunciated the clatter of Dr. Sue's heels and accentuated the squeak in Merritt's shoes. They sounded like an un-oiled machine. Sue greeted passing assistants in the hall with curt words, loud plastic smiles and her nervous head panning the doorways that flanked their route.

Yesterday, she had met with the Mayor. He was his usual convivial political persona, and she felt especially encouraged at getting in to see him at a moment's notice. His response to her pleading concerns of conservative residents readying for the onslaught of amoral, sex-seething gay men, women and whatever seemed genuine. He was patient, kind and responded to her cues. He had even told her he would be glad to appear on the show. She was so elated, that she ran back to her place, freshened up and headed straight to Big Al's with her news. Perhaps it was fortunate that she never got to tell him, because this morning, the Mayor's appointment administrator called with regrets. Damn, she had had to call Merritt Smears for Plan B. She was all the more determined to claw her way up another rung on the ladder in Al's eyes.

Lost in thought, she continued to drag Merritt down the hall. Her stomach became nervous and giddy the closer they got to the sound stage. Before they reached the summit, they had to pass Al's office. Her neck and head began to flush. Steps from the doorway, she slowed down, hoping to pass unnoticed. With herself and Smears planted on the set to start the show, it would be no turning back. She would hold the reins.

"Barrymore! I can hear you clomping from a mile away. Wait a MINUTE, Smears?" Al's bark preceded his bite. His short stout girth entered from his office. Sue stopped in her tracks and gasped. Merritt stumbled into Sue. Al's face reddened before anyone could shift into damage control. Al's interrogation superseded all other reaction. "Smears! What the hell are you doing here? Where's the damn Mayor?"

At the same time, Dr. Sue managed to squeeze in, "Al! That SNIVELING excuse for a Mayor STIFFED us. Thank God Merritt Smears was good enough to fill in for today's show."

Merritt choked up on a phlegm ball.

The assistant producer screamed from the stage door, "Dr. Barrymore! Fifteen seconds!"

She grabbed Merritt's arm and pulled him toward the set. It was not a good idea to cross Al's bullshitting rages, but Dr. Sue was determined to assert her lusty mettle against Siegel's fiery ego. "STUFF IT AL," she shrieked. As they clicked and squeaked away, Al stood planted to the floor with fists clenched stiffly at his sides.

Sue made it to her seat of power and commanded the submissive Smears to sit, just in time for the start of the theme music to Town Hall, LIVE! The announcer began his introduction, and Dr. Sue Barrymore turned in her chair to deliver today's exceptionally forced signature smile to the camera.

With the chaos of the flooded Mission behind her, thanks to the kind hands of Mr. Parker and Mr. Luke, Reverend Blanche Pickens walked the short distance home reassured. She flopped down in the parlor of the pastor's modest row house next to the church. It was the kind of room one expected inside the painted brick Federal style, narrower than most, with a haphazard collection of un-antique old furniture and threadbare oriental upholstery. The hand work on the doilies and curtains provided her with a hobby, not that she had time for one really. She tossed her feathered hat down beside her in exhaustion and hit the remote.

The theme music to Town Hall, LIVE! struck up and Dr. Sue smiled. Blanche released a disgusted snort. "That woman make my skin crawl," she declared out loud.

The TV theme song revved to its churning finale and the start of the announcer's voice over. "*Tuesday, October 29th. Good Afternoon and welcome to Town Hall, LIVE! Today's Topic? Transvestite Triathlon: The Mayor's Response. We'll be right back after this commercial message.*" Dr. Sue leaned in toward Merritt, placing a friendly grip on his forearm and rewarding an even glossier smile to the side of his newly shaved head.

At that moment, the phone rang. "Yes," she told the caller, "I am watchin' the show." With that, Blanche hardly got a word in edgewise for three minutes. "Well Jibbers," she countered finally, "she sure got your dander up. A good thing you didn't appear. It's an abomination, objectin' to a few men dressin' up like women. They are God's children tryin' to help our community." And then, "Sure, I can be at your office at five this afternoon. Take care of my niece now! Yes, I will see you tomorrow. Bye now!"

"Good Afternoon, welcome to Town Hall, LIVE! I'm Dr. Sue Barrymore and today we continue to discuss the travails our citizens will have to endure IF they are besieged with this Transvestite Triathlon. As I mentioned yesterday, I went straight from this show to our Mayor's office on YOUR behalf. We spoke at great length, and he even agreed to come on today's show. Of course OTHER pressing matters seemed to develop this morning preventing his appearance. But the Triathlon IS a pressing matter here in Ward District 4. To that end, we welcome today's guest, the Ward 4 Business District Bureau of Development director, Merritt Smears."

Dr. Sue turned from the camera, can-canning one leg over the other as she turned to face her guest. "Merritt, what is your opinion regarding the state of torment the citizens in your neighborhood feel toward the upcoming revelry this Thursday night?"

Merritt sat in his chair, unsure whether to glance at Sue or stare at the camera. He did both, repeatedly. When Dr. Sue softly gripped his forearm to stir him to speak, he twitched. "Merritt?"

"Yes, yes, first of all, thank you Dr. Sue for having me on your program today. It is indeed a rare privilege. My honest opinion of the Triathlon situation is that we will have citizens forced to lock themselves in their homes and business owners in fear of looting and vandalism. This is not right. I would like to beseech the Mayor to look into this matter and its gravity, enlist a task force and put the police department on alert with riot containment squads." He sat back in his chair like a zombie in slow motion, folded his arms, and smiled with the pleasure of finishing a bowel movement.

"Task force?" Dr. Sue sneered. "It will be Groundhog's Day before the Mayor approves a task force. What's at stake here is not a drag queen's choice of appropriate heels. We are talking about gangs of hoodlums. HOMO-sexual and trans-VESTite HOODLUMS. They will turn our fair northwest neighborhood into a war zone like northeast! All that rampant disrespect! It will be like the slums of Harlem. HARLEM!" At that point she was shaking Merritt's arm with such force, he was holding onto his chair as if it were a bronco bull.

Dr. Sue broke her hold on Merritt and tried to compose herself, back across the line she had just crossed. "If these people really wanted to be of service, they would put on a bake sale. They could start a clothing drive. They could stay off the streets and make their donations to the churches from the privacy of their own back yards. After all, these people don't have children. They don't have to spend time teaching phonics. They've come out of their closets and have filled them with more clothes. They have the time to bake cakes and play with make-up! I say they should put these addictions to better use helping their community, well away from our impressionable children. I urge all the citizens of this city to call or e-mail the Mayor's office. Tell him to put his foot down and STOP their hedonism." Back on the other side of the line, Dr. Sue had managed to dig a much deeper hole.

Blanche Pickens fell back into her seat, hands aloft like a hold-up. "OH NO she didn't! Not only did she slander our families in northeast, she had to take that bus ride all the way up to Harlem. Oh she is in for some BIG surprise this time. That baggy-butt whitey don't know who she's up against!" She high-fived the couch in anticipation of her visit to City Hall.

Jack was planted in front of the TV at Hudson Grille, steaming as usual from the lunchtime antics. "Riots from transvestites? The only riot will be from two drag queens fighting over the last set of press-on nails down at Trina's House of Beautee! I'll give her a CLOSET! And a friggin' CAKE!"

ELEVEN

Luke had waited all morning for the return of his knight in shining 'amour.' He had recounted for Jack every moment in the basement of the Mission with Parker. Jack sat on the edge of the barstool through every drip, twist and slosh, and was duly impressed by Luke's dive over the crate to fetch the rag for his wanting master. It was like sharing the hopes, dreams and drives of kindred sisters. They giggled and squealed as if in the very presence of a pseudo-Menudo pop star.

Except for a brief tirade with Dr. Sue, Jack kept up a supportive muster through the lunch shift, assuring Luke that Parker Fox had not fallen into competing clutches down at City Hall. By 2:30, he had to reassure Luke that Parker had not moved to Burma with a religious cult or disappeared like some Incan god from Machu Picchu, settling on the more likely jaunt to 7-11 for a Slurpee. Luke was in a desperate fever, when at 3:34 his he-man arrived in time for a late lunch.

Inside, Luke was like a tossed salad. He wanted to gush at Parker, ask him if the permit inspectors had tied him down, flayed open his shirt, clamped on electrodes and served him a permit where he least expected. Instead the wiser Luke stayed calm and said, "Hey man, how'd it go?"

Parker pulled up to the bar, straddled the seat with flanks of denim thigh and crossed his forearms to work up some extra cleavage for Luke. "Smooth," he replied. "Too smooth in fact. Kinda Stepford even. Whatever. I got the permit. How about a Heiny?"

Luke caught the beer request a quarter second too late. His mind had dragged Parker back into the stockroom for late lunch. Parker felt the electric jolt from Luke's facial expression, but neither had the chance to elaborate. Jerry Callahan walked by the front window of the Grille and entered.

The ricochet of introductions and dialog that ensued wove wonder amongst the four until they unraveled themselves back into understanding. Jerry outlined the mystery meetings, suspicious behaviors and sketchy tales he had overheard, and with the evidence of the address he had just delivered the plans to, they put together the pieces of the puzzle. It did not paint a pretty picture.

Luke was scared. Jack was incensed, and Jerry secured the admiration of Jack. Parker, after giving Luke a goodbye hug that Jack promptly imitated with Jerry, went off to report to his boss Jon Miller. He realized he was not sure how to approach that discussion. His boss was a business partner of one of their suspects, and the holder of a permit issued by another.

The granite steps trembled under Reverend Pickens as she made her way to the Mayor's office with Slim and Gilbert in tow. She had insisted on them giving her moral support. Blanche Pickens huffed, a little out of breath, "That fool Dr. Sue, she has no idea who she's dealin' with around here." Slim and Gilbert caught up with her and took an arm on either side.

"Grandma Pickens, you are the bomb," Slim charmed.

"Dr. Sue, start singin' a psalm, Rev'ren Pickens gonna ignite her napalm with no qualm," Gilbert quipped, his eloquence surprising everyone.

Blanche's influence in this place had substance. It lay in the fact that she grew up with the Mayor in the very neighborhood she was defending. While the Mayor carefully played his cards between all parties alike, his marriage to Blanche's niece racked up more points than some watery third rate TV show, no matter what the ratings. Blanche didn't like doing it often, but when really and truly riled up, she could rattle the cage of kin.

As the motley trio stepped onto the marble floor, it was reduced to a duo. Gilbert had come this far, he said, but he did not feel comfortable in such places. Blanche shrugged. She could probably do as well without the scruffy authenticity that Gilbert provided. She walked up to the security guard and asked how his mother was doing with the flu before she and Slim took the elevator ride up to the fifth floor. She marched herself and her young bodyguard past an astonished assistant and through the Mayor's office door without pause.

The Mayor rose from his chair to meet Blanche halfway before they clasped hands. "Bee-zy," he declared, "How good to see you! You made it here in record time. Didn't break any speed limits, did you?"

"Jibbers, there ain't no speed limits for the broom I'm on today, but I nearly broke an ankle on all them steps outside! I might just sue the city and build myself a new church and mission! Slim here is one of my flock. I take it you saw the rest of that WOMAN yesterday?"

"Eh-hem." A man seated in front of the Mayor's desk stopped the family conversation. Greg Thicke rose from his chair and joined the small crowd before him. "Reverend Pickens, how good to see you. The Mayor and I were just talking about that woman…"

"Greg Thicke, what a surprise. Recoverin' from your appearance on Town Hall, LIVE! yesterday?" Blanche surveyed the man with mock concern.

"A very close call. I don't know what my campaign manager was thinking. I stopped by to discuss it with the Mayor, and I understand he called you. Frankly, Dr. Barrymore scares me in the worst way."

The Mayor went back to have a seat at his desk. He sat in the swivel chair and looked out over folded hands. "This darn race has been running every Halloween for years. The people love it, and it always raises thousands of dollars for the local church charities. This is the first year Dr. Barrymore has decided to stir up a conservative backlash, but I am not going to risk irritating the moderate voters as well as the gays, blacks, elderly and the other half of the business community by calling it off. I've received a total of one e-mail since the end of the show today, and that was from Dr. Sue."

The Reverend seized her cue. "I am sick to death of these news people stirrin' up petty issues for the sake of ratings. As if it isn't hard enough out there dealin' with real issues. Now, I don't pretend to understand why these men enjoy playing dress-up, but if they want to raise some money to help neighborhood programs, I say we should cheer them on at the finish line."

"Maybe we can show our solidarity by dressing up with high heels and marching on Town Hall, LIVE! tomorrow." Everyone turned to look at Greg Thicke like he just ate a toad.

"Greg, re-engage your brain," cautioned the Mayor.

Slim looked around awkwardly, not sure what to say.

Blanche was the only one holding her tongue for a moment of thought. "Mr. Thicke, that is one smart idea. Wednesdays are Open Forum on Town Hall, LIVE! I think I will invite myself and a few friends on her show tomorrow! I might even lend them some clothes and shoes if you catch my drift. Mayor, Greg? If you'd like to join in…"

The Mayor looked at Reverend Blanche. "Beezy, you know I support you and all your work. You all know I try to maintain a live and let live policy in even with the most extreme of my constituents. But you have to understand, this is my living. I have to get those voters back in two years, and well, Greg has to get them in less than a week. I think we had better toe the line and sit this one out. Besides, what would your niece have to say if she found me rooting through her closets?"

Before Blanche had a chance to respond, the Mayor's assistant paged him on the intercom.

"Mayor, Jon Miller for you on line six." By lifting the phone, the mayor had escaped some fiery napalm.

"Jon, good to hear from you. I hope you aren't calling me about that Barrymore show." He paused to listen, raised his eyes to the ceiling, let his mouth dance around in grimace and ran a hand up his forehead to scratch the crown of his hair. "I see. This sounds unfortunate. Give me a day and I will get back to you. Yes, thank you for calling. I'll see what I can find out." The Mayor hung up the phone and returned to the conversation before him in a more serious mood.

But Blanche beat him to it. "Mr. Jon Miller? He owns our Mercy Mission buildin'. What's he want?"

"Blanche, Slim my boy, it's nothing for you to worry about. But something has come up that I have to attend to, and it sounds like you need to get going to ramp up your, um, storming of the studios?"

"Oh Jibbers, you always have to attend to somethin'. Anyway thanks for sidin' with us about Barrymore and the triathalon and lettin' me blow off a little steam." She walked over to the Mayor for a short hug and goodbye.

When Greg turned to shake the Mayor's hand and leave also, the Mayor spoke to him softly to one side. "Greg, if you have a moment, there's something we need to discuss."

TWELVE

He had already asked for explanations of purple chicco, purple potatoes, taro, yarrow and chevre. Now Jerry risked the machete madness of Jack at work by posing yet another query. "And what's that green stuff over there?" Jack, nearly whistling Dixie, smartly told him all about the true subtleties of mache. Such was love in those provocative stages before early, long before surly.

Dinner rush was winding down. It was a happily busy Tuesday at the Grille. There was lots of slicing, slinging and flinging. Jack was slicing. Luke was slinging. Jerry was flinging. It was a merry madhouse for mid-week. Waiters for now only appeared on weekends, and they were friends and acquaintances picking up tips and minimum wage for what still seemed like a party. The Hudson-Betz magic had yet to lure Jerry into the fold.

"Speaking of mache, the cat just dragged in. Hi Liz, how's our girl tonight?" Jack tried to be as nice as his pride would allow. Aside from her cash register ringing more quickly, Liz had an uncanny knack for bagging more men than Jack. It was almost as bad as being assured that her hair always looked better. Of course she did own a hair salon. Bitch.

"Is that Jack Betz, soon to be the *Washingtonian*'s Best New Chef of the Year speaking to me?" Liz tried to be as nice as her pride would allow. There was nothing worse that being out-best-girlfriended by a boy. And thanks to Jack, she and Luke went shopping a whole lot less these days. Of course she did own a hair salon now. Their schedules were as different as night and day.

Liz stood looking very uptown in this very downtown neighborhood. Her freshly tossed mid-length hair, each strand frosted to look unnaturally natural in honey, strawberry blonde and mocha shadow; a perfectly pressed pale olive linen suit contrasting well with a mellow tan and make-up highlights behind enviable eyeglasses along with nails and lips in ruby presented itself as a well wrapped package. So did the rich camel clutch and simple gold ear discs. The sensational shoes were a whole other story.

"The girl is fine tonight, thank you." She sat down on a stool at the Chef's Table before Jack's culinary pulpit. "It looks like you guys worked up quite a storm this evening. Mnn. Mache." She naughtily snuck a few leaves for a quick taste. "So when do I get to hear why Luke commanded me to come down to the hinterlands?"

Jack tossed a salad along with his hip and eyelashes. "Oh, let's wait till the master and his tight sphincter can join us for a big pow-wow. No use going through it all twice. Why don't you provide some comic relief from my whittling with some good bad hair stories."

"As a matter of fact," Liz bubbled, "I have QUITE a few. Today is one for the OZ annals! First, I arrive to break in another new receptionist. I wasn't sure if I should call him Alberto or Alberta. He can barely speak a word of clear English, but I think Enrique taught him just enough to get on my good side. He 'lubs' the lighting, he 'lubs' my perfume and he would 'keel' for my Manolo Blahnik shoes. Then, do you remember that schlub, Merritt Smears, who helped you guys get your permits after I schmoozed him up at that party? Well there is Alberto, handling Merritt throwing a fit, with more snob appeal than I could pull off in a week. I could have kissed him! Of course while he was playing the little bad guy, I get to come on like the good guy to smooth things over. Something wrong?"

Jack stood and Jerry sat frozen in place. They were too stunned to reply.

"Anyway, I start calming Merritt down. Enrique somehow manages to chop off his comb-over and give him a CREW CUT!" Liz roared with glee.

She turned toward Jerry who started choking on his taro chip, poured him a glass of water from the pitcher on the counter and continued. "So, as I was saying, here's the Ferret freaking out at the sight of his crew cut, which actually looked pretty damn good compared to the comb-over. I complement him on how handsome he looks and he starts to calm down a bit. He tells me it was Enrique's idea. So out of no where, the devil in me comes out and I say, Oh, Enrique worked you over with his clippers? Then, softly to his side, I nudge him and tell him that Dr. Sue Barrymore once told me that she would absolutely cream herself if she had one night with Enrique and his clippers. Especially if he would do her lover while she watched... Merritt Smears turned redder than my nail polish! I thought he was going to squirt blood from his ears."

Jerry continued with his coughing fit. "Honey, honey..." Liz reached over to give Jerry a few stiff whacks on his back, "Jack, did you put cayenne pepper on those chips or something?"

"Liz," Jack said smiling ear to ear, "I'd like to introduce you to a special friend of mine. Jerry Callahan, this is Luke's BEST friend in the ENTIRE world, Liz Osbourne. Liz, feel free to remind me of this moment the next time I give you any shit, of just how much we love you. Guess who my friend, Jerry, works for in this best of all possible worlds."

Liz looked at Jerry with lips that spelled out the "O" in mortified. "Well, it can't be Alberto, so that leaves, oh no, not Merritt Smears. Jack, just hand me a knife, any knife. I'm going to open a vein."

Jerry jumped up from his chair to put an arm around Liz. "No, no, no. I haven't been that choked up with good reason for years. By the way, those are great eye glasses, but seriously—you're telling me my asshole boss goes to Salon OZ for a haircut? I thought he just stuck his head a ceiling fan every few weeks. I'd never think of him as vain."

Liz looked relieved. "I think he keeps coming to chat up the rich dames. I certainly won't turn away his forty-five bucks as long as he keeps his pants zipped. Did you hear, Jack? Jerry likes my glasses. Keep him. And what do you mean Jerry's 'special', mnn?" Liz, chatting this way and that, settled her pursed lips toward Jack.

Jack feigned embarrassment. It was a small melodrama from the man who was never embarrassed. "Oh, you know, special enough to sit here and keep me company. Maybe he's just into knives and fresh vegetables or something."

Jerry was quick to erase the moment of awkward interrogation. "Actually, I like watching Jack play with his zucchini and purple potatoes. It's so much better than TV. I just hope he isn't prone to slice and dice all the root vegetables he encounters. That might dampen a friendship."

"Quick and cute. Keep that knife in your pocket, Jack. Make sure you keep this guy simmering."

Jack brought his saber down with a loud thwack. "Yes, mother. And Luke, don't look so worried: Liz and I aren't bitching at each other or scheming about you. Jerry here is pining over Liz's eyewear, and Liz wants Jerry and me to give her nephews and nieces. And by the way, Liz has replaced you as my new best friend, so move over buddy. There. Does that about sum it up for everyone?"

Luke looked bemused but relieved. "Jeez, how'd you two manage to cram in twelve years of psycho-analysis and couples therapy? Liz just got here ten minutes ago!"

"Liz slipped Merritt Smears a quickie little bit of MISS-information and I have rewarded her the title of Goddess." Jack beamed as he wiped his cutting board clean.

"Of course we haven't yet told her what the asshole may be plotting for these parts of town. I think she would be a little less inclined to toy with him," added Jerry.

Luke was quick to hold up his hands and reply. "Well, let's just wait and see about all that. It wouldn't be the first time a gaggle of queens got all up in arms over a bunch of coincidences. Next thing you know, we'll be all wrapped up in antics like a cheesy gay novel."

"Oh my yes," said Liz, "so many wanna-be Maupins, so little time. And then, there are all those so called 'gay-themed' movies sanitized for our protection out of Hollywood. Anne Heche would never be able to play me. I'm straight and it would be too confusing for anyone in the jello-belt."

Jack pointed with his knife. "I love cheesy gay novels. I love novel cheeses. Novel and gay, is that redundant or cliché?" He blinked and winced, then added, "Shut up Jack. SO. Now that we're all here, Luke wants to tell ya'll he is going to run in the Triathlon on Thursday, incognito of course, as a black drag queen and win us the thousand dollars so we can stay in business another month."

"Well Liz," Luke said calmly, "Didn't I tell you? Will somebody call Betty Ford? Jack is having another episode."

Jack screeched so high he nearly broke wine glasses. He ejected his reply so quickly the sound waves could topple chairs. "I am NOT having an episode! It's another one of my brilliant ideas."

"Brilliant for who Jack? If it's so brilliant, why aren't you the one to run down the street in black makeup and heels?" Luke sounded angry, but he had long ago come to enjoy their rationalizations. He knew he was going to run in the race. It had been a long time since he even thought about doing anything outrageous, camp and fun like the old days. He just didn't know why he was going to run the race. Not yet anyway. Part of the game was frustrating Jack, watching his conniving brain at work and all the machinations he would go through to reach the goal. To that end, Luke tossed back the hot potato. "After all Jack, you were the hurdler in high school. If anyone should run the race, it should be you!"

"Which makes me all the more prone to varicose veins. Are you trying to cut me down in my prime? And don't give me that 'after all' business, after all, it does say HUDSON Grille. It doesn't say Betz's Barbeque Pit, now does it?"

Liz was rifling through her clutch, "Where's my Blackberry. Here it is. Okay everyone. I keep this picture of Luke last year at Halloween. You remember Dr. Frankenfurter. Well here is Lukenfurter. I keep it to remind myself how not to 'over-do' an outfit, but look at this! Isn't he cute? Look at those legs!"

Jerry grabbed the device. "Whew, daddy! You want to ramp up business? Just do your maitre d' thing dressed up like this. Why are you hidin' your stuff in those khakis? Look at them dimples!"

"See? You could be our infamous major domo homo!" Jack said. "Not only could you win us some much needed cash, you would help out places like the Mercy Mission AND put your assets to work in community service."

Luke laid out his hand demanding the Blackberry. Looking at the screen, he tried to hide his self appreciating grin behind fake embarrassment. "Don't everyone get your hopes up. If Dr. Sue has her way, there won't BE any triathlon. Nobody's gonna get to see anyone's ass, let alone mine, if that comes down."

"She ain't gonna stop shit," spat Jack. "Which reminds me, I think we need to be closed tomorrow at lunch."

"Closed? What do you mean, closed?" Luke asked. "It's nearly the end of the month and we barely have three-quarters of this month's rent."

"Tomorrow is that open forum thing on Town Hall, LIVE! " said Jack. "If you want the thousand bucks for winning, then we have to make sure we raise a stink against dear Dr. Sue. The Reverend Pickens has already called, asking for a bunch of people to start a rally."

"Jack, we can't close. Running a restaurant isn't a hobby, it's a business," Luke sounded tart.

"Okay, okay, you can stay here. Jerry and I will hit the show, and I'll set you up with a 'make-your-own lunch line.' We could have a 'Phoebe Buffet Day' at the Grille. The lesbians will love it! I'll make sure I can get you some help." Jack had likely been scheming all evening on this one. Liz and Jerry sat rapt in the ping-pong playing itself out between Luke and Jack.

Jerry was surprised that Jack expected him to take the day off. "Hey Jack, I have a job to keep too. Can you imagine that A-hole Smears if he saw me on TV hawking the rights of drag queens?"

"We'll keep you in the back with a big sign," Jack said. "Come on now people! This is serious! All this nay, nay, nay. We can't let someone like Dr. Sue run our lives. We need to put her DOWN and fight for our trans-feminine and trans-racial freedom! Come on Liz. How about you? Isn't there some she-he-she affinity you need to support?"

"Oh Jack, I really have to wean my new baby receptionist. It's his second day and I can't go fire another one so soon. I'll lose my mind. Maybe I can pop over for a few minutes, but I'll really have to get back quick. Make sure you give me a big sign too. I don't want to lose any stodgy customers over this."

"HELLO, over here!" Luke demanded. "Has anyone heard me agree to any of this yet?"

"Luke, just give it up honey," Liz remarked. "We both know you aren't going to win this one. You know Jack. I've already resigned myself to schlep back here tomorrow with my Lukenfurter bustier and a bag of goodies so you guys can play dress up. Now, what's it take to get a salad around here?"

THIRTEEN

Like decade-old cheese in Pavlov's rat trap, Dr. Sue sat facing the empty chair where she had knelt the previous evening. The thin cloud of cigar smoke hung waist high in the room and recalled nausea from the pit of her stomach. While last night's sensation was borne of disgust and scotch, this bout was laced with fear and worry.

After today's show, she would have to eat some mighty humble pie. She hadn't bagged the Mayor, which might have worked to fire up the ratings. His stand-in had rambled on in administrator-speak about enlisting a task force, for chrissakes. And then there was the Harlem faux pas. There would be hell to pay and Al would relish seeing her squirm.

When she arrived at the appointed hour, he welcomed her with calm and cool small talk. She followed him upstairs in silence as he chomped on his bit of cigar regaling her with bellows of stench. When they entered the room he pointed to the chair and she obediently sat to accept her due.

She flinched as he began, but was surprised that he remained calm. "Sue, Sue Sue. Last night I was considering the possibilities of national syndication. But one more trick like the ones you pulled today and we'll have to suspend the show. I had to spend most of the afternoon fielding irate calls from half the city. And yeah, yeah, yeah, I know you'll threaten to walk out. But, you're still under contract. And, you still have to pay off a little more of your debt from our Georgetown days. Besides that, I certainly don't need to remind you about our little home movies, do I? The networks would have a field day with those. Now if you'll excuse me for a moment, I will leave you to think about that while I tend to some business. I'll be back to discuss how you're going to dig us out of your mess in a few minutes." He turned and left the room, shutting the door on Sue with a loud crack.

"Oh, he's good," she thought, and then her fear hit with another wave. Al's uncharacteristic calm surrounded her like looming walls of iron spikes waiting to close in before the floor dropped out to leave her gored psyche dripping with blood in a slow painful torture. She knew there had to be a secret lever to stop the fatal crush and her brain raced in desperation to find it.

Dr. Sue grabbed her purse and ripped at the zipper. In a nervous, frantic search, various unwanted dreck fell to the floor. She paused in relief, and held out the cell phone, then resumed to punch the buttons with the intensity of video game madness.

Al Siegel had left the room to grin with sinister delight. Sue Barrymore seemed to enjoy the perverse pleasure and excitement of squirming in and out of tight spots with reckless fear. He knew he played the 'soft touch' to the hilt and was giddy in setting the plot of events like a sadistic master. He would take great joy putting her back in place through humiliation and psychological bondage. Of course, these crafty electrical synapses sparked around his brain without any true conscious understanding.

He plodded down the steps in thought with the ponderous swing of a beauty queen lacking any element of beauty. Then inspiration struck. The problem of Dr. Sue upstairs, and that of his business project downstairs could be solved, one with the other. He could bring Sue down a few steps, like twenty-four, and introduce her to his secret money maker. It would be a marriage made in hell, and offered the possibilities of clipping the wings of a whole flock of feisty birds with one brilliant idea.

He turned around and headed back up the stairs to get Sue. As he came back toward the door, he heard her talking. She was on the phone. "She should be talking to a priest, making her final confession," he thought. As he reached the door and grasped the knob, he could hear her clearly.

"...no honey, I don't think you came off inadequately. It was me. I just got so hot inside, I don't know what I was saying. Either I wanted to show off to Al or I was so steamed up over your handsome new military look, that I—"

Hearing Sue smarm on the phone with some other dick brought Al's plan into clearer focus. He turned the doorknob and cut off her conversation in mid-heat.

Sue's head whipped toward the sound of the door, and her heart nearly leapt out of her left bra cup. She flipped the lid of the phone shut on Merritt and asked, "Back so soon?"

"Don't look so innocent, Barrymore. I heard just about all I needed. Sounds like you're whoring in front as well as behind me. Well, follow me babe. I'm going to give you a taste of where you'll end up if you ever decide to screw with any of my business again. Come on. Get your fat ass up and march it downstairs. I have a surprise for you."

Annoyed at the interruption, she led the way and went down the steps, driving every footfall into the staircase like a pouting eleven-year-old forbidden from a slumber party or navel piercing. Al kept chomping on his cigar and puffing out a rattle of "heh heh, mumble, cross me again, mumble, gonna love this, mumble, Dr. Sue ain't gonna be worth a fuckin' nickel in this town." Sue ground her teeth and sneered, walking farther down the stairway.

Once they were on the main floor, Al took the lead and Sue's wrist, steering them through the dining room and kitchen toward the basement door. Few lights were on in each of the spaces, creating a path of shapes and dim corners. Sue just rolled lid-heavy eyes with impatience, but her interest revived when she heard what sounded like the muffled voices of a party below them.

Al opened the door and the noise of conversation was more apparent. Several animated voices were speaking at once, but obviously not amongst themselves. As they reached the bottom of the stairs, Al turned on another light and reached to key in a code on the door pad. The noise that came from behind the door perplexed Sue, stirring curiosity, excitement and fear.

"Now, be quiet. I have some broads working in here." Before he opened the door he turned to Sue and announced, "Welcome to Miss Sallie's Hot Lines."

As the door opened, Sue was stunned. Inside, the room was the color of blood. Three black women in extreme sizes (narrow, wad, and extra-wad) sat in their black lacy slips with phone headsets that seemed like accessories in their swirling, beaded or braided hair sculptures. Dr. Sue held her breath and listened.

"I can feel your big strong thighs and daddy slidin' his big strong meat between my breast-a-siz. Oh yeah, slide it baby, slide it home to your momma."

Al spoke softly, leaning toward Dr. Sue. "I like to call them my Courvoisier Girls. Broads always ready to pop anyone's cork. Like a good drink, smooth going down. Pack a wallop on the finish. The big, big one there is Tanka Rae. The wide, big one is Kahlua. That skinny thing is Chardonay Courvoisier. Hard to believe they are sisters. I don't know if you remember them from your go-go days. They've filled out a bit and you of course were in such a different league. Heh!"

Sue was at once mortified and titillated listening to this scene. She tried to focus on the one Al called Kahlua, who sat in the middle, her long tongue flicking and licking the mouth piece knob before her. "I'm flickin' my Bic under your nuts. Yeah, you scared white honky. Momma's gonna singe your furry nuts. Momma's strokin' your stick, roastin' your giblets, basting your turkey. Cum on momma, squirt that turkey you honky." Kahlua smiled and nodded at Sue, her big gold tooth twinkling in the light.

The skinny little one, Chardonay, sat in her corner, shapely legs crossed, filing her nails. Her delivery did not match the other tirades. In a soft breathy voice, she let her client drive. She simply sat, filling in agreement, "mm-hmn, oh yeah, mm-hmn, mm-hmn, yeah, ok." Looking at Sue she batted big brown pony eyes. Tanka Rae on the other hand, glared at the white bitch intruder.

The Courvoisier Girls were notorious among some circles of the Capital City. After all, it was a city of notorious circles. There were the interns who met under the desks of famous politicians baring flanks. There were the lobbyists who met around tables of smoky porterhouse greasing palms at the Plam. And then, there were the Courvoisier Girls offering rump roast around the notorious circles of Logan, Dupont and Washington. Although these were traffic circles, the girls were not part of L'Enfant's master plan.

Tanka Rae was probably the largest of the girls, and also the meanest. The only thing bigger and meaner than her mouth was her butt. It was her biggest asset on many fronts, especially behind the scenes with many a man into 'that', and even more so on the semi-professional whipped cream wrestling tour. A good ballast serves one well in that slick and slippery underworld, whipped cream or otherwise.

Kahlua, her less physical sister, made up for prowess with her loud mouth, quick vicious brain and ample width. Many a man liked that too, as long as he was deaf. And, if he wasn't before, he certainly was after, when Kahlua blew off a big one. Then, all that mouth from Kahlua was reduced to good vibrations in his central park, so to speak.

Finally, there was Chardonay, Courvoisier sister number three. All the outsize genes must have been assigned to the first two, because Chardonay was a sprite at best. Petite, excessively fashionable and very nearly mute, her lip-gloss was louder than her voice. It wasn't that she didn't try, but most of her audible energy was expressed in action. A simple hello started with her 'loudly' mouthing the word, followed with a big smile and a sway of the single plume of hair spraying straight out from the top of her head. The big finish was her dip at the knee better than any Playboy bunny serving a cocktail. The ritual was punctuated by the extension of a long bejeweled index finger that declared her benefactor as "the One." Strapping studs at the clubs she frequented were usually on their knees after her dipsy-dumb greeting. She was the strong, silent type.

Dr. Sue Barrymore knew she was out of her league. That of course, never stopped her. However, as willing as she was on some fronts (mostly her back or knees), there were a few things she refused to stoop for and this was tawdry even for her. After all, she was a public figure! While some people ridiculed her for passionate views, she considered herself a bastion of conservative standard and opinion. Well, at least that was her public persona. What she did in private was her own business. It was the foundation of the Constitution. A woman had to deal with the stress of celebrity somehow, but even she couldn't go down this deep.

Al stirred Sue from her consideration, "Well doll, what do you think? This could be your new home. Make me some money with that natural phone talent I overheard upstairs. Let this be your warning. One more slip, babe, and it won't be a pink one. It will be black and lace."

Outside, parked across the street, the midnight blue panel van filled space as innocently as scores of other vehicles up and down the dark narrow block. Inside the van, an array of signal lights, dials and frequency indicators barely lit the man at watch. His arm reached to adjust the sensitive instruments. He brought his hand up and cupped the headset on his right ear to catch a nuance. The small snake tattoo perched on his forearm lurked in the shadows for the long late watch, while the sordid sounds of the Siegel soap operas provided more than enough entertainment. Armed with patience, what Detective Rollins really needed now was another bag of donuts and some hard evidence.

FOURTEEN

"OKAY PEOPLE, settle down, settle down, look at the face, look at the face." Jack was standing in back of a parked pick-up truck performing starched stewardess arm motions, guiding the crowd's gaze toward his face as they milled around on the sidewalk. "Neighbors, friends of Mercy Mission follow Reverend Blanche. Business owners and Friends of Hudson Grille—come in and have some breakfast. Plumbing contractors, please see Parker Fox. Let's all PULL THE PLUG on Dr. Sue!" Jack then jumped out of the truck raising his arms for the dismount.

Parker was standing near Luke, helping to man the coffee-pots. It was another crisp, clear fall day, and the crowd on the sidewalk buzzed with the positive energy of a Mary Kay meeting. Except for the plumbers, who didn't have a clue about Mary Kay.

Parker was filling Luke in on the simultaneous happening before them. Jack's contingent materialized as a result of his cell phone speed dialing. They traveled in packs, hopping on any opportunity to cruise in the same way they never missed a trunk sale at Nordstrom, or for lesbian supporters, a free class at Home Depot.

Luke was taking in everything that Parker had to non-verbally communicate. The wet shampoo aroma carried itself on the crisp breeze from tossed damp hair. The potential chafe from a day old unshaved square jaw played in Luke's daydream. The glow of fine hairs on the nape of his neck nearly made his stomach growl out loud. Luke fought back the urge to ask Parker where he spent last evening, his whole body wanting to wrap itself around the taut t-shirt beside him.

Parker wrecked Luke's train of sensual thought, nudging him as he asked, "You need another cup of coffee or something?"

"No, no," Luke looked over with lazy eyelids, "I'm just enjoying the fall breeze. This is really my favorite time of the year. So, go on, don't let my reveling interrupt you." He nudged his shoulder back into Parker's and busied himself with nonchalant coffee-pot care. All this new pal interplay was going to kill him!

Parker went on to tell Luke about meeting with Jon after he left the Grille yesterday afternoon. At the news of the conspiratorial behaviors Jerry Callahan had observed, and Parker's experience of walking out of City Hall, permit in hand, unscathed, Jon had looked worried. "Let's not tell Blanche Perkins about any of this," he had quickly said. He didn't want to "rev up the Rev" based solely on early suspicions about Merritt Smears, Al Siegel and Lou Thicke. She had already bugged him again about progress of the permit and plumbing work at the Mercy Mission. In fact she was going to gather neighbors from various Mission houses to pack the audience at Town Hall, LIVE!, of all things. "But," he offered, "I will call up the Mayor and see if I can get any inkling of what those stooges might be up to." That was yesterday and Parker had heard no more from Jon yet.

"So-o-o," Parker continued, his report apparently concluded, "let me get over and start these plumbers to work at the Mission. I will check in with you later. If you see any of our Keystone Cops lurking around, give me a call on my cell." He found a pen in a side thigh pocket and wrote the number down on a napkin.

Luke took the napkin with an uncontrollable smile and a rush of excitement. "You mean you'll come and save me if I get kidnapped?"

"Maybe you should stuff your pants with croutons so you can leave us a trail just in case." Parker toyed with the lip of Luke's pocket with a tentative finger.

Luke pushed Parker's hand away with a friendly hip. "Get out of here. I have to get back to work and pull together this mess with Jack. And watch out for those humpy plumbers. If you're not back in a half hour, I'm coming down there to join you!"

Parker was already steps away, but looked back over his shoulder with a sly grin and suggestive wink. "Give me ten minutes, we'll be ready for you."

After milling around and cavorting with friends, Jack made his way over to Luke. "I see you and Parker are getting cozy. Do you feel lucky and stiff? And don't give me that 'I don't know what you're talking about' look. It's all over your face. I haven't seen you smiling like this since, well yesterday. And, Parker was there for that too. Of course you know I can't possibly come up with your triathlon costume, bridesmaid dresses and something for mother of the bride on such short notice. You're just going to have to take cold showers with him till I am ready."

"We haven't even made it to the front door yet, let alone the altar, but I bet even a cold shower wouldn't diminish my—outlook. And did you see some of those plumbers?" Luke fanned himself with the back of his hand.

Jack slapped Luke's shoulder. "You're nearly engaged. I'll not have you eying tradesmen, or for that matter any of my contingent. Not a bad turn out though huh? In natural light it's so much easier to see which of these guys works the bottle bronzer. It smells like the Clinique counter at Nieman Marcus out here." He turned to address his admirers.

"Okay, MARINES. I thought that would get your attention. Everybody into Hudson Grille."

"By the way Luke, Roz and Mannie said they would help you sling hash at lunch for the Phoebe Buffet today. Gilbert even offered to work the bar, but I thought that was a bad idea for a recovering alcoholic. I'm sure we can get some of the guys to get things ready for you before we head up to the Studios. You're not mad at me for ditching you at lunch, are you?"

"Jack, I've been through twenty years of your bouffant hair-brained schemes. This invasion may actually turn out to do some good. Except, I don't think it's going to get me out of running in this race. Which, may I remind you, I haven't agreed to run. Maybe if I break a heel, I won't have to do the mud wrestling part. Even if I did get to the finish line first or second, do you have any idea who I might have to wrestle? Really now. I could get creamed!"

"I've been telling you, don't worry about it. Let's get this coffee stuff back inside and this little cavalcade in gear. Just remember Luke, that thousand bucks will help get us through the month. You get that cute ass to that finish line and you'll have the one thing up your boa that no other contestant will."

"What's that, a ten pound cast iron skillet?" Luke surmised.

"Nope, you got me babe. Never underestimate the ingenuity of Jack Betz and his industrial surplus catalog. In fact, I was up till two this morning—working. And before you jump to conclusions including me, Jerry and industrial surplus, I want you to know we shared a little 'pec' before I sent him home so I could get to work on your secret weapon-wear."

Instead of continuing a diatribe, Jack threw Luke a smile that all but said, "So there. You're my best friend. I'm not going to leave you stranded in a mud pit, and believe it or not, Jack Betz doesn't jump every pair of khakis on the block. Sometimes popping rivets is more important than popping another load. Besides, I think I might take a lesson from you and take it slow with Jerry."

Luke hooked an arm around Jack's neck and replied with an understanding hug.

FIFTEEN

While the groups at the Grille and Mission planned their en-
counter with the wicked witch of Northwest Washington, D.C., little
Alberto sat at his desk in OZ painting his nails a pale shade of lavender.
He let out frustrated snorts each time the phone rang, and had to pick up
the receiver with fingers splayed like asterisks. The awkward task didn't
bother him as much as the interruption. He was trying to watch *The View*
with rapt attention while Barbara Walters empathetically interrogated
prodigal guest Star Jones who was supplying intimate details of her
eyebrow shaping rituals. The vital information was shared with fervid
intensity hoping to save countless victims from Paramus to Larchmont
from looking like a gorilla. Alberto wondered if Ms. Osbourne would
mind him waxing and tweezing his lush Latin brows at the front desk for
the sake of peer-pressured beauty.

Dr. Sue Barrymore pried open the salon behind the veil of her
glamour-sized Oscar de la Renta tortoise-shell eye armor. It must have
been the day Oscar felt quirky and used an entire tortoise shell for each
lens. Instead of enabling incognito, the glasses drew so much attention
that she was either recognized as the infamous talk show host or a pimp
with big tits. The whole deal was gaudy and obvious.

Since she had found OZ, Sue seemed wickedly drawn to the
place. She opened the glass door, snorting a fix of air conditioned peroxide and hair spray, deciding that an addiction to daily beauty uppers was
better than the early morning vodka gargle she had considered. It had
been a demeaning evening with Al, and she felt desperate to cleanse her
morale to regain some sense of dignity. The slips of her tongue on-air and
on Al had left her wanting for the bottle, but Sue realized she had better
toe the line rather than fall over it into the clutches of his outsized phone
sex kittens.

Alberto caught his breath as Dr. Sue entered the salon. In spite of
the large glasses, he sensed fame before him and skipped a beat while
figuring out how to react. His brain ran a quick search and scan to put a
name to the face which remained unrecognizable until the apricot lips
bloomed into a plastic smile. His mind flashed vivid images of Enrique
screaming "PUTA" to this face on the TV. His stomach soured and his

tawny button nose wrinkled involuntarily. He caught a whiff of her unpleasant perfume and braced himself to deal with the infamous Sue Barrymore.

With tacky fingernails still outstretched, Alberto leaned his elbows on the desk and brought his palms together as if to pray, telling Dr. Sue to "wait a moment" with voluptuously exaggerated but silent lips. When he finally caught the very last detail of the Star Jones eyebrow waxing method, he returned another plastic smile back at Sue. Now that he knew who the devil was before him, his high boyish voice slid down the harmonic scale as he snidely asked, "Jew hab an ap-point-ment?" The final syllable was delivered with a remarkable croaking bass.

Dr. Sue's teeth clenched and her lips tightened with impatience. "Is Enrique in?" she demanded.

Alberto clicked his chin down a notch to peer at Dr. Sue and slid his voice right back up the harmonic scale. He spoke more slowly this time, in case English might not be her native language. "Jeww- hahhb-ahnn ap-POINT-ment?"

Eyelids closed to slits, she inhaled audibly and admitted, "No, I do not. But, I would most certainly appreciate it, if you could let Enrique know that I am here." She didn't add the "piss-ant chimichanga" she was thinking.

None the less, Alberto's antennae picked up the signal loud and clear. He noticed that she noticed and left her to stew for an uncomfortable moment before delivering his next punch. When he was good and ready, he delivered the slow and breathy, "And Jeww aaar?"

"I am Dr. Sue Barrymore -"

He cut her off to stare down at the appointment book on the desk, and continued, "Oh, Enrique will be in after lunch. Would you like if Ms. Osbourn-eh could see jeww?" Little Alberto tipped lavender nails at his new boss, standing in the distance looking like Munch's Scream. He stepped up the velocity of his waving fingers, commanding her appearance with the air of a maitre d'. Liz, never one to be commanded to anything, quickly considered cutting off the little runt's shoe allowance, but could only be pleased with his dealing with Sue.

Liz approached the situation with her 'good cop' poise before Sue could blast the little guy with any venomous spew. She felt like Starsky to his Hutch, working their familiar routine to deal with unpleasant customers. The tone with which Dr. Sue asked Liz "where did she find that receptionist" warmed her heart. Even though she would now have to personally attend to the witch, she was proud of the little munchkin and his ability to rattle the not-so-good Doctor.

"Well, we all have a few rough spots to take care of, now don't we," Liz assuaged. "And feel free to take off your sunglasses; I think the girls recognize you."

Liz led the way across the tile floor like a geisha floating on rice paper. Sue followed like a Clydesdale. They passed the crystal cone-head domes that bobbed and weaved like a Greek chorus of graying morning doves. The matrons hadn't had this much upper body exercise since Monica was in town.

Their wizened facial expressions telegraphed the overall tenor of their discussion. Dr. Sue was always a ripe specimen for dissection. They fed on everything from the color of her pedicure polish (apricot), to the depth of her visible panty line featured in her too tight taupe pant suit, right up to the hair which was experiencing technical difficulties. They paused as Sue snuggled her way into the foie gras colored leather styling chair. After simultaneous sips of their International Coffees, they re-sumed knitting those tangled webs of conjecture.

Dr. Sue looked in the mirror and pursed her lips and eyes as though she had just bit into the most succulent ripe stone fruit, savoring the sweet with one eye and a tart surprise with the other. "So. I want something fresh and new. And clean and now. Something Oprah won't get to until next year. Do you think you can do that? What do you think?" Sue continued winking at herself in the mirror, imagining.

Liz had to bite her lip from the inside, lest she reveal to Dr. Sue what really crossed her mind. Liz immediately envisioned a complete disregard for all the fussy snipping and layering of most styles. Liz very much wanted a single "fresh, clean cut" at the neck. But it would be a little hard to up-sell all the extra bottles of shampoo, rinse, conditioner, finishing spray, holding spray and UV sparkle, so she regained her senses. With a brief description, Liz sold Sue on a "Congressional Page-Boy." Sue indeed believed that it would be "youthful" and was nearly begging to begin after hearing it would "shed ten years and ten pounds from her old self."

Liz was determined to give Sue exactly what she deserved, the stylist's ultimate weapon of revenge: the haircut that looked good on the way out, but devil possessed after the first home washing. Liz was always so tickled that everyone, including Dr. Sue, could be amused with, ooh—thinning shears. Little did they know that with a simple flick of the wrist, an unmanageable haircut was just waiting to happen. By tomorrow, Dr.

Sue's hair would look like a weeping willow tree. There would be bonus points if it were humid.

Liz started to chat her victim to distraction. "So, Dr. Sue, I'm sure Enrique will be heartbroken that he missed you. He felt so privileged to work with you when you were in the other day. He talked of nothing else for the rest of his shift. Oh, and then yesterday when Merritt—oh, perhaps I shouldn't tell secrets?"

Dr. Sue scooched up an inch and asked, "Merritt? Merritt who?"

"Why Merritt Smears. I believe you two ran into each other here, the other day. Oh my, Dr. Sue! The two of them are such dirty boys! The stories Enrique told me nearly curled my hair. It seems that Merritt is far more adventuresome than he looks. Of course Enrique is risque, but even he was surprised."

Sue wiggled her fat butt in the chair and begged for details. Liz went on to fabricate about Merritt's fictitious fantasy. "Well, it starts out predictably enough for a man: Merritt is at the center of a threesome. But the other two are you and...Enrique!" Sue gasped, so Liz pressed on. "Then the tit man and the butt boy turn their attentions on you! And Enrique has his nasty clippers roving EVERYwhere!" She spritzed and snipped at the head before her, filling it with just enough tale to set Sue loose with her own imagination. Riveted, Sue squirmed in the chair, utterly distracted from the blitz of thinning and shearing. The weeping willow hairdo would be wailing by morning.

Down at the Development office building, Greg Thicke was in the lobby waiting for the elevator. The Mayor had drawn him aside to warn him darkly of some unnamed dubious activity his unnamed relative might possibly be involved in. "Wouldn't want complications for your election next week," blah blah. So Greg decided to pay his brother a visit. All Greg had to do was talk about his campaign, bring up the Mission and if his brother started scratching the back of his scalp, Greg would know something was awry. Since they were kids, Greg knew Lou was lying or hiding something with this involuntary tic. It then remained to prise out what this activity was.

Not that he and his brother didn't get along well, but on the ride up in the elevator, Greg felt a little uneasy going into what might be hostile territory. Greg was always on hand to take care of his lug witted brother, who had been dealt more than a fair share of lumps over the years. Lou had been dropped on his head too many times in high school wrestling matches, and wasn't as quick as most to play along with others around him. With a secure bureaucrat job it was easier, but if he was mixed up in anything nefarious, there was no telling how hard he might fall from the outcome. Someday the pieces of that block head would be harder to pick up and put back together again.

As Greg turned the knob to the business office area, the door opened with a groan. He entered the office and saw his brother hovering over Jerry's desk. The two of them looking startled at the intrusion. Lou nodded to his brother and told him he'd be with him in a minute, then went on directing Jerry with some task.

Greg had been to the office countless times before, and had come to know Jerry in passing or in brief phone conversations when he would be calling his brother. He always considered Jerry diligent and polite for a city employee. He felt somewhat concerned with the current look on Jerry's face. It bore a sense of awkward tension and resistance. Probably just another heap of work at the grind, but Greg realized that if he didn't get a scratch out of Lou, that maybe he could get some details from Jerry.

Lou came over and shook his brother's hand and led him back into his office as they talked. Jerry sat at his desk steaming and worried. Lou had just asked him to pull up some business license records for the Mercy Mission and the Hudson Grille. Jerry was steamed because he was still waiting for his show-up-sometime boss. Merritt could be out for most of the day. Jerry was getting antsy to go meet up with Jack before the show but couldn't leave until there was someone manning the phones and reception area. In the meantime, Jerry was at wits' end, having to pull yet more documents for the Grille. It certainly couldn't lead to anything pleasant. Nobody in any city office did anything because it was pleasant.

Jerry was in the middle of a phone call explaining the labyrinthine requirements of the permitting process to a novice homeowner when Greg and Lou emerged from the office. Jerry found it even odder-than-usual behavior for Lou, who was using both hands like garden hoes to gnash at the back of his head. He shook off the incident and returned to concentrate on the dizzy spin of questions from his caller. As he finished, Lou was reminding Greg to leave a quarter for the cup of coffee before he left out the groaning door.

Greg walked over to Jerry's desk, steaming cup in hand. When Jerry looked up, he found Greg smiling at him the way a scientist peers into a microscope, raising one eye to admire a specimen slide. It made Jerry somewhat uncomfortable.

When silence invaded their space, Jerry could feel his head begin to tingle, fingers of warmth envelope his throat and the flush of blood rushing to his cheeks. Greg started to make small talk. He complimented Jerry's shirt. (Men don't compliment men on their apparel.) He asked Jerry if he was going to the Triathlon race. (A question usually reserved among 'family' members, gay family, that is.) Jerry's butt sat rock solid, glued to his chair. He was nervously self-conscious, and positive that his face was now glowing neon red.

While he had passing conversations with Greg, they were always efficient and polite, respectful to their mutual stations in life. Jerry wondered why Greg seemed to be crossing into personal boundaries. Most politicians were usually too busy and self-absorbed to pay attention to clerks, although sometimes they were known to abduct an intern. Jerry gulped.

It was then that Greg popped the question, with a breeze that ruffled the short hairs on the back of Jerry's neck. "Ever been to Hudson Grille?" Jerry's forearms fell to his desk with a soft thud. They tried to cover a coincidental pile of permits and licenses.

SIXTEEN

The crowd began gathering outside the entrance to Siegel Studios. There was both exuberance and pandemonium in the air. Reverend Blanche had pulled out all the stops and delivered a van full of mission denizens all dressed up in their Sunday best. She herself, looking adorable, led her friends in a sing and sway. She was wearing men's pinstripe pants, cinched up around her bosom with a big belt, along with a matching jacket, a fedora and a press-on mustache. It was very much madcap Lucy Ricardo at her best. Mrs. Oates looked like she was ready to go fox hunting, and Mr. Atkins in a fluffy feather stretch cap and flowered house coat, looked like any other elderly black woman in need of some facial hair removal. Slim was on hand, feeling thankfully taller in a set of black rubber flip-flops with six inch thick soles and an awesome black cowboy hat that he sweet-talked off some guy with muscles. Even Gilbert, who would normally be snoozing off this part of the day, showed up not so much in drag, though someone had tied a rainbow of ribbons to his tambourine, which he rattled to emphasize someone's catty remark.

Gilbert stood smiling at the raucous group. He hoisted Slim up on his shoulders for a better view and they looked on. "Great day, Reverend, isn't it?" asked Gilbert.

Blanche replied, "All these people here to help out places like the Mission." She threw her arms wide in excitement. There was no doubting her knack in rallying young and old with authority. Details didn't escape her either. Looking down she added, "Maybe we can scrape together some change and buy a pair of new boots for them big feet of yours. Don't expect we have any size 13's in the donation box, huh Gilbert?"

"No ma'am. Don't expect so. We'll be all right, won't we Slim?"

As the crowd grew, Blanche confidently gave her flock their directions for the day. They now included a contingent of business owners from the Triathlon Corridor, some wearing an array of brightly colored feather boas. And finally, there was Jack, who had jumped up on top of a bike rack to address his troops. 'Friends of Jack' stood out from the rest of the pack, not only because they where cheering him on, but because all of them wore identical Marilyn Monroe masks. It was hard to tell which were men or women by dresses or pants, high voices or low since everything was a mixed mess behind the same silly lipstick grin. Jack cleared his throat theatrically to get attention, "Will the real Marilyn Monroe please sit on my face?"

Several Marilyns raised their hands and squealed.

Jack continued taunting, "Will one of you Marilyns sit on Dr. Sue's face?" All the Marilyns and quite a few others began to boo, hiss and grumble crude adjectives. "Okay Christian Soldiers, only fifteen minutes before they should open the doors to let us in and take on the Wicked Witch of the Northwest!"

Jack dismounted, again with the flourish and aplomb of an aquacade star, and asked one of the Marilyns, "Have you seen Jerry yet?"

One of the other Marilyns answered in sing-song, "Jack has lost his honey, Jack has lost his honey..."

Jack whipped around surprised. "Liz! You made it!

"Just in the nick of time. I traded my big floppy hat for this Marilyn mask. It was a defining moment of sisterhood. I can't wait to catch up with you guys tonight to tell you my latest! I can't get into all the gory details now, but Dr. Sue left the salon right before me. If my timing is right, half-way through today's show, the hair on that bitch is gonna look like Sally Struthers in an Annie wig."

Jack gave Liz a hug and said, "I can't even imagine why we took so long to like each other. Do you think our new status is going to freak out Luke?"

"Oh come on now, don't you think he'd be happy? But just in case, later on, I may have to disagree with you on some details of your Triathlon plans to make it seem like I'm still on his side. Don't hold it against me, okay?"

"Liz, you are so evil! How do you expect me to ever trust you?"

"Honey, EVIL is waiting for us inside. I'm just trying to be diplomatic."

Precisely at 11:50 a.m., the attendant opened the doors for the studio audience and was mowed down as if in the way at the start of the Boston Marathon or the rush of shoppers for the Pre-Winter fur sale at Filene's Bargain Basement. It depended on which side of the fence you cruised. Sue and Merritt, already seated on stage dropped their jaws and gasped, he louder than her. Al stood off to one side of the stage and mumbled a "JesusMary'n'Joseph" under his breath.

The Marilyns raced down the aisles like banshees, clawing their way to make it to the front row. Jack and Liz hung out in the middle, the seat next to Jack quickly filled by—thank God—Jerry, in a gorilla mask.

"Don't look at me that way Jack. I didn't have time to shave!"

Jack turned and kissed his gorilla on the lips. He settled back in his seat, only to find himself being stared down by the googly-eyed glare of Merritt Smears. It took the man an interminably long time to look away in disgust. It gave Jack the creeps.

The audience seating filled quickly. All around the room were colorful splashes of Triathlon supporters, behaving boisterously. The conservative audience huddled together in one small section, gravitating together like prayer beads of silver mercury.

Dr. Sue opened the show with her usual spiel, smiling and turning in time to her theme music. The announcer reminded the TV audience that it was Wednesday, Open Forum Day at Town Hall, LIVE! Dr. Sue got up from her chair and walked the small stage, trying to appear carefree and sassy in spite of boos and catcalls from the audience, which the technician drowned with canned applause.

The front row of Marilyns crossed their legs in a can-can sequence, performed a squealing rise and fall wave from their seats and for a finale, turned, flipped up their skirts toward the audience. The roar of laughter from the audience upstaged Dr. Sue. The Marilyns turned to reveal their little white tap pants decorated with the infamous iron-on smile of Dr. Sue.

Dr. Sue scowled. "Thank you, I guess, for your 'tribute.' I see we have a rather passionate audience with us today!" Applause and whoops. "I also see from the small number of conservative members of our audience, that many others are already in fear, having locked themselves at home or have already fled the city!" Shouts of glee. Sue stopped smugly and declared, "Well, I for one am not afraid of a man in a boa!" She seemed quite proud of herself.

Someone shouted from the audience, "YOU look like a man in a boa! What's up with the hair?"

Liz slunk down in her seat, and nudged Jack's elbow. "Told you. Now that she's getting steamed up, her hair is starting to frizz. Ten more minutes and we can start singing for the sun to come out!"

Dr. Sue stood tall and kept her composure. She didn't have to dig deep to retrieve strengths gleaned from other such indignities. "Thank you, thank you. I figure you have a big loud hole on your other end too?" Dr. Sue accepted a well deserved round of applause, and even started clapping for herself. She brought up her hand to settle down the audience. "Thank you, thank you. I'd like to welcome to the stage a paragon of our community, the Reverend Blanche Pickens."

Reverend Blanche stood in the audience to thunderous applause, and proceeded to go up on stage. When she arrived, Dr. Sue met her with outstretched arms and a warm hug between 'sisters.' As they hugged one side and then the other, the audience got a clear view of Blanche rolling her eyes in disbelief. The audience calmed and readied themselves to deliver the respect the Reverend deserved. She removed herself from Sue's clutches with braced arms and turned to audience for a half bow. She brought her hands together as if to pray before them. "Children of God. For that's what we are, all of us. We must find the way in our hearts to respect each other, and allow for times that bring disagreement. I am here to demonstrate this respect, but I am also deeply sorry for some of our neighbors who are wrapped so tight in their unneighborly beliefs that they cannot see the greater good of havin' some fun while helpin' out the less fortunate." The audience burst out clapping, and the front row of Marilyns reached for the sky with a shaking sea of red-tipped nails.

Reverend Blanche turned and joined Merritt and Sue in an empty seat to their right. Before she sat, she made sure the Doctor didn't pull the chair out from behind her. The good doctor just sat smiling. Merritt looked worried. He realized that his horniness had found him a place in the center of Dr. Sue's stage, but now he felt exposed under the spotlight. Merritt Smears began to perspire like a mineral oil lamp. He clutched the arms of his chair to hang on for the ride.

As the rowdy applause subsided, Dr. Sue raised a finger to make a point, but had to wait a moment to be heard. Her face tensed before she could begin. "Wrapped too tight or not, our more conservative neighbors have their rights too, to live in peace and quiet. They shouldn't be subjected to moral perverts." Someone heckled "PULL HER PLUG!!"

Reverend Blanche nervously adjusted her hat to make sure it was securely placed on her head or to symbolically batten down the hatch. "If these people were true friends of the neighborhood, and if they were more generous with their wealth, perhaps we wouldn't have to hold such events as the Triathlon."

Dr. Sue raised an eyebrow to volley, "If your people would try and get more jobs—"

Blanche raised her voice over Dr. Sue, "If your people would get down off their high horses—"

"Speaking of high horses, look at yourselves!" Sue twisted her head to stare at Blanche. "What I see too often is black people and gays playing the martyrs of how you are treated. Do you have any idea how it is to be subjected to these behaviors as a white person?"

Reverend Blanche waited a moment before dignifying such a statement with an answer. She began again calm, soft and steady. "If you would take a moment to look out of your eyes instead of that pin hole at the other end, you might see that the black people and the gay people aren't tryin' to change you people who happen to be white. We are behavin' this way to get your attention. We are white and black and many colors, men and women, human beings in the eyes of God, tryin' to show you that we are also lovin' partners and carin' people who deserve to be treated equally. We are here today to claim the right to have the Triathlon event to raise money for the elderly and less fortunate whether they are black, white, rainbow or polka dot. And my question to Dr. Sue is: When do you think Jesus climbed down off the cross to make you queen?"

Dr. Sue knew she had been pegged, and she hissed like a cat in a corner. Instead of gracefully springing onto the next subject, she stood up and flung her sheaf of notes at the Reverend like a cloud of industrial-sized confetti. The entire audience gasped and the front row of Marilyns slid in unison to the edge of their seats.

Al Siegel stood in the wings, wringing his hands. He couldn't decide if what might happen next would improve ratings or backfire in controversy. He stood ready to pull the plug and was counting the seconds to the next commercial break. He'd have to throw cold water on those two. As for Smears, Al was glad the goon had the good sense to keep his mouth shut.

Dr. Sue was left standing, head turned away from the audience in a pregnant pause. The moment truly seemed to last a full nine months until Jack Betz jumped to his feet and screamed, "Cat finally got your tongue Dr. Sue?" The audience roared with more applause and Jack took his bows. It was a moment he had practiced in front of the TV at the Grille for many months. Merritt Smears, having nothing better to do, gave Jack some more oogly-googly mojo.

Finally Dr. Sue turned to the audience in tears. The dam had opened. "YOU should be ashamed! Heathens and cowards, hiding behind masks. Reverend Blanche here to defend sinners. THIS is what the world is coming to, and it will only bring on the fires of HELL!" Dr. Sue paced the small stage in front of her styrofoam set, pointing at her audience. They started to boo.

Reverend Blanche leaned forward in her chair and continued to provide contrast to her hysterical opponent. With dignified calm she asked, "Dr. Barrymore, what kind of doctor are you anyway? Surely you're not a medical doctor, nor could you be a doctor of humanity. It seems to me, the only thing wrong with the world, are people like you on shows like this, creatin' circuses in the media to stir up rage. There is no love in your heart, no room for anyone different and no possibility to care for your neighbor. You are the Spin Doctor of Doom."

The audience went nuts. Applause was amplified with stomping feet and shouting, "Doom, doom, doom!" Dr. Sue covered her ears. Reverend Blanche started clapping in rhythm, hands over her head. Merritt looked off stage trying to find Al and the means to escape. The sweat dripped off his chin to blacken his necktie.

Sue held up her hand to quiet the crowd to no avail. She walked back upstage toward Reverend Blanche and raised her hand as though she would deliver a slap to be heard around the world. Instead, she grabbed Blanche's bright pink fedora and flung it into the audience like a frisbee. She stood planted on the stage yelling "Heathens!" but the mob engulfed her ranting with their shouts of "Doom."

Al Siegel gave the signal to cut to a commercial, and wondered how he was going convince Reverend Blanche to become the new host of Town Hall, LIVE!

SEVENTEEN

After the incident, Sue ran off stage and down the hall to her Halloween lair of a dressing room. As she lay on her lounge in tears, Town Hall, LIVE! returned from commercial break without her. Reverend Blanche held court with Merritt Smears who had changed his stripes and tune for the benefit of saving face, smoothing discord and to keep from sounding like a total ass. After the Dr. Sue spectacle, he wasn't going to be that stupid.

The conservative members of the audience shuddered as the festive fags and friends called for the head of Dr. Doom. It took some time for Reverend Blanche to calm them down. The "open forum" segment filled out the hour with members of the audience touting the Triathlon, its munificent works and good natured fun. Mrs. Oates stood up and shared the tales of joy places like the Mercy Mission brought to the elderly, filling voids of loneliness and the help it gave the less fortunate. Slim was there to hold her hand.

Many others shared as well but the real heart-pounder came from one of the obvious conservatives who put Merritt Smears on the spot. Mrs. Conservative admitted that she felt so shallow, so wrapped up in her own little world of tea parties, shopping and days at the beauty salon, that she never conceived of less happy days for the unfortunate. When she asked how the city and more specifically, how Ward 4 Business Development might help them help the Missions, the spotlight was turned on the Director. It was Merritt who had to admit that while we (referring to the conservative contingent) may not understand or relish the antics of our more "colorful" citizens, that we should look beyond that and to the help that they provide to the community as a whole.

He pledged to look into the matter. (Political-speak for a big fat 'maybe' in a couple of months or years depending on excess pork fund availability.) But, for better or worse, it made him look reasonably good at the moment and saved him from being lynched by a Mongol horde of Marilyns.

Al Siegel entered Dr. Sue's chamber without knocking. "Well, you blew it this time babe, and I'm not talking about Big Al."

Sue sniffed and yanked another tissue from the Romanov style tissue decanter. She blew her nose with startlingly loud flatulence. The wounded doctor meekly tried to wrest some pity out of Al. She knew he held all of her cards, and was convinced the royal face cards were conspiring behind her back. The coup was imminent.

"Oh Al, I am so sorry. But, certainly you can't expect me to let such personal attacks slide off my back. Couldn't we invite Reverend Blanche back tomorrow for a formal apology episode? We could even bring on the Mayor to witness. It would be a moment cable TV could never forget. Please Al, couldn't we..."

"The Courvoisier girls need the day off tomorrow. You'll cover their shift. Let's say about—noon tomorrow, okay? We'll run a Town Hall or two without you, and then some re-runs. Maybe we'll bring you back in a month or two after all this shit dies down. We'll pretend it never happened. Work the phones or I bring out the videos of your Georgetown days right when you're in the headlines. You won't get the show here or anywhere. I'm sure the tabloids would love this. You and Merritt—it would be like Jim and Tammy Faye all over again." He left the room without any other mercy, and smiled as he walked down the hall to the tunes of a sobbing Sue.

It wasn't a moment after Al returned to his office and desk that Merritt Smears appeared at the door. "Quite a show we put on today, wasn't it?"

Al looked up at Merritt and smirked. "Put your new girlfriend through the ringer. Shouldn't you be down the hall consoling her? Talk about a big piece of ass. You really know how to pick 'em. And tell me, did you get scalped for her too?" Al was definitely miffed at Merritt for bringing up the rear on his 'territory'. Dr. Sue may have been pressing his boxers, but today she was being tossed out like so much dirty laundry. It was time for Al to turn the screw. "It certainly wouldn't look too good for your office if the gossips found out you were hooked up with our Dr. Sue, would it? Which reminds me, thanks for the utility maps. Now that I've studied them, it seems there are a couple of properties on that block worth looking into."

Merritt Smears felt the forceps at his temples. He knew he was being pulled into Al's scheme deeper that he would have chosen. At some point he'd have to find a way to get back behind the wheel. For now though, he'd be a well-behaved passenger along for the ride. It was time to offer up some platitudes.

"Barrymore's of little consequence to our plans though, heh heh, isn't she? But let me tell you, Al, before the show I saw that fag from the restaurant next to the Mission in the audience. He was the one who started goading Dr. Sue halfway through the show. You'll be glad to hear I've already stuck Lou on their trail, checking into permit compliance. We're even going to arrange some surprise health inspections. You know how nasty that can get. Don't worry about me Al. I'm in this with you through thick and thin."

Al studied Merritt's face for a long moment until he felt Smears squirm somewhere deep inside. Al had played the game far more often than his haphazard crony and could rely on his innate ability to draw out and work the perspiring fear of an opponent or ally. After a suitably unnerving pause, he brushed aside Merritt's obsequious overture with a "Yeah, whatever." Then, he rewarded his lapdog with "Good idea on the health inspections though." Al would toy, tug and tempt this way and that until he got what he really wanted.

EIGHTEEN

That night at the Hudson Grille, things were back in gear after the scandalous Sue show and the grueling lines at the Phoebe Buffet. Jack was back to manning the range while Luke managed a full house. After the show, spirits were high and they had arranged to celebrate over dinner. Some tables had been grouped in the center of the room for a party of victorious friends against Dr. Sue. Luke and Jack took a break from their duties to lead the table in a toast. Ironically, they saluted Dr. Sue. "If she hadn't been as evil, we wouldn't be having such a celebration."

Reverend Blanche, seated at the head of the table, was undoubtedly the heroine of the moment. Everyone was suggesting she run for public office. Liz, Slim, Gilbert, Jerry, and Parker as well as a few other Mercy Missioners and numerous business owners held court around the table. Jack was pulling out the stops with festive fare, plate after plate of tapas with a theme. There was Blackened Big Mouth Bass stuffed with Whipped Butter Squash Mousseline, Sacrificial Lamb Medallions and Crab Not-So-Imperial Anymore. There were several others along the same vein, but the pièce de résistance was a cake bearing the likeness of Dr. Sue's head, severed at a bloody neck with a chocolate covered pastry dildo stuck in her mouth. This garnered loud kudos and everyone thought Jack should open a side business. (It's never good to give Jack any more ideas, but more on that later...) Reverend Blanche acted appalled at the cake's arrival, but she was the first to lay claim to the chocolate goodie. After all, even the religious are allowed to crave chocolate.

At one point during the dessert course, Luke came back to the table of honor, waving the evening edition of the *Washington Post*, exclaiming excitement on making it to the front page. It was the front page of the Style and Entertainment section, but a worthy front page none the less. There were even a few small pictures, one of the Marilyns and another featuring a close-up of Reverend Blanche's mug, in her smart hat and eyes throwing darts at Dr. Sue. The headline read, "Dr. Sue or Dr. Doom?"

Luke handed it off to Liz for a dramatic reading. She adjusted yet another pair of fashionable eyeglasses and began:

Tempers flared on today's edition of Town Hall, LIVE! Wednesday's Open Forum drew a record audience of citizens from the Ward 4 neighborhood and surrounding areas to rally for and against the running of this year's Transvestite Triathlon. The popular event is a fund raiser for local charities...

A passionate audience obviously rattled the nerves of the usually candid, stalwart conservative host, Dr. Sue Barrymore, well known to Washington audiences for her staunch, moral-minded opinions. Leading the counterpoint view of today's discussion was the civic and religious personality, Reverend Blanche Pickens. Reverend Pickens is well respected in the city for her work in assisting various community missions, recreation centers and shelters for the elderly and less fortunate, providing meals, day care and education programs in their neighborhoods.

Reverend Pickens remained calm and steadfast in her opinions and statements which provided contrast to Dr. Sue Barrymore's fervor. Excitement and enthusiasm grew as each opponent rallied their point of view, culminating with Reverend Pickens questioning Dr. Sue Barrymore's credentials. In a bold statement, the Reverend labeled Sue Barrymore as Dr. Doom, which lead to tears, tense moments and hysterical reaction as Sue raised a hand to her guest and flung the Reverend's hat into the jubilant audience.

Our available research indicates that Sue Barrymore does not hold any doctoral degrees or licenses, though she has touted herself with that title for several years. For now, Dr. Doom may be a more appropriate title in an arena where people behaved more like World Wrestling Entertainment than the American Medical Association.

The representative of the City offered no firm endorsement or disapproval of the event. Consequently, concerned citizens and Halloween revelers alike are expected to witness another Transvestite Triathlon, set to run tomorrow evening on U Street, beginning at nine o'clock p.m."

Everyone cheered and clapped at the announcement that the Triathlon would take place without any more interference.

During coffee, the kitchen was declared closed and Jack joined everyone at the table. He made one side slide down so he could squeeze in a chair next to Jerry. "Hi handsome," Jack leaned in close to his new pal, "I'm sorry we haven't had much time to play. Maybe after the race and all these inspectors we can catch a movie or play show and tell?"

Jerry leaned over toward Jack in agreement, and for the rest of the evening they were prone to play touch, that cute, early-stage show of affection, where shoulders nuzzled, hands had a tendency to touch and knees knocked in jest. Blanche Pickens kept throwing them winks and wrinkles of her nose, coaxing them on like a proud mother. Slim sat by casting an "ew" comment into the ring now and then. Gilbert, in an especially tattered, wrinkled shirt, came and went and came, keeping mostly quiet. He seemed happy enough to be fed course after course of foods he had never been able to enjoy.

Luke, busy boy that he was, did not go through the night unrewarded. His every smirk and double-take reached Parker like electricity by way of an infatuation hot line. The fun was watching Fox squirm, determined that the sparks would not embarrass his butch façade. But it was futile for both of them, and each blush felt like heavenly sunshine.

Somewhat closer to earth Liz was happy for her boys, but a twinge of jealousy jolted her to a hastened assessment of her options. Both left and right, successful business owners graced her with all the right compliments. She batted back with smiling eye lashings and winks. Perhaps for an offer of the perfect pair of shoes or glasses she might consider a three-way—but she figured she would be left to watch, while they played dress-up together. Her laugh began to form but caught, when a third option dawned across the table. She adjusted her horn rims to focus on the potential investment property and decided in short order that yes—Jon Miller might be worth developing.

The whole evening continued with a sustained buzz of energy at the Hudson Grille. It was like a merry-go-round of swirling highlights, mirror-bright smiles and rolling waves of dancing laughter. Everyone was having a sparkling time at the carnival on the night before All Hallows Eve.

Luke was at the bar fixing a tray of shooters. It was the first time in the past few months of worry and struggle that work seemed like play. He felt like the busy host of a popular soirée. Through the large front window of the Grille, the pedestrian street traffic was busier than usual, especially for a late Wednesday night in this part of town. Evidently, the area was growing more popular, but it didn't hurt that it was Halloween when friends of friends came into town to enjoy the festivities. Luke imagined the throng of queens who would collectively spend a year of hours this very night to finish up their outrageous creations for the following evening. It wasn't enough to pump up at the gym: this was the occasion to add feathers, sequins and spectacle to those mounds of muscle.

The door to the restaurant opened, jarring Luke from his images of deliciously feathered mounds. He caught his breath as though the cash drawer had flown open and punched him square in his gut. The sound of silence whip-lashed through the long narrow room. In the front of the room stood three men in black, chomping on stinking cigars.

Merritt Smears, Lou Thicke and Al Siegel looked like pasty, punchy and paunchy in respective order. Not even black could flatter them. To think it was only today when the revelers had just finished burying Dr. Doom, now these goombahs decided to show up for the reception.

Liz was chatting with Parker across the table. She stopped mid-sentence as Jon Miller stood up in haste. When Parker moved to follow, Jon authoritatively placed a restraining hand on Parker's shoulder. Without further hesitation, Jon walked coolly toward the group and greeted Al, his business partner, with camaraderie. Al responded with the businessman's routine hearty backslap and handshake. Jon then turned to Lou, smiling convincingly. "Thanks a bunch Lou, for the permit for work next door. Lemme buy you a drink." As Lou grinned vapidly, Parker wondered again where Jon's loyalties lay. More than a day had gone by and Jon had said nothing more about his discussion with the Mayor. Luke stood silent with a flood of premonitions taking control of his already tense body.

The grease that coated their unctuous conversation could be scooped up with a ladle. It was unusual to see the gang of three socializing after hours and even more unlikely that they would be remotely interested in seeing "how business was doing" at a gay-owned establishment. While Jon dutifully kept on bullshitting them, the goons ordered beers at the bar.

Luke and Jerry shared a knowing look as they witnessed the obvious stare-down connecting Merritt Smears' pumpkin head and Jack's fiery lantern eyes.

NINETEEN

"And absolutely, not one fucking word from ANYone about this to Parker Fox, or I will personally take long chocolate pastries and shove them in places other than your big mouths! I don't know if he'd care about this or not but I just don't want to go there with him before our first date-date. Jack, no hints. Jerry, no innuendo, and Liz, no facial expressions. Just be a cadaver and lie there! How we ever got through this evening without you all blabbering on—thank you Dr. Sue and the three stooges for keeping everyone preoccupied."

The Grille was closed and Luke stood toward the back of the dining room ranting, wearing only fish net stockings, black satin panties and a bustier. It was the remnants of his Dr. Frankenfurter costume and the start of his get-up for tomorrow night's race. He modestly hid most of his better attributes by day under a standard uniform of khakis and sedate shirts, layered with a t-shirt, sometimes two to add some bulk. But, what he kept so secret was enticing to some, such as Parker, and consisted of some strong legs, a tight butt (with dimples), a hairy chest and arms defined enough, but seen in a gym only on occasion. He didn't seem to have any problem prancing around at the moment though, with all the attributes accentuated by the hose, short pants, cinched waist and cleavage enhancing bondage. Perhaps he was just feeling divine.

Jack was the first to test the waters after Luke's sermon of strictures. "Suppose I were to ask Parker if he liked his meat dark or white?"

"NO!" boomed Luke.

Liz stepped up for the spike, "Can I ask him if he'd be interested in one of my black stylists? By the way Luke, Parker is really quite charming. I can see why you're in such a mood. He even felt up my hand bag, said he once had a saddle just as smooth. Can you imagine him on a horse? Even I got a little bothered."

Luke stood there in disbelief. "Stop it. You two are gonna drive me crazy!" Luke played up his exasperation and wiggled his fanny for emphasis.

Jerry, new to the group, was more tactful. "He did seem to enjoy his slice of the chocolate dildo. I don't think you have to worry about this black thing."

"E-nough already. Okay, let's get back to more serious matters. What the hell is up with that Merritt Smears? Casing the joint with his cronies tonight? God, he is creepy."

"Well Merritt's been acting pretty wound up lately," Jerry offered. "I know for a fact they have something going down. I have pulled every plat plan, utility drawing and diagram, permit and license for this whole block. I have even personally delivered copies to Al Siegel's door. And by the way," he confided, "you better get ready for a surprise health inspection, probably tomorrow."

As the insider tips spilled out, Luke became increasingly horrified . "Jesus Christ! A health inspection, tomorrow! I'll end up wetting my best running panties. Jack, fill every last every soap dispenser, label everything in the cooler twice, put out all the fly traps from the stock room, we have our time and temperature logs and Jack, don't forget to whip up a batch of that -"

"Got it."

"- that smells like heaven. No matter who the fucking health department sends us, they say they can't accept 'tokens' of appreciation, but with that stuff of yours they always end up staying for lunch. God DAMN that smarmy, filthy Merritt Smears. He was staring at you today on TV, Jack. Even the cameraman was picking it up. And then again tonight at the Grille."

Jack tried to shrug it off. "What is he going to do? Abduct me? Ew, do you think we should find a body guard? I'd love to interview a few hundred bodyguard applicants. I mean we wouldn't have to hire one. Just keep'em coming through the door, so I am always surrounded!"

Jerry laughed half-heartedly. Still more clouds were gathering in his mind. "Guys, that's the last undercover info I'm likely to be able to give you. Now that Merritt saw me in the middle of your restaurant celebrating, I am sure my ass has seen the last of my job come tomorrow. And, if that weren't enough, I think Greg Thicke is in on this too. That was his brother who showed up tonight. He was the big stupid looking one in the middle. Anyway, I know you're not going to believe this, but I think Greg was coming on to me today at the office."

Jack interrupted, "Greg Thicke, a queen? No way! Ever since Ellen and Rosie came out, everyone wants to be gay. Shit. I'd expect him to be a crook, but a homo? No, no way. But now, do we vote for him or not? Jerry, you better be careful, he even looks like Anderson Cooper."

"Yeah, I know. All this is getting to be a bit much. Do you think you guys can use a full-time waiter? Hell, I'll even wash a dish or two."

Luke set out to bring back sanity. "At this point, I would believe just about anything. If that asshole Smears even tries to fire you, let him. I'm sure we can sue, especially if he's the crook we think he is. And Greg Thicke too? Jeez. If you do get fired, it's probably not a bad thing anyway. I certainly think we can bring on a waiter if business keeps up like it has for the past few days. It will give me more time to work on marketing and advertising. "

"Ex-actly now," Liz barged in. "Luke honey, listen to me gurrl." She started bobbing her head around, chewing a big hunk of imaginary bubble gum. She inched her glasses down on the edge of her nose and pursed up her red lips into a kissable wad. "It's time to start marketing our big black beauty girl for tomorrow night!"

Liz stood and addressed her delighted band of admirers. "Who was it that said there isn't much difference between a black woman and a gay male? So I've been thinking of some names. Girl's gotta have a good name for a Triathlon race. I'm sure Judy Jetson Jackson Jessie Kersey Mercy Joyner is gonna be taken already. This is an ath-let-ic event after all. And you can't use Flo Jo Mojo HoJo or whatever because she passed away. So, I've been thinking of some other NASTY names like Juwanna VulvaSalada or Tae Smilina Bacon. But then, but then—" Liz started getting giddy with herself, and the guys were glued in—"then there are the less rank and vile names, things like Betina Barbarosa or Hissy-Fitz-Gerald. They're too Long Island skank and Hampton's hussy. So how about, and this one is very D.C., how about LaChuChuWanda Watkins? It's the kind of name you can really say with your hips!"

Jack jumped up and squealed, "That's it. I love it. Luke loves it. Don't you Luke? I mean LaChuChuWanda, servin' up a fine piece of caboose now. Talk about gurrl-friend?" Jack caught himself, "and what were you saying about black women and gay men?"

"Eh-hem? Do I get to vote around here?" asked Luke. "This is my manhood I'm giving up here."

"Believe me, you're manhood is going to be well protected." Jack got up and ran around to his cooking pulpit, and produced a large orange trash bag printed to look like a pumpkin. He shook the bag of evidence to puzzle his tempted, curious audience. "And, this is just one of your secret weapons. Here Luke, try this on for size. LaChuChuWanda is going to be better equipped than 007. Which makes me 'Q', and we know what that stands for!"

Everyone marveled while Luke strapped himself into Jack's latest creation. They considered possibilities and necessary adjustments. Luke finally began to ease into his role, pantomiming Charlie's Angel moves while Jack tried to sing snippets of *I'm A Survivor*. At the big event tomorrow, with a little black face, Luke would look like a member of Destiny's Child.

TWENTY

Jerry dragged his butt to work the next morning with the fear and loathing usually reserved for an HIV test. When he arrived at the office, he braced himself for the familiar groan of the reception door. As he opened it, he surmised that it would probably be his last time to wince at the Pavlovian sound. The door might not be open as he got booted back out.

His senses were heightened as he entered the area. He could smell the grimy cream pea walls, and almost feel the tacky touch of the shellac-like film from decades of cigar smoke that clung to all the dull surfaces. He imagined the sorry families of mites that tried to survive in the worn upholsteries and carpet. The entire place bore the bleak desolate strand of hope that hung on trying to survive some microscopic chemical catastrophe. He started to look forward with relief at being freed from the place. It could only be better for his health. He took a short breath to brace himself for confrontation, and walked the short distance to the safe haven of his desk.

The door to Merritt's office was shut, but there was no doubt he had already arrived. Jerry shuddered at the sounds of a domineering blow hole. He thanked God he had fully functional, loving parents because his boss sounded like a fully dysfunctional father type. While he couldn't understand everything Merritt was saying, the loud tones were heavy with belittling and condescending vibrations. Jerry hadn't had much to drink the night before, but with little sleep, the whole affair around him enhanced the queasy nausea from his mild hangover.

He opened his Xando bag containing breakfast and a decent cup of coffee, and began to eat the cherry filled croissant for relief. As he was fixing the pop-up lid on his coffee, Merritt boomed on the intercom, "Callahan?" The hot coffee flew all over his desk.

Greg Thicke had called Merritt Smears to arrange an early morning appointment. It had been exactly like calling on the devil. Basically, he needed more information. He didn't see that he had any other choice but to smoke Smears out. Yet he knew that he had to be on guard for the political flame that could bite him on the ass. The election was only days away, and while he wasn't doing poorly in the polls, coming up with some dirt that affected constituents could potentially either work in his favor, or, if his dumb brother Lou was involved and was outed, be spun against him.

The Mayor, his long time friend and supporter, had given him an inkling that something was awry in the Development office. Greg still held out hope for Lou, but when it came down to this election, the chips were going to have to fall where they may. Between Greg's election and Lou's job there was little choice. He had to risk a confrontation with Merritt Smears.

Greg sat before Smears' desk surrounded by the man's ridiculous array of golfing apparatus. The place seemed more like some cheap amusement booth on a beach boardwalk, than it did a place of official business. It did not surprise him. He had been here before, but the equipment had multiplied since his last visit.

Merritt was already on his second cigar before Greg got a word in edgewise. Greg claimed he wanted to discuss with Merritt areas of neighborhood development, upcoming projects, sites that could be put to better use. Potentially Greg could speak to these in his final round of campaign speeches. Smears managed to skirt very clear of mentioning any areas near the Hudson Grille or Mercy Mission. He did however effectively double the amount of air pollution in the voting district, not only from the cigar, but also from all the hot air expelled in blowing his own horn.

Just about when Greg was considering running from the cloudy room and any more boring drivel from Smears, Merritt threw him a curveball. He mentioned Lou in a tone that intimated a warning. Merritt informed Greg that he was concerned with Lou, that he couldn't be sure if he was on the take from developers, and that Greg should be concerned, considering his political hopes. This information told Greg everything. If there was really something going on inside this man's limited bureaucratic domain, he would do what ever it took to save his neck. Merritt was willing to shop Lou, and if necessary sink Greg at the same time.

While Greg was considering his awkward position, Merritt applied a further squeeze. He had called Jerry Callahan into the office. Then, even though Greg had been to the office before, Smears went through the act of formally introducing him to Jerry. Greg found himself locking eyes with Jerry in a distracting moment. Merritt, as if calling in a witness, asked Jerry if he had recently noticed any strange behavior from Lou Thicke. He stared pointedly at Jerry. Jerry withered and tried to get a grip on himself. What was the answer Smears was looking for, and that his job might depend on? All of Lou's behavior was strange. And was Greg trying to pick him up? He prayed that his reply was non-committal.

"No."

Smears let the suspense hang while he smeared the other half of his bagel. Finally, he told Jerry to keep his eyes open and to let him know, because Greg would certainly appreciate any information. Jerry, in some relief, realized that Merritt was scamming Greg. There could be no other reason that Merritt would include him on any other dealing or details.

As Greg was leaving, he shook Jerry's hand with both of his, thanking him and hoped for his vote. Jerry hoped that was all he wanted.

Merritt asked Jerry to hang on a minute after Greg had left. "You think you know that I know you know, but you don't. So what you have to do around here is city business, and while we're not the CIA, it is business, and information isn't to be discussed outside the office. Understand? We are trying to maintain agendas for the good of the public's welfare."

Jerry realized that Merritt did not mention any disciplinary files, grounds for termination or interpretation of events. It was either because he had no real grounds, or because he wanted the situation to crawl back under the mite infested carpet. He was sure Merritt would be much more careful, and at some point soon suggest a transfer. Jerry knew that Merritt knew that Jerry knew about the trio's machinations. That much had been made semi-clear. So while Jerry may have survived the chopping block this time, his wings had been sharply clipped.

Merritt dismissed Jerry with all the charm of a cranky, constipated high school principal. Then he got on the phone to call Big Al, and let him know that everything had gone off as planned.

TWENTY-ONE

Everything hit the proverbial fan at the Hudson Grille as well as Mercy Mission. It was obvious to everyone that Merritt Smears had pulled out all the stops and had gone on attack. Lou Thicke and another inspector had shown up at Mercy Mission. Inspectors NEVER showed up unless one called for an appointment, and even then it was dubious that they would ever arrive on schedule.

Reverend Pickens nearly had a virgin birth when faced with the likes of inspectors, and she promptly made a hysterical call to her landlord Jon Miller. Jon called Parker Fox, who was in the middle of a shower, and told him to get over to the Mission even before he dried off. Luke would have enjoyed the scene of Parker standing in the middle of his bedroom, shining, dripping wet from head, to chest, to butt and calf. He gave one good shake like a race-horse ridding his body of a gallon of spraying water droplets. He emerged fully dressed in another tight t-shirt and butt hugging jeans, with bare feet that morphed into black high-top running shoes as he raced out the door, gallantly responding to the deacon in distress.

Infinitely less glamorous, the health inspector was now waiting at the door of Hudson Grille. Luke, approaching from a block away, could tell something was unusual. Gilbert was out front, but he wasn't snoozing by the doorstep. Instead, he was sitting alert on the sidewalk, his back propped up against the paneling below the front window. He was staring up at a short, potato-shaped woman. From a distance, she stood like a dusty, tweeded, reddish-brown orb, with snarly ivory eyes. She quarter-turned in each direction, looked up and down the street but mostly away from the scraggly looking Gilbert. She then held up her briefcase-laden hand to check a watch on the other wrist.

After all the scrutiny and mind-numbing explanations required by the virago's multiple inquisitions, Luke, Jack and Parker gathered at the bar of the Grille to compare notes. The air between them was tense with pressure. They were angered at the utter gall of the inspections, their timing, and the ridiculous hurdles that were being imposed.

While the Grille and Mission had momentarily escaped their respective fatal bullets, the two inspectors had left their mark of irksome fear as well as long lists of non-compliant issues that needed to be corrected within twenty-four hours. All the items split hairs with the codes, finding crooks and chinks in their muddled interpretation. Unfortunately it was the way the system worked, and the way it would have to be played out if they didn't want to suspend operation. It sucked big time and to top it all off, the potato bitch didn't even stay for lunch!

Parker figured he could call up Jon and together they could band together a crew of help. The basement had to be cleaned from standing water, the drain pipes had to be renewed because their diameter was not up to code, and all "hazardous" broken tile on the main floor had to be replaced. It was a wonder they hadn't pulled out the asbestos card, but that was an eight letter word. Lou and his sidekick had enough difficulty with pipe and drip.

Luke and Jack had smaller stuff to rectify than Parker. It would be no great pain to put up an extra hand-washing sign and to better separate the storage of chicken and beef. But for chrissakes, how were they supposed to know that their ice crystals were too large? Did she really expect them to inspect every damn can for a bulge or a flawed seam? Luke was pretty sure these items had been checked off just for their annoyance value.

"Now now, honey," chided Jack, "To work! You don't want caught with a flawed SEAM in twenty-four hours' time, do you?" He suggestively stroked Luke's tight jean hip pocket.

"Hey I want that job," Parker broke in, grinning as he reached to fondle the other pocket. Luke's heart skipped a beat.

"Seriously guys," he said, brushing all their hands aside, "I think we have no alternative but to close for dinner tonight. We have a shitload of busy work to do for the bitch, we've already missed the breakfast shift, and there's the lunch shift to run. Then we—uh—" Luke paused, wondering what Parker would think of his soon to be 'maybe boyfriend' as a tube-topped, afro-headed, beaded and braided black drag queen.

Fortunately, Jack caught on. "Sure. Yes, yes, we should close. Most of our would-be patrons tonight will be out there whooping it up, and we are a block too far away to be one of the Triathlon bar stops anyway."

Jack kept up a nervous chatter, moving on to a scathing commentary that further diminished the stature of Mrs. Potato the health inspector. After his tirade, he winked at Luke, mimed a sigh of relief and then volunteered to get back to the task at hand. "OK I'm just dying to go test some cleaning solvents for parts-per-million ratios, as prescribed by that friggin' yam." It was one of the more affectionate, less objectionable nicknames he had called her.

Luke and Parker were left alone at the bar. They looked into each other's eyes, took a tandem breath and shared a weak smile. One was Jeanette McDonald to the other's Nelson Eddy. Both of them felt like they had just been in a car wreck, glad to be unhurt but dismayed at having to deal with all the fallout. Luke knew that Parker had to be on his way, but really didn't want him to leave, so he started up a conversation.

"So how was the Reverend Pickens after all those goons tore up at the Mission?"

"She was brave and got kind of pissy. She probably felt kind of helpless, her fort under attack. I had to calm her down and keep her out of the way. I should be able to get everything done so they can't shut the place down. If not, we can always call in a TV crew. That should fix 'em."

Luke reached out to touch Parker's hand, but ended up drumming his fingers on the bar. Parker noticed Luke's change of course, but did not mention it. Instead he asked, "So, I don't know if we'll be finished in time, but I was wondering if you were going to watch the race tonight."

Luke's drumming fingers slowed down and stopped. "Oh, after our clean-up and chores, I promised Jack I would help him help a-uh friend of his who plans to enter." He winced with apology.

Parker looked disappointed and tried to let Luke off the hook. "Ah, I'll probably be at the Mission till late anyway. But, you never know, maybe I will see you there." Parker got up from his barstool as Luke replied with an awkward "Maybe."

Before he went out the door, Parker turned back to Luke with renewed enthusiasm. He kind of skipped as he turned. "If not kiddo, drop by the Mission after the race. If I am still there, maybe you can help me check out some pipe diameters in the basement!"

TWENTY-TWO

It was a gray overcast morning, chilly and damp. Dr. Sue parked her cream colored pearlescent Acura (with an apricot cast) on one of the side residential streets that hid itself between the north-south numbers and the east-west letters of L'Enfant's master plan of Washington, D.C. The master plan did not intend for the neighborhood to be half abandoned, disheveled or littered with overturned stripped cars, garbage, needles or used condoms. It made Sue wish for the safety of her own street, much farther north and west in lovely Glover Park. She stepped around the steaming manhole cover, not only to avoid the steam, but to steer clear of the snoring bundle of rags that curled up close to the rusty holes for warmth.

Al suggested she use the back alley to come to his house, as it would be easier to find a parking space, but more likely to conceal her arrival from nosey neighbors. What ever the reason, she felt better using the rear door in spite of feeling like hired help. The alley was empty at this hour from the truant street urchins, pimps, hookers or aggressive drug dealers that might accost her at night. By day, business was more plentiful on the more heavily traveled thoroughfares.

The alley was the same grungy path she had used to escape from the perverted episode with Al a few nights before. It seemed all her waking hours were becoming filled with demeaning, regrettable or compromising incidents. She wondered if there was a twelve step program for moral zealots who were corrupted by ingesting sin and sundry other degradations.

She stopped abruptly as she saw a man ahead in the alley. "Jesus Christ," she thought, "just what I need is to get mugged on my way to be a phone sex tramp. Wouldn't that be par for the fucking course?"

He stood, wearing a dark, knee-length ill-fitting coat, loitering around in circles, talking on a cell phone. She wondered how anyone would rather throw money away on a cell phone bill, than try and save what they could to dig out of living in a hovel.

As he got off the phone, Sue felt relieved. The man got into an old midnight blue van that was parked tightly in a crowd of overgrown weeds, a half dead tree strangled with ivy and stalks of sumac laden with pods of poison fruit.

Sue hastened her pace and walked toward the van with absent-minded determination and passed it with the notion that reaching her destination was more important than fretting about some van hiding out in a secluded alley. In this way she suppressed the fear of having to confront some thug who relished roughing up anyone for a wad of cash and their next fix.

She strode quickly, looking over her shoulder to make sure the man in the coat wasn't hanging out of the window of the van sizing her up for the kill. As she confirmed that her stalker paid her no interest, she cursed herself for wearing an expensive pair of open-toed flats to trudge down the muddy lane.

By the time she raised her hand to pound on Al's back door for the third time her impatience was growing. The cold damp air was giving her an uncomfortable chill and she jiggled up and down to alleviate an urgent need to pee. "Really now," she asked, "can't those bitches downstairs hike their fat asses up some steps to let me in?" She hoped Al had remembered to tell them she was coming in around noon.

Finally the curtain on the back door parted to reveal the big white eyes of Kahlua Courvoisier, which grew even larger when she recognized Dr. Sue. The door opened and Sue exhaled in relief, feeling the warmer air from the house grab at her cold limbs. The cold, drizzly air from the outside hung with the scent of garbage and fetid standing pothole water. It was replaced by a heavy tropical fog hanging around Kahlua like a humid cloud. The passion-fruity cigarette-smoky miasma caused Sue to recoil briefly on the stoop.

"Missus Barrymore, hi baby. Come on in, come on in. Certainly din't expec-to be seein' you again so soon... When Mr. Al told us the famous Dr. Sue was our old pal Suzette, we had a fit. Those was good old times girl. It's been ten years. You look so—so different. I mean we all put on a few pounds. What I mean is you look real refine now."

Sue was barely listening to Kahlua as she tried to wrestle her way out of the metallic melon-colored vinyl car coat. Kahlua hovered around Sue and tried to assist, but Sue swung from side to side, walking through the kitchen, dropping her bag on the floor, intent on making it to the bathroom under the stair before she wet her pants.

Kahlua just kept talking right along, oblivious to the fact that Sue was ignoring her attempt at hospitality. Sue reached the room and slammed the door in the bubbling bundle's face which kept chatting at her through the closed door. Kahlua in her black lacy slip raised her bare arm, black and fatty, to rest a palm on the door jamb. Her other fist came to rest on an ample hip as she continued praising Missus Barrymore, gold tooth flashing like a pen light while she spoke. "Why Suzette, I mean Dr. Sue, anyway, weez all so happy when Mr. Al told us you'd be coming by today. We've been trying to talk him into giving us today off for a coupla weeks now. He kept ignoring us even when we told him we didn't need this sorry ass job and for him to go fuck himself. Then this morning, he came in all sweet and nice—ain't seen him this happy EV-ah you know. We nearly knocked him over on the way out, except he told us to hang around, treat you nice and warm you up on the phones before we left."

The toilet paper roll rumbled as it spun, the toilet flushed and the sink water turned on with a rush, then as quickly turned off. The handle to the door rattled as it was being unlocked before the door swung open for a perturbed looking Sue. Her face grimaced at the sight of Kahlua's fuzzy armpit stretching to greet her.

"Okay sweetheart, follow me," said Kahlua. Once you get used to letting yourself go, well, I know I sure have a good time down here everyday!"

Sue followed the big Dixie cup as she waddled her fat thighs around each other. She pulled her chin back in distaste as she watched the huge beach ball mounds of rump shuffle under Kahlua's shiny black slip. Sue had nothing to say as her troop leader traipsed down the steps on one piglet-like hoof then the other, filling the stairwell with her width and incessant rambling.

"Mr. Al says we are gonna be moving operations real soon out of this basement. Somewhere's over on U Street. He says we'll have a whole lot more room, we may be bringing on more girls and maybe even some guys. Wouldn't that be fun? He also says we may be expanding beyond the phone business and starting to make movies! He can be such an asshole sometimes, but I gotta think twice now, maybe Kahlua is gonna become a movie star! Wouldn't that be slammin'? Sure would help me out trying to feed my kids, two of 'em now. My momma's taking care of 'em, along with Tanka Rae's three, she 'bout to lose her mind. Thank God Chardonay's saving hers..."

Sue was glad they had reached the bottom of the stair, the door to the room, and the cipher lock. It took all of Kahlua's capacity to handle each, and shut up. While Sue wasn't looking forward to the next step in her 'adventure', at least these small hurdles gave her a moment of silence to regain her wits.

As the door opened on the dim room, Sue looked to heaven for perseverance. All she received back was a wall clock reading twelve, and the start of Town Hall, LIVE! on a small TV high in the corner. The sound was on mute, but that did nothing to alleviate the slap to her ego. It was HER show, and instead of the signature smile the camera zoomed in on Reverend Blanche's fussy Sunday hat. Blanche was flanked by Greg Thicke, both of them laughing and having a good time. Sue was sure they must have been laughing at her folly.

Irritated, Sue snapped, "Could you—" and then changed her hostile tone. "Would you please do me a favor and turn off the TV?" Chardonay aimed the remote, pushed the button and nodded her head like *I Dream of Jeannie.*

Tanka Rae, who the evening before was looking fierce, especially in the looks she flung at Sue, seemed friendlier today. She was glad to see the woman that would enable them to take off an odd day in the middle of the week. Yes, there were other shifts of girls, but they too wanted off for Halloween, either to party or to take their kids trick and treating. Sue was surprised when Tanka Rae opened up her heart and mind to thank her. "Doctor Barrymore, I thought you'd be some stuck-up white bitch looking down her nose like we was a bunch of sorry ass trash. It really make me think twice about bustin' your fuckin' jaw when I heard you was really Suzette and gonna get us a day off. Idda be nice to get out of this shit-hole. So how you been girl?"

Sue was left to nod her head, speechless for once.

Chardonay fluttered the tip of her middle finger in a tiny fairy wave which led Kahlua to pipe up and fill the silent void. "OKAY Momma, sit cho white ass down here. We's gonna teach you how to be HOT and bother up some mens!"

The phone rang and Tanka Rae answered in a sexy breathy voice that belied her sturdy oil-tanker build. "Miss Sallie's Hot Lines." Their credit card number entered to gain access to live chat, Tanka Rae was ready to perform her service. "This is Aquarius. I am all wet and wild for YOU honey..."

Another phone rang and Kahlua slid on her headset and answered deep and throaty, "Miss Sallie's Hot Lines, this is Capricorn. I am gonna let you ride my ass baby—OH! Sorry Mr. Al. Sue? Oh yeah honey, she here. Yeah, hang on. Sue, baby, it's the boss man. He wants to talk wit you."

Sue walked over to take the handset, rolling her eyes and ready for the indignity. "Hello. Hi Al. No, I'm not wearing the slip. I'll answer the damn phone, but I'm not gonna—Okay already—ALONE? I can't manage these phones a-lone!" He hung up on her which allowed her to vent freely. "That God damned ASSHOLE! Really now."

Chardonay looked embarrassed in the corner so Sue put a lid on her foul mouth. Sue hitched her bra and commanded, "Okay Kahlua, take the next caller. Gemini is ready to unleash her twins!" Kahlua punched the blinking light with her rhinestone studded nail tip.

The girls had left with hugs and air kisses and Sue had managed not to screw up too badly. She only hung up on two callers that seemed more like violent molesters than they did your ordinary phone sex pervert. She sat in her slip, lit another cigarette and watched the phones with lights blinking. They all seemed to be screaming, "Do me, do me!" She had finally realized that being only one person, she could only take one call at a time. She had tried two at once and things were a little too dicey. They would have to sit there on hold, listening to some cunt recording, begging them to hang on to their loads before they had to start paying by the minute. What a racket. She looked at the flashing lights with disdain, and told them aloud to "Fuck Off!" She needed a break, much deserved after an hour of fake panting, cooing and snarling lewd suggestions to the retards on the other end of the line. She put the headset back on and punched a few numbers and waited for the other end to answer. She got voice mail but pressed on nonetheless.

"Hello, my name is Gemini and I'm here with my huge, strapping, naked Latino stud. He has these big electric hair clippers vibrating up against his ten inch hard-on. He's threatening me with his clippers, just ready and waiting to shave me down to my bare skin. It's going to be soo smooth for you. All wet and bare and slippery for my Merritt..."

TWENTY-THREE

They checked off their health department lists, item by item as each task was completed, in between flipping tuna steaks, slinging menus, drinks and dessert plates. Their adrenaline pumped, fueled by expelling their annoyance and the steady ringing of the cash register. A manic effort in multi-tasking sped up their pace and ability to hustle their customers with friendly and efficient manners. At the close of the lunch shift they had turned more tables than usual, and they high-fived a salute to their success.

"That sack of spuds is no match for us. If she has the nerve to find anything else wrong with this place, I'm gonna toss her in the cooler and flush the key. I am one tired—chef." Jack caught himself before Luke could reply and continued, "How about I meet you back at your place in an hour and a half. Then we can pull LaChuChuWanda together."

"Sounds good," said Luke. "Give me time to call Liz, take a hot shower and a nap. I'll see you around four-thirty."

They parted ways and Luke was tempted to seek out Parker next door, but he was tired. He called Liz from the bar before heading home.

On his way down the street, he started to get excited and nervous about the race tonight. Liz had proudly told him that his wig was complete. It was a "veritable masterpiece," but she warned, that as glorious as it was, it would certainly draw some attention if he made it to the winner's circle. This amused him, but he was so exhausted, he was sure LaChuChuWanda would hobble off the course before she made it to her second shooter. He could see himself sitting at the bar, all black and bitchin', screaming at the bartender like some Fox Network harlot, slinging back cocktails without a care in the world.

When he finally hit the shower, his black diva fantasies had subsided to make way for dreams of kneading his soapy fingers into the thick muscles of Parker's shoulders and back. It took him less than a minute to grab onto his balls and stroke off, shooting a load to his master. Spent, he set an alarm, crawled back into bed, and ground another hard-on into a pillow between his legs. Fatigue was delicious that way, especially thinking of Fox.

A delicious hour later, Luke got out of bed still dreaming of his man while he made a fresh cup of coffee. He ran around the simple room, gathering up newspapers, magazines and tossed mail. He slid the coffee table out of the way without toppling his collection of obelisks to make room for Jack, and ran a quick swipe of the duster across more obvious surfaces. He always confided with himself that he didn't have to care about what Jack thought of the place, but he did.

He opened the gray flannel drapes and hoisted up the aluminum colored blinds. There was only a gray sky beyond so he released the cord and adjusted the slats half open. He didn't want to give the whole neighborhood a show of Jack's extravaganza anyway. He ran back to the bath, slicked back his hair and tucked himself into the fishnets and panties. With a nap behind him, he was feeling more positive about the night, and picked up the bustier. In the middle of inhaling and binding, the doorbell rang. He skipped the rest of the lacing and pranced on tip toe out to the door. As he caught a glance of his ass in the mirror, he gave it a smack and flashed a smile at himself.

"Mn child, zat my plumber coming home to LaChuChuWanda?" Luke spoke at the door, praying it was Jack on the other side.

"Open the door you black bitch, I got packages!"

Luke smiled as he opened the door, and was surprised not to see much of Jack. Before him were two jeaned legs with stuffed blue Ikea bags hanging from each shoulder. A pair of arms held a tool caddy, Jack's infamous box of small power tools, all topped with a large Balducci's bag in front of his face.

"We're in luck! I had my neighbor downstairs get us dinner. I caught him on the phone just before he was ready to leave the store. Well, just don't stand there, help me already."

Jack unstacked finally said, "LaChuChuWanda lookin' fine!" They shuffled the bags, boxes, totes and tools off to one side of the room when the doorbell rang again.

"Let's try this one more time." Luke hoisted his wire framed tits, stuck out his butt and walked back to the door on the balls of his feet. His hips swung like a runway model. Jack was glad to see his partner finally getting into the act after so much resistance.

"Mn child. Zat you Ozzie? LaChuChuWanda got a surprise for you!" He opened the door for Liz.

"Surprise, I'll give you a surprise. I should have brought Parker along. That would have been a surprise. Here, help me with this wig box."

Jack gasped, "The wig, the wig, show us the wig!"

Liz paused for a proud second before she unzipped the enormous round black patent leather case. What she unveiled would have stopped traffic clear across the Pennsylvania Avenue Bridge. Tall, with braids, sparkling beads, shimmering metallic strands, twisted and swirled. Liz had employed every trick out of the Ebony Jet bible.

"Wait a minute, we're not done yet." From another satchel, she pulled out a large multi-pronged pinwheel that she secured to the back of the wig with several wing-nuts. "You're not the only crafty one, Jack. You see here? This clear strap goes under your chin. Ain't nobody gonna rip this sucker off your head. And, with this wire here, there's a switch we can mount to the belt thing Jack had you try on last night. A flick of the switch and voilà!" The pinwheel started to turn on the back of the wig with surprising velocity. The metallic fins reflected off built-in flashing lights and created a whirling halo of light. "This thing has the power of a hand-held circular saw! Enrique helped me rework it from one of his hair show exhibits. I mean it won't chop off a finger or anything, but hell, I certainly wouldn't get near it."

Jack let out a whoop. "Miss Thing, you make it up to the finish line and we'll just hold you up and mow them down!"

Luke tried on the wig and doubled over in hysterics every time he flipped on the switch. On, off, on, off. The three of them were in a fit of giggles.

"I thought I'm supposed to go from store to store, finding things as I go to add to my costume?"

Jack held up a list. "Here's the sequence of stores. While you're slugging down shooters, I'll be running to the next shop and have every-thing ready for you to buy. I've already scoped everything out. I'll be at the front door of every one. When I have to help you install something, Jerry will be on up ahead. Liz, go get the make-up. Luke, break open the food. I told him to get lots of carbs. Here is the strategy..."

"So here is the strategy."

They were gathered around the table looking at the map of colored grids on the block that was home to Mercy Mission and Hudson Grille. Al, Lou and Merritt along with some utility workers with well greased palms. They had their bases covered from gas and electric to telephone and cable.

"We don't need to get into the building tonight. You can access the lines from the street." Al chomped on his cigar and paused to stoke up a good cloud of smoke. "Get the truck in place around eight. That will be an hour before the race. It is a commercial street, so everything will be closed. The only all-night shop is at the far end of the block. Just do what little you have to, so these buildings here need to be evacuated."

TWENTY-FOUR

Luke had to dip when leaving his apartment, getting on and off the elevator and through the vestibule door. The wig was spectacular. It also added a foot to his black diva-ness. He caught another glimpse of himself in the front glass doors and was reasonably confident with his disguise. It was hard to get past the outrageous hair, large tinted glasses and his ruby red mouth accentuated like collagen lips. At the moment he was wearing "sensible" running shoes to get him to the start of the race, and according to Jack's plan, three-quarters of the way to victory before a purchase of some "fierce, shit-kickin', mud-slingin' women's size 13 boots" on hold at the Pic 'N Pay en route.

He navigated his way through the front doors to his apartment building and presented himself to the night. Passers-by looked up at him in all his glory as he stood on the wide stone landing under a lit wire-glass canopy. One leather-clad couple and "the Village People" merged to form a small crowd at the base of the steps. They stopped in awe to witness Luke's entrance.

"Hey sweetheart, I gotta sling for that pretty black ass." The leather man bellowed as he lobbed an arm over his partner's shoulder to leer. The ridiculously attractive couple, wearing black studded title sashes from some contest victory, whistled up at Luke.

He managed not to fall to his knees, instead turning his butt Vargas style toward them, and blew a kiss over his shoulder.

"Well, she isn't having any problem in the spotlight now, is she." Jack remarked to Liz as they stood behind their creation.

"I heard that. LaChuChuWanda is ready, willing and able, especially for the likes of those two!"

"Oh look! There's Parker!" Liz hammed.

"Bitch." Luke retorted.

A third party joined the crowd that stood below, one in sixties-a-go-go, swinging a mod flowered tote blaring Pet Shop Boys. LaChuChu-Wanda picked up the beat for a bit of show-off dancing before gloriously descending the stairs to his cheering fans. He paused for a few flash shots with and without Jack and Liz mugging behind him.

They headed south to P Street to get themselves in the thick of things, a growing parade of party boys, girls, everything and anything in between.

They walked south then west past the Whole Foods store, each of them taking in the splendors in front, in the shape of six near-naked men in Mylar harnesses and feathered angel wings. "Jesus Christ," said Jack, "there are more packed boxes out here than inside the market!"

"Oh look. It's CooCoo for Cocoa Puff! And boy, am I ever!" Liz was pointing to a black hunk with ninety-five percent of his costume devoted to a bobbing cereal box headdress.

In front of the coffee bar window, Luke/LaChuChuWanda wiggled some tail and switched on the pinwheel halo canted above his braids. The three of them encored another round of giggles from the faces that sat ringside watching the throng of costumes. The two dykes dressed as a seat from a roller coaster were out again for another year, along with the usual array of dildoed flashers and political masks. Luke smiled as he spotted a Mark Foley mask surrounded by a retinue with "Mark Foley's page" labels strung around their necks.

The Triathlon began at 17th and P Streets, a tradition that started with the former "High Heel Race." Dupont Circle, past its days of revival and gentrification, was no longer on the bohemian fringe that had held a seductive appeal as the gay epicenter. New commercial ventures on Connecticut Avenue resembled the much straighter Georgetown (the former, former epicenter). So the race followed the latest in-crowd: east on P Street, north on 14th, west on U and back south on 17th, ending at JR's Bar, now an institution for the terminally gay socialite.

Luke, Jack and Liz picked up Jerry on the way over, and proceeded to the starting block. When Luke registered at the sign-up table as Miss LaChuChuWanda Watkins, he was presented with a numbered armband, 221, which Jack thought a good omen of odds. After Jack had finished kneading Luke's shoulders in a pre-race warm-up, giving him pep talk hints and anecdotes to ease nervousness, LaChuChuWanda walked over to join his costumed comrades.

A dog-collared Reverend Ted Haggard seemed unrepentant, arm-in-arm with his toy-boy. He brandished his wedding ring, a big box labeled "Methamphetamine" and his trademark inane grin. There were miscellaneous Connie's—Chung, Francis and one Lingus; and some westerners—the big gun gals or knock-offs of Dolly. While LaChuChu-Wanda saw several black sisters, she was probably better categorized in the "Fancy Division," those contestants with excessively clever costume gimmicks. Nothing quite stood up to the whirly-gig halo, not even the Dunkin'Donut mustached matron with the tassled fluorescent traffic-cones.

"Ladies and broads," began the announcer, "Welcome to the third annual Transvestite Triathlon! It looks like we are coming up on seven thousand, eight hundred dollars in donations, and we still will have to tally proceeds from our participating businesses and totals from the contestant raffle. So, if you haven't bet on your favorite Tri-athlete, come on down and place your donation on a winning number! We'll be starting in five minutes, so get into positions! Everybody not running in the race, stand way the heck back, it looks like we're shaping up for quite a stampede tonight!"

LaChuChuWanda stood in the middle of her mostly bass and baritone brethren anxiously awaiting the next few minutes to pass. Just moments ago, emboldened by flattering catcalls and wicked delighted revelers, Luke had a final moment to realize that once again, he had juiced himself up on Jack's enthusiastic scheming. His nervousness subdued, he proudly foresaw his destiny in terms of white and black. LaChuChuWanda had to run her fuckin' ass off!

"Running, Shopping and Swilling for the Grand Prize of One Thousand Dollars, Transvestite Tri-athletes get READ-y, get SET—" BAM went the starting pistol and the three hundred and some girls were off like a shot. Elbows, headdresses, boas and plumes, bangles, spangles, heels, fishnets and a flurry of feathers stomped en masse past gawking voyeurs twenty deep on either side.

The myriad of mascara'ed ostriches, frumpy baubled penguins, tutu'ed tiara'ed bears, black sequined lionesses, and nail-tipped tassled toucans herded off and up the street. They were like a clamoring mongrel menagerie at feeding time.

"Get off me bitch! Don't go there girl. You skanky whore. Oh no, she di'int. I'm gonna beat yo butt. Madonna my asshole, you look more like Roseanne Barr, faggot..." accompanied the manic circus of late night starlets scrambling for positions ahead. They flooded the door of the first bar like a tsunami, passed through a gauntlet of screaming, cheering Abercrombie and Fitches, and bolted to a bar lined with hundreds of little plastic shooter cups. The bartenders braced for the onslaught and watched the sea of little liquid pools slosh up when the wave hit.

LaChuChuWanda was among the first slam of twenty or so to hit the beachhead. The exhilaration to scramble and claw to the front was then eclipsed by the undertow that yanked them back through the next waves of runners barreling up behind them. They had to employ every available ounce of survival instinct to wade back, out and off onto the next venue. Shopping!

It must have taken an enormous amount of courage for any shopkeeper or bar to sign up for this kind of beating. There's nothing more frightening that a drag queen driven to extremes supporting her bead and sequin fund. It was a niche addiction several steps up from shoe hoarding. Take three hundred of them, all with various vices, all trying to keep up with the Joan'ses, all vying for another source of disposable income, and you got big trouble. Good causes and guerrilla marketing aside, all of the participating businesses would have a major mess to clean up tomorrow.

"Girl, that my thong. I had it first. It too small for you anyway you cow..." And so on.

"Good grief," said Luke, glad to see Jack and Jerry. "We got some mean mammas out running tonight." They were at the hardware store, of all places, one of Jack's favorite haunts. "Here," screamed Jack, "the bungee cords. You remember? Around the waist!" Jerry gave Luke the exact amount. Jack was holding a place in line. "Come ON, 'ChuChu," they urged.

And so on. They scrambled to the Caribbean Hut for a cargo net shawl, to the Black Cat for shooters and Shareena's House of Beautee for applicator bottles and hair sheen goop. More shooters, more effects. Jerry and Jack's system kept Luke ahead in the pack. Then came the hiccup.

They were at the Pic 'N Pay, LaChuChuWanda purchasing Jack's well-chosen sturdy heeled boots. Jack and Jerry were holding the door for their racehorse. But LaChuChuWanda's blackened ruby-lipped mug came to a complete stop, her bustier a step and a half ahead. She turned for a double-take and headed back down an aisle, instead of to the exit door where Jack and Jerry screamed in horror.

"LUKE! We'll come back tomorrow!" Jack turned to Jerry, "Get her back out here! We ain't got time for any more SHOE shopping!"

But LaChuChuWanda was stomping down the aisle toward a saucer-eyed Slim, caught in the act of shoving a tempting pair of basketball shoes into his backpack. In mid-zipper, Luke was upon him and hissed, "SLIM! What the HECK are you DOING!" Slim froze at the sight of the tall black chorus girl charging upon him.

Jerry was a step behind but had a limited view of the act. He grabbed LaChuChuWanda's arm and yanked in the opposite direction. "Oh no you don't 'ChuChu, back in the race!" Jerry pulled on Luke, but Luke grabbed on to Slim and back up the aisle they went.

Jerry was oblivious of all but his quarry LaChuChuWanda in tow. Slim hanging on to his pack finally asked his kidnapper, "Luke? Is that YOU?"

The 'ChuChu train headed toward a yelling Jack stationed at the door. Everyone about stared—contestants in line, the cashiers and a store manager with watchful eye. The startled manager yelled "Stop!"

As they made it to the door and barreled outside, Jack and Jerry flung LaChuChuWanda back into the race as he/she screamed at Slim, "DROP IT!" The backpack fell to the sidewalk as LaChuChuWanda held on to Slim, both now running in the throng of contestants.

As Luke ran, he shouted at Slim, "What the hell were you doing?"

Slim, running, skipping and tripping behind LaChuChuWanda, yelled back, "What am I doing? Me? You're dressed like a girl! A BLACK girl!"

"Never mind about me, Snot Nose. You were stealing!"

Back in front of the shoe-store, Jack knew better than Luke that, whether there were stolen goods in it or not, they could not abandon the backpack. He snatched it up and jogged to catch up with Jerry already ahead. It was slow going for both of them. Jerry turned his head back toward Jack while still in stride, pawing his way through the crowd. "What the heck was all that about?" They both ran to catch up with LaChuChuWanda. "I see his hair! I can see the halo!"

They were headed back down 17th Street toward the finish. Walking fast, skipping, running as the crowd would allow, Jack and Jerry kept reporting sightings of LaChuChuWanda as they tried to keep up. At the finish line, the frenzy of yelling and cheering indicated that the winners were close.

Against the pitch black backdrop of night, the streetlights cast harsh beacons of light down onto a sea of cheering, partying heads. Clouds of exhaled breath billowed in the cold night as the air filled with a fine drizzle. Speakers on the podium began to blare "Ride of the Valkyries," and the Master of Ceremonies lumbered toward the microphone.

"Jack, Jerry!" A block and a half from the line, they turned to see Liz hopping up and down in the crowd. Sliding sideways, hand clinging to hand, they worked their way toward her, arriving surprised, stumbling and relieved.

"Look who I found," said Liz, her arm hooked through Parker's for safe keeping.

"Hey!" said Parker. Bare forearms were shoved into his pockets; he leaned into Liz for warmth. His tensed muscles suggested a chill beneath the thin damp cotton t-shirt, white against the night and matching his broad friendly smile.

Jack hugged Liz, bussed Parker's cheek and took a step back in their huddle. His gaze fell transfixed for an instant on the Hudson Grille logo, mounded pec and hard nipple.

"Did you see who won yet?" asked Parker.

Jack awoke and quickly turned toward the platform a half block away. "No, not yet, but hey, Liz, I think I see the wig!"

"Somebody lift me up!" said Liz. Maybe I can see! Come O-h!"

Parker had pushed down on her waist and hoisted her up on the rebound so she sat in his strong arms at waist level. She strained and peered into the distance declaring, "Oh yeah, that's it alright. I can see the halo. He turned on the halo! It's LU-LaChuChuWanda!"

Jack screamed and slapped at Liz's thigh, then turned to throw his arms around Jerry. "Come on, come on, we gotta get up there!" Liz's dilemma was how to get close enough to see LaChuChuWanda while keeping Parker far enough away so he didn't recognize Luke.

"Go, go," said Liz, "We'll catch up behind you."

Jack grabbed Jerry's hand as they re-entered the fray, tightening the straps on the backpack as they squeezed through the dense crowd.

Jerry and Jack were delighted to see their pal on top of the platform. The Master of Ceremonies was standing at the mike, fondly tapping the head of the black phallus to test the sound. "Ladies, trans-ladies, gentle women and the rest of you straight men out there—we have some WINNERS! In second place, number 221. Come over here and tell us your name and where you're from."

Luke walked over to the microphone holding a hand over his sun-glasses to shield his face from the glare of the spotlight.

Parker shouted to Liz leading him by the hand, "'Zat Jack's friend who placed, then?"

"Parker, doll, this crowd is just too much for me," she yelled back. "How about we just hang off the side here."

"My name is," all out of breath, Luke managed, "Miss LaChu-ChuWanda Watkins. I am a, I am a proud trans-racial transvestite from Northwest Washington, DC!"

The street applauded and the gush of cheering and whooping rolled toward the stage. Jack began to chant "Chu, chu, chu, chu," which led a good body of the fans to pick up the rhythm. "Choo, choo-choo, choo-choo-choo-choochoo!"

The MC came back to the mike. "In first position and ready to wrestle in the final round of the Triathlon against LaChuChuWanda, LAST YEAR'S WINNER—Miss Tanka Rae Courvoisier!" She and her sisters leapt about wildly, making quite a scene.

The crowd went mad once again. "Tanka Rae, Tanka Rae," they chorused.

"She ain't no Transvestite!" someone yelled. "She ain't no Drag King," said another.

Tanka Rae grabbed the mike from the MC. "Thank you, thank you. And you shut up mister! I am Tanka Rae Courvoisier, and as I TOLD you all LAST year when I WON, I am a naturally engendered trans-lesbian-gay-vestite WHAT-EV-AH! Get over yourself." She snapped her fingers at 'twelve and three' then stomped off to the side.

The MC wrestled the mike from Tanka Rae with some effort. "O-Kay now. She ran her ass off with the best of them—whatever she wants to be. Now it's time for the real show!"

Luke had retreated back to the side of the stage near Slim to observe the antics. He was kind of woozy from all the shooters and started to see life flashing before his eyes. Fear welled in his stomach with the power and mass of a medicine-ball. Across the stage, he saw the Michelin Amazon woman in sumo stance, joining her pals the Cocoa Pillsbury Dough Girl and an Afro-American Gidget doll. They rallied and danced with hands in the air doing the Bump. The tons of flesh, the mounds of hip and thigh nearly tossed little Luke off the stage. He imagined his thin frame and beautiful heap of wig squashed under the weight of his opponent. "They won't be able to make out the difference between my remains and the mud slop," he confided to little Slim beside him. They traded grimaces.

"LaChuChuWanda!" Jack was on the steps to the platform with Jerry behind him. Luke got back into LaChuChuWanda's head and stepped back to make room for Jack who flung his arms around to hug, jump and swing around her.

"Am I glad to see you!" said Luke.

"You ready for Loada FatAss over there?" asked Jack.

"Can I just tell them to give her the check, NOW?"

"Don't talk like that! We got a few more tricks up our sleeve, remember?"

Down and far enough away, Liz was sitting on Parker's broad shoulders giving him a play by play. "Jack just made it to the stage. He's hugging his uh-friend, so it looks like he's one of the finalists!"

"Meez Os-bourn-eh!"

"Oh my Jesus Christ," Liz rasped, her voice getting hoarse from all the shouting. "Enrique, Alberto!" Liz wiggled, signaling Parker to let her down. "Parker, this is Enrique and Alberto from my salon."

There they stood, dressed up like cowboys with plaid shirts and leather vests open to their navels, along with temptingly well-tailored chaps that would give any well deserving horny ranch hand a big stud in his pants. The two Latinas, a symphony in Mary Kay pink, twirled for admiration of their assets.

Enrique, curtsying into Liz, did not hide his shy embarrassed approval of Parker. "Ay-ay-yi, Meez Leez, where chew find deez lovely man?"

Liz, trying to stifle a squeal behind her smile, realized she should not encourage Enrique's interest. She retaliated with her own question, "What are you two doing here? Alberto! You look—like—quite the little cowboy—man—something, now don't you? Did you run in the race?"

Alberto stood miffed and lop-sided, looking like a broken Latino Wild Wild West doll.

"Heez heel, it fall off." said Enrique forlornly.

"Well, Lu—LaChuChuWanda and JACK, and Jack made it to the finish line! Enrique, why don't you get up to the stage and we'll stay here with Alberto. GO! GO!" she urged, and before he had a chance to question. "GO! Quick!" she commanded.

He fought into the crowd rewarding them with a view of his million buck butt and looked back wistfully at Parker a few times before disappearing.

Half the crowd was chanting "ChuChu!" the other "Tanka Rae!" As they got in sync, the shouting volleyed into "ChuChu -Tanka Rae." The carpet of heads and costumes echoed one name or the other like a block-long steam-powered piano. The drizzling mist above was of little consequence as the massive machine gained energy.

The air horn blared for blocks to hear. The mud wrestling began, and the to and fro chanting became chaotic. The spotlight focused on the two opponents, one short and squat; the other tall, skinny and bewigged. The drizzle spread its slow diagonal sheen across the highlighted pit on the large platform.

The MC barked decisive moves into the mike, maintaining an exaggerated level of excitement for the crowd out of view. The roar of ews and aws from the front rows mimicked themselves down the street, cheering and booing like plebeians at the Coliseum.

"AW, that was a good one!" yelled the MC. "EW! That must have hurt." The audience was drawn to the spectacle as if the Rock and Hulk Hogan were at it.

Ringside, things were a lot more frenetic and grueling. Mud wrestling is not very pretty and much worse when you are being mowed down by the bull, dyke or what ever she claimed to be. Tanka Rae had a clear advantage, even down to the way her width eclipsed the spotlight, throwing the pit into darkness every time she went for the body slam. But LaChuChuWanda was always quick for the roll, driving her opponent to a powerful belly flop and a spray of mud on to the front row.

"EW!" they shrieked. "AW!" they went, as Tanka Rae rose again to her feet.

The air horn blared again and the MC sent the opponents to their corners for the end of Round One. He milked and taunted the fired-up crowd, stoking their frenzy as if it were a Monster Truck Rally.

In their corner, Jack and Slim were tag-teaming like ace paramedics at a disaster scene. They hauled out Jack's crafty riggings and zipped up LaChuChu for the next onslaught. Meanwhile Slim squirted water at Luke's gasping mouth from a nozzled bottle.

"MEESTER JACK!" Enrique shrieked.

Jack turned, startled, then in one sweeping motion hauled him up on the platform. "Holy Halle Booty girl!" He admiredthe view of lush South America before he started barking orders, "Here Enrique! Help us!"

Jack delved deeper into the backpack with gusto. Around Luke's knees and wrists he had Enrique strap on belts, to which were attached a contraption of non-slip bath-mat pieces and industrial-size suction cups— one on each knee, one on each wrist. Every time Enrique squealed at a near broken nail or spatter of mud, Jack and Jerry took pleasurable turns in smacking his ass and wise-cracking about his girly sniffles. It was a short minute of bedlam before the team of four had equipped and pumped up their lanky black charge again, ready to take on the formidable Tanka Rae.

Jack, Jerry, Enrique and Slim worked at stage-side with gusto. They lobbed condom water balloons at Tanka Rae, causing her to slip and fall butt first back into the mud. Kahlua (Dough Girl) and Chardonay worked their own tag team, but they had not come strategically equipped like Jack and crew. Jack and Jerry's bungee cord lassos snagged Tanka Rae in mid-lunge. Kahlua's response was to spend precious moments commanding Chardonay to take off her black lycra pants to use as a sling-shot. Jerry tangled up Tanka Rae with the cargo net shawl and held on, while Jack pumped gobs of hair sheen goo on her head. LaChuChu-Wanda managed a good shove while she was mopping mud and slime out of her eyes.

Kahlua, leering greedily, wound up Chardonay's mud-filled lycra sling-shot and let fly at LaChuChuWanda with a wild whoop. It missed, but the full force of a direct hit caught Enrique on his pretty Latin ass. He burst into a snorting rage. Slim, quick to react, reached into his back pack, retrieved the size 13 basketball shoes and catapulted them across the ring. Their laces tied, they wrapped themselves ballistically around Kahlua's ankles and felled her like a stone, slamming her onto the mat. Up went another spray of mud, spattering Enrique once more. Strutting around like a flamenco flamingo, he began to wail "AiYiYiYiYiYiYi," like a banshee.

Back in the main fight and catching her breath during the distraction, LaChuChuWanda hunched ready with elbows braced on her knees.

She watched her opponent approaching through heavily eyelashed slits. They faced off and walked slowly in a circle. Luke wiped the corner of his mouth as he stalked Tanka Rae around, taunting her. He then flipped the switch for his swirling finned halo and quietly gave the nod.

Slim yelled "Tanka Rae! CATCH!" Tanka looked left. As LaChuChuWanda dropped onto suction cupped knees, the backpack thrown by Jack hit Tanka Rae in the back of the thighs, breaking her stance. She fell before Luke in a flurry of slippery arms, fending off the halo that was spitting mud, her face wracked with horror. LaChuChu-Wanda simply inclined forward, slammed her wrists to the wet mud mat and lynched for the pin.

She and the suction cups held on for dear life as Tanka Rae began to flail and squirm. The MC started the ten-count countdown and the audience shouted "Chu Chu Chu Chu" in unison.

"...NINE, TEN! LaChuChuRhonda! LaChuChuRhonda is the WINNER!" screamed the excited MC. "LaChuChuRhonda , One THOUSAND dollars! Let's ALL HEAR IT for LaChuChuRhonda!"

The wig wasn't pretty any more, and the four comrades felt whipped as well, but they cheered and hugged excitedly at their success. It took Enrique and Jack, both now covered in mud, a moment to un-buckle LaChuChuWanda from the suction cups, which also gave Tanka Rae time to cuss up a storm. Kahlua sloshed through the mud to calm her sister and slung a few disgusted globs back down into the pit as she approached. "Tanka Rae, shut your mouth. Your ass been whipped, just shut your mouth now."

"Wanda, it's Waahn-duh, not Rhonda—LaChuChuWanda," said Jack to the MC, who got back on his mike to the audience. "Ladies and Gentlemen! This year's winner of the Transvestite Triathalon, Miss LaChuChuWanda Watkins!"

LaChuChuWanda stood up with the help of Slim and walked toward the front of the platform. The MC held her arm up, high in the air for victory, while Jack, Jerry and Enrique stood behind them. Luke switched on the halo, to great effect. It whipped a spray of mud off to the sides and toward a ducking MC.

"Hey, it's the Black Madonna and Child!" yelled someone from the front row.

With Slim in hand, a muddy LaChuChuWanda stood proud in front of the cheering crowd. The streetlight behind the whirling halo wig sparkled with drizzle. Luke lifted his bustier bosom in triumph.

"And now, for the presentation of the one thousand dollar check, don't get it muddy now!"

Luke noticed a commotion coming through the crowd toward the stage. He nudged Slim to look up ahead. Approaching was the Pic 'N Pay manager looking none too happy, pointing and shouting toward the stage. He couldn't quite be heard over the partying crowd.

The MC boomed into the mike, "Are we ready for the pictures now?"

"HEY YOU! Kid on stage!" The manager was now closer to the platform.

"Just say CHEESE!" yelled the MC.

"They stole from my store!" screamed the manager.

As the flash went off for the picture, there was an unexpected loud boom in the distance. Two more flashes for a bit more 'cheese' were followed by two more booms sounding a whole lot closer. The crowd began to stir and then scramble.

"FIRE!" someone yelled, and then all hell broke loose.

"THIEF!" shouted the manager, as everyone started screaming and running.

Luke and Slim ran down the steps followed by the MC, Jack, the group and squealing 'girls'.

"What asshole shouted a fire alarm for chrissakes?" bitched Jack.

"Get away! The MANHOLE just BLEW!"

TWENTY-FIVE

"No, I'm not gonna let go of your hand. I may not know what to do about this mess, but letting you run off isn't in the picture, bud." LaChuChuWanda, half dismantled, rushed through the wet street with Slim, dodging around the dispersing crowd.

As he trailed behind a man wearing fishnet stockings, bustier, platform army boots and a black face, all of which were coated in mud, Slim knew he was in trouble. Enough of the real Luke was apparent, with the wig in his other hand like the head of St. John the Baptist, and most of Jack's gizmos and armatures shoved into the pack. The drizzle had turned to rain, further diluting what was left of LaChuChuWanda. They dragged themselves through the rainy night, a pissed-off semi-black Madonna with criminal child.

There was silence between them, up the steps, through the doors, in the elevator and hall. The wig sat on the floor in a rejected lump as Luke angrily unlocked the door to his apartment. His other hand stayed glued to the kid's.

"In!" snapped Luke. He swung Slim inside, raked the wig in with his foot, and turned to shut the door. The turn of two deadbolts and toss of a security chain spoke louder than words.

"Alright Snot-nose, explain yourself!"

Slim hedged, tried to look innocent and started with, "I wasn't—" Bad move.

"Don't tell me you weren't NUTHIN'! You stole that pair of shoes. Why?"

"Gilbert. They're for Gilbert. Have you seen his shoes? They're full of holes."

"For Gilbert? What were you going to tell him, what were you going to tell the Reverend? That you found a pair of brand new size thirteen basketball shoes somewhere?"

"Well -" Slim hesitated.

"Well WHAT?" asked Luke.

"Well, I wasn't gonna lie, I just wasn't gonna tell the whole truth. You once said—"

"Oh for crying out loud." Luke's palm came up to push at his temple, a weak attempt to keep his head from exploding.

The phone rang and startled them both. Luke turned and walked toward the incessant buzz with two-second intervals. "I'm coming already!" Annoyed, unhurried, Luke's knot of exasperation unleashed itself as he ripped the little black phone from its cradle. "WHAT!" he snapped.

Luke paused to listen. Slim looked over, hearing the rattle of hasty chatter, and slowly sank to have a seat. He clenched his teeth and froze as he watched Luke's eyes roll up into white.

"Oh...shit," said Luke. "Slim's here. Lemme wash up. I'll be right over." He hung up the phone with a snap.

"There was a manhole explosion in front of Mercy Mission and the Grille. I have to go. You WILL be here when I get back. Understand?"

He was out the door in less than five seconds, having substituted force for thoroughness in his scrubbing. Hands were shoved in jacket pockets, shoulders hunched to brace against the spitting rain. He walked determinedly and fast, then broke into a jog. He ran up the dim residential street fording the rutted and broken paving, dodging branches and trash tubs. The brick federal facades and stoops rolled by on his right; the unmoving line of cars on his left, beaded and shiny; trees shook from gusts of wind throwing leaves and flushes of downpour upon him.

He emerged on to U Street, where streetlights blared by the dozen, as did cars with horns standing impatiently in the intersection. The light was stuck on green. Signs blinked "Don't Walk." A crowd up ahead was gathered to enjoy a ringside view of a Pepco utility truck, two fire engines askew, and a scurry of helmets and hoses under hot white work lights.

In the cold wet night air, Luke could smell the idling exhausts, taste the acrid smoke and steam ahead, and feel the weight of trouble looming above.

"Jack, what happened?" Luke was grave.

"Some utility worker down in the manhole started a fire, which set off an explosion. That strained the system and set off other explosions. There were explosions as far over as the race on P Street. They've evacuated the buildings. Most of these shops were closed, but the Mission... Reverend Blanche was somewhere at the race. She's a bit of a wreck. She's already left. You say Slim was with you?"

"He's back at my place. Our little criminal. Stole a pair of shoes for Gilbert. Don't ask. Maybe I can keep him till they can get back into the Mission. Where's Liz and Jerry?"

"Coming back with some hot coffee, but there isn't any use standing around here. By the way, Parker is with them. He's going to find Jon Miller on his way down here. Jeez, what else—Parker was at the race, but Liz kept him occupied. I don't think he knows it was you up there as 'ChuChu, but he isn't your ordinary dumb queen. Get ready if he pops the question."

"And what question do you think that might be?" Luke inquired. "God, what a mess."

"I don't know, maybe he'll be kind and ask to see if your cute ass is black too? Mmn, you missed cleaning some spots, hon." Jack wet a finger and rubbed at Luke's neck.

"Well, at least I have the check! I worked for every damn penny of it too." Luke put an arm around Jack's waist while they stood and looked at the recovery work before them.

"Luke, there you are honey," Liz said as she came up alongside, leading her troops.

Next was Parker who came up from behind and wrapped his big arms around Luke's shoulders. "Where you been hiding all night handsome?"

"I was helping Jack, where you been?" Luke didn't say that he was helping Jack through another bout of lame-brained manifestation of creative fantasy, with himself being the black Barbie doll stuck in a madcap tea party. No. Then Parker really would have thought he was crazy. Swept up in a Jack-a-thon was one thing, admitting to it was quite another.

"Finished my list at the Mission. Ran into Liz on my way home, that and the little mob on 17th street." With arms still wrapped, Parker felt his crotch fill up against Luke's butt. Inhaling, he noticed that the smell of soap did not fully mask another, the remnant of waxy make-up and hair spray. This made him smile and chuckle inside as he held on to the thought. It warmed him as much as the man in his arms.

The rain still spat but it did not dampen Jon and Liz's pleasure at running into each other. Despite today's grave situation, they advanced their breezy conversation of the other evening—which Al and the stooges had interrupted—into one that was heartfelt and sincere. Liz thanked heaven for the chance to legitimately console, pat and clutch—and especially to extend an offer to help in any way along with her business card. (Surely a good haircut was a reasonable solace for the woes of exploding manhole covers? Happily stunned, Jon certainly seemed to think so.)

Jack and Jerry arrived conjoined. "Hey," said Luke to them all, "There's nothing more we can do here till morning. How about we go back to my place and warm up. I need y'all's help with a little problem I have sitting in my living room."

As they left to walk the few blocks, Luke managed to tell the story of Slim's errant ways without mentioning LaChuChuWanda. As far as he was concerned, she was last seen doing the backstroke over on 17th Street in some mud pit.

Luke opened his door. "Okay, you little monster. Say hello to company. I brought all these people back here so we can act like old people, parents and crap. Put the fear of God in ya."

Slim sat in the chair looking up at the contingent filing in, and switched off the TV smartly.

The wise and worldly head of Jon conveyed the most weight, though everyone had something to say. Jack however was the kindest, and could not help approving of a perfectly healthy yen for footwear. Oh Jack.

Slim, who sat quiet and overwhelmed, finally cracked a smile at this. Liz, who took on the role of Earth Mother, decided it was getting late and that she would keep Slim, "for the night." She would call Reverend Blanche, keep the criminal incident to herself, and hope the police weren't cracking down on shoplifters for the moment. Jack and Jerry, still seamlessly conjoined at this point, echoed the mutual fatigue and the need to head home. No one asked which, letting them leave with a smile and a hope that tonight was the night.

At the door, Parker patted Jon on the back, maneuvering to let his boss leave for the night without appearing rude. As Luke hugged Liz goodnight, she spoke in his ear. "You're letting the Fox stay for breakfast, I hope." It was just loud enough to get her a little shove out the door. Usually so composed, it was funny to see her scamper and giggle mischievously.

"GIT!" commanded Luke. "Jon, make sure she exits the building! And don't let her return with surveillance cameras!" When Jon scooped up her arm in his, Luke was both relieved and amused. Notions of double weddings already flashed through his head.

Luke bolted the door and turned to find Parker very much in his personal space. With fists resting on either side of the dim narrow hallway; his face hung with a lazy grin. The stretched wall of T-shirt and muscle blocked any exit, so Luke licked at his lips, set his own magnet on high, then put a leg-lock on his stud.

TWENTY-SIX

Uptown, Liz was in the kitchen fixing her coffee while keeping an eye on Slim. He was sitting in the living room watching the morning news.

She thought back to the previous night's festivities with a mixture of fondness and regret. Their horse had won the race, for heaven's sake! It was a triumph for her favorite gelding, whoops no, her colt, the one she had lovingly named and coiffed, the one Jack had assiduously trained and dressed. Even Enrique and Slim had helped to hobble the rival nag. But the gang had barely celebrated their victory at all!

And all because Parker was not allowed to be in the know. What a farce. Luke had to get a grip on his self-confidence.

Well actually, not only because of that. There was the minor distraction of the explosions. And that damned stupid behavior by the kid.

The evening had ended well enough though. Jon had been the perfect gentleman, finding the cab for her and Slim, and even paying for it. In climbing into it, had she, perhaps just a little, flashed her thighs at him? He sure enough had checked them out. Could be interesting...

With a sudden start, she was back in the present. The screen behind the TV reporter bore the caption "MANHOLE MESS."

"... the center of the explosion was in front of the Mercy Mission on U Street, Northwest. Damage to the front of the building has closed the facility and members of the Mission have been relocated to other facilities around town. The explosion has left scores of fiery manholes smoking in Dupont Circle and adjacent neighborhoods to the east, all in the vicinity of last night's Halloween festivities.

In a related story, police are on the look out for the winner of last night's Transvestite Triathlon as well as one of his mud wrestling counterparts, now dubbed as the "Black Madonna and Child." Police have taken a complaint from one of the participating shop owners claiming that there was merchandise stolen from his property by suspects identified as the winning contestants. The merchant claims the juvenile may have had a gun..."

"Ahhgh," screamed Liz.

"Gun, I didn't have no gun," yelled Slim.

Liz was already dialing Jack's number.

Jack had to raise his voice over Liz and her incoherent rambling. "Calm, I said calm down honey. CALM DOWN. All that mud and dim lighting, you can barely tell it is Luke. So listen, Jerry and I are talking about going over to check out all those Smoking Fiery Manholes. HA! Did you see those hunky firemen? NO, I am not trying to change the subject—"

Liz came to a stop but then let loose again. "JACK! It's, well it's, yes, it's shoplifting. It's bad, but there wasn't a gun, it's not like it was a stick-up, can you imagine they are making this big a deal out of a pair of shoes? They're giving any bad spin they can to the Triathlon. They have the Manhole Mess, why can't they settle on that for a while. They make it sound like some rampage of costumed looting and pillaging. What the heck am I gonna do now? Maybe I can take him to work with me and hide him behind the peroxide bottles or something..."

Farther downtown, early morning glowed at the open window and gentle gusts of cool fall air danced on the plain white curtain teasing Luke from his slumber. The chill to his face was in contrast to the heat of the body pressed against his back. He took his hand to clutch Parker's arm closer to his heart and sighed to record the moment of bliss.

Luke rocked his hips, nodding his attention into Parker's other hand. "If you would let go down there, I could get up and make us some coffee."

Parker's grasp tightened around his prey. "You are up." He let his words and lips lick across the nape of Luke's neck.

Luke tried to roll over but was bound in Parker's arms. "Mr. Fox, I think something of yours has come between us."

Parker smirked, "A good friend of mine. We're very attached."

Luke half-heartedly tried to roll again. "Oh yeah. I think I dreamt about him last night. Don't think he liked me though. That fathead spat right in my face."

Parker nuzzled more at Luke's neck. "Well, what did you expect? First you rough him up and start wringing his neck. Then you had to go and give him that fierce licking. Actually though, I think he liked you. He only spits that much on guys he wants to impress."

Luke volleyed, "First impressions are very important, but I'm afraid I'm going to need a lot more convincing."

Parker's interest continued to rise and Luke ground in closer. Parker's hand continued its ride and their breathing quickened.

Luke whispered, "You keep that up and we'll have fresh squeezed juice to go with that coffee."

Words didn't follow, only a stronger intensity between them. Their friction was more audible amid steady gasps.

Parker asserted his grip. "I prefer cream."

Luke inhaled deeply and held his breath. Parker's hand twisted on the up stroke. "It's my house bud," Luke rasped. "Gotta work for your cream." He stretched toward the night stand. "Put on this mitt and butter up. I make a terrific turnover."

They showered together and after Parker rinsed him, Luke left Parker to finish. He was drying with a towel when the phone rang. Luke sprang to the other side of the bed and gasped at the sight. With his foot, he pushed the telltale ratty Wanda wig under the bed, while grabbing the phone before the third ring.

A few blocks away, Jack was on the other end of the line with Jerry curled up in the crook of his arm. "That whore. I bet you I'm going to find him a frickin' mess—Oh hi Luke, so how BIG was it? Mn, yeah, you most certainly do know what I'm talking about. Is that a shower I hear running? So I guess you can talk. So we WON honey, we won! Now we can pay our bills. You haven't turned on the TV- no? Well don't. You'll just get upset. The news is calling you the Black Madonna and Child. But I swear—we can barely tell it's you in the picture. Anyway the whole city is in an uproar. UPROAR! Manhole explosions, delinquent store-robbing child with gun—God knows where they came up with the gun. That babbling shoe-store owner, can't understand a WORD he's saying. Liz called, she's gone ballistic. Slim is still with her, and they were about to call around to find Reverend Pickens. The Mission's closed up for now, and they moved the old folk to other shelters. Reverend Blanche was actually on the tube calling for her Slim to turn himself in! SO—who was the top and who was the bottom—like I need to ask. Don't take that tone of voice with me girl. Oh, and Jon Miller called. Are you fit to walk your way to work today or should I send a car? At least you won't have to sit down much on the job. I'm, well no, I'm not sorry. OKAY, be that way. I'll see you in an hour? Good. Later." He turned off the phone with a deliberate press of his thumb, and rolled on top of Jerry. "Well, piss on that one."

"Maybe you should have waited to tell him, like, all the news that will give him fits." Jerry put his arms around Jack.

Jack pondered. "Mn, maybe. Now where were we?" He stroked the hair at Jerry's temple with a finger tip, then leaned his head down to distract the conversation ready on Jerry's lips. "Mn, you taste good. I think the house chef is going to scramble you up before breakfast. Luke will be fine. Better I work up his lather before he starts blaming us for getting him into this mess."

"What do you mean 'us'?" asked Jerry.

"You know, 'us', as in like maybe we'll have to use 'us' a few more times so you get what I mean. Jack took a slow and measured dive into Jerry's lips once again with a delighted hunger. Jerry encouraged him by lacing ankles and calves around Jack's back while kneading insistently.

They spent a long moment gently wrestling and toyed with the electricity between them, developing firm and mutual understandings. Their hearts began to race, then thighs tensed and toes curled. They flipped so that each met his match, then jaws strained, heads shook and eyes rolled. Their rhythms pumped, mutually demanding and reciprocating a fever of sweat and flesh, mouths and tongues. In a moment they froze, held a gasp, then willed a crescendo of agonizing escape from somewhere deep within. With abandon came blasts and stars, swallows and gulps, followed by the giddy exhale of satisfaction.

"God-damn," said Jerry, "Now that's what I call Jacking off."

"We can do that, any - time - you - want." Jack licked the corner of his mouth. "I really didn't think you government boys had it in you."

"That's next," said Jerry, "but I'll give you a minute."

TWENTY-SEVEN

"Luke, Parker! Over here!" Jack waved to the couple as they approached the crowd gathered around the utility sawhorses that blocked off the area in front of the Mercy Mission. He and Jerry were standing with Enrique and Alberto all armed with more cups of steaming coffee.

The early morning sky was still gray and cloudy threatening to rain again. Faces in the crowd were similarly overcast, and some of those who once found refuge at the Mission were close to tears. Reverend Blanche Pickens tried to console and encourage the flock.

Along the barricades, the crowd spilled out onto the street, which was further blocked by the parked Pepco van, a fire truck and pair of TV station vehicles. Reporters, cameramen, intermittent flash bulbs and the rumble of conversation surrounded the barking commands of those in charge. A plume of steam and smoke rising from the manhole served as a focus for all the gravity and activity.

"Nothing like a herd of hunky firemen inspecting their manholes to draw out a crowd, heh?" Jack hugged Luke as he joined them.

"I'm glad to see you two still with your afterglow," he added, while giving a second hug to Parker.

Enrique and Alberto, pointing and straining to review each and every man in uniform, turned to greet Luke and Parker. Alberto's smile widened as he recognized Luke from the night before, but he was struck by shyness again before the broad shoulders of gray sweatshirt beneath Parker's million-dollar grin.

"Oooh, Meester Luke," squealed Enrique in admiration, "Eet eez an honor to—oowch!"

At that moment, Jack had firmly planted his size eleven Reebok on Enrique's toe. "Enrique was just going to get us some more coffee. I'm buying. Anybody want some coffee?" His eyes locked with Enrique's and communicated a laser beam of stern intent.

The pregnant pause loomed like a ton of nails over the group of six. Eyes darted as they traded question marks. The brief second was a minute too long before Enrique could respond. "Cream and sugars?"

Everyone exhaled in unison except Parker who inhaled, trying to act nonchalant.

"Come Alberto. We get the coffees?" Enrique grabbed Alberto's hand and the two pair of flame red, extra tight, racing stripe sweat pants peeled off the edge of the crowd.

Parker's jaw rose as he looked out over the heads, "S'cuse me guys, I see my boss over there. I better go check in with him. He looks pretty worried."

"Well no wonder," observed Luke. "Jon Miller right now owns a cordoned-off battered façade with no utility connection, poor guy."

"And Jon was supposed to hear back from the Mayor on Wednesday. I'll go find out what's up." Parker squeezed Luke's hand and the lingering hold broke in mid-air.

"Boy, that was close," Luke whispered. "I owe you one Jack."

A knowing smile washed over Jerry's face as he nudged Jack's arm to commiserate. "Aw, parting is such sweet sorrow. Think we all came about the same time this morning?"

Jack's mug grimaced. "EW! Jerry, that's so disgusting. But, I like it. It's so perverted."

Luke stood there dumbfounded with embarrassment. "You guys are sick. SICK! Perfect for each other."

"If you only knew. Even I'm too shy to share all the details." Jack was nearly blushing. "Later though," he added with a wink.

"So what the hell is this with the gun? Parker and I raced aver here before we could catch the news on TV." Luke stood, bracing himself for the bomb.

"All I know," Jack started, "is that the TV reporter ended her re-cap with the notion that the shoe-store guy thought there was a gun. And then, they flashed him on screen being questioned by a cop in his store. Damn media. Like the picture is supposed to accurately tell the whole story?"

"But it's so untrue!" Luke hissed. "And keep your voice down. Do you want everyone here to start screaming for the police? Maybe I should go over to the shoe-store, return the shoes and see if I can make this go away."

Jerry hunched and whispered into the huddle. "Don't you think he might recognize you?"

"Oh come on now Jerry," Jack exclaimed. "Mary here looks like fucking John Wayne compared to the way she was rigged up last night. Hell, in that flannel shirt, someone would probably mistake him for a genuine lesbian!"

"Come on, I'm not that butch. But I think it may be worth a shot, oops—I mean try, worth a try. But if you guys would come along for moral support..." Luke was starting to dither.

"Gotta get back soon to the hell-hole office," piped Jerry.

"Restaurant—remember?" said Jack. "We have a restaurant to run?"

"Honey, sweets, we have a closed restaurant, and we have a fugitive—" Luke stopped and lowered his voice to whisper "—child stashed—oh my God, LIZ!" he hissed. "You said you talked to Liz? How's she doing? She is going to kill—KILL me this time."

"Calm down," urged Jack. "She's a bit wigged out, hee hee, but she's going to hide him at work behind the peroxide bottles. WELL, that's what she said. Christ, this is really starting to sound like a Cheech & Chong movie."

"Mr. Luke! Luke!" The shouts came from the crowd, followed by the dove grey wool suit and matching hat of Reverend Blanche Pickens. "Luke," she launched in frantically, "do you know where my Slim is? He hasn't been home all night!"

"Oh Blanche, I'm so sorry. He's safe with Liz and she tried to call you to tell you that." Blanche sighed audibly with relief. "He's hiding out while I, uh, carry out the Grand Plan to get us out of this."

"But you know they are saying..."

"Yes yes, we know. Jack saw your appeal on TV. But the gun thing is a total fiction, blown up by the media. Don't worry, and don't say anything more to ANYONE. At least for an hour or two." He felt a sharp pang from the hook he was truly skewered on now.

"Oh my God," interrupted Jerry, "here comes Greg Thicke."

Everyone ceased their hushed conversation and waited. Greg approached with the gleam in his eye and outstretched hand expected of the politician. "Reverend Pickens. AND Jerry Callahan—this is a surprise. Good to see you, son." Greg shook Blanche's hand normally, and then Jerry's as if expecting water to gush.

Luke and Jack exchanged a simultaneous look that spelled "weird."

Jerry reciprocated the smarminess as he introduced Luke and Jack.

"Greg Thicke, our favorite political candidate, this is Jack Betz and Luke Hudson who own the Hudson Grille here."

"Darn lucky you two," said Greg. "I hear they will be letting everything on the street re-open, except for the Mission, in an hour or so."

"Mr. Thicke," Blanche chimed in nervously, "do you have any news on the Mission re-opening? I do hope..."

Greg shook his head. "I'm afraid there's too much damage to the front of the building Reverend, and they are going to keep the power off till..."

"What are we to do with all these folks who depend on the Mission for shelter? I haven't called the Mayor yet. We've been so busy with them this mornin'." To Luke's relief and pride, she sounded more distraught as she continued, "And if that's not enough, my youngster Slim is missin'."

"Reverend Blanche, I know, I know. I'm sure the police will find him—AND that Black Madonna winner they've been talking about—"

"I just don't know what we're goin' to DO..." Her voice was well practiced in wailing.

"We can host a BENEFIT!" squealed Jack, to get off the subject.

Luke's eyes nearly bugged out of their sockets. Greg and Blanche, at first surprised by the shriek, warmed in expression as the thought took hold. Jerry beamed at his lover. "Cool idea dude."

"Yes, at the Hudson Grille, tomorrow, Saturday night. We'd be more than happy to help our neighbors," Jack added. His enthusiasm nearly turned all the power back on.

"Jack?" Luke began.

"Luke and I," Jack continued, "think it would be a marvelous idea. And of course, a little publicity couldn't hurt now, could it?"

"Well. I'm goin' on Town Hall, LIVE! this afternoon," said Blanche.

"I have some TV interviews scheduled at the polling places tonight," said Greg.

"Oooh, we'd certainly appreciate any mention you could give us." coo'ed Jack.

Jerry placed his hand on Luke's shoulder, as much to hold him up as to suggest moral support.

"Let's make it a dessert party! Maybe 8 to 10 pm. $10 or so at the door. All profits to benefit the Mercy Mission. We can probably cover the cost of ingredients with what we'll make at the bar. How's that sound?"

"Like a miracle," said Blanche, "you sound like quite the businessman."

"You bet, I'll be sure to mention it tonight," said Greg. "Thank you guys, thank you very much. You are a credit to the community. And we'll see you later Jerry. Very good to see you again." He shook Jerry's hand again and left the four of them to work the crowd.

"JACK! Are you out of your mind?" barked Luke.

"Luke—it's camouflage. A smoke-screen. It will distract them while looking for LaChuChu Madonna. It will at least give you some points when you are standing before a judge. Not only that, it will be great publicity!"

"Like how hard is it going to be, tracking down LaChuChu-Wanda? They only have to follow my cashed check." Luke looked doomed.

"Well, you haven't cashed the check yet. Have you?" asked Jack.

"No. But the end of the month was yesterday. What are we going to pay bills with? Desserts?" asked Luke.

"We have a few days. It will work out, somehow." Jack took hold of Luke's other shoulder.

"So, Jerry," asked Jack, "that Greg certainly knows how to lay it on as thick as his name, doesn't he?

"Didn't I tell you? He really gives me the creeps." Jerry quivered.

"Let's see if we can get into the Grille," said Luke. "I have got to talk to Liz."

Jerry at that moment caught sight of Merritt Smears being interviewed by a TV reporter. Whoops, he really couldn't delay going to the office any longer. He gave Jack a subdued hug and left.

Across the way, Merritt Smears had finished with the TV reporter. (In reality, she was completely finished with him and his rash of smarmy innuendo.) Greg Thicke saw his chance opening and made his way over. Merritt was wiping the greasy dew from his crew cut forehead and locked a defensive eye on Greg.

"Well, Greg Thicke. Are you here at Mercy Mission trying to squeeze out a few more votes from the grief stricken masses?" Merritt wadded up his hanky and shoved it in his back pocket. He then reached to shake Greg's hand. Greg recoiled with no other choice, and locked in the moist warm grip. He smelled an unpleasant after-shave that he was sure would linger.

"Merritt. Calming down the crowd are you? I came down here right away. Right after I picked up Lou this morning. From the hospital. He claims he had an accident at home. You wouldn't know anything more about that now would you?"

"Greg! That's awful. No, I haven't heard from Lou at all this morning. I had no idea. What happened to him? How would I know what happens to him at home?" Merritt fidgeted around in various pockets, hunting for a match to re-light his stub of a cigar.

"Burns, Merritt," said Greg, "some pretty nasty burns on his hands and arms. I think you know as well as I do, my brother Lou is only good for a few things. Cooking and initiative are not two of them. He pretty much follows orders and carries out the grunt work. That's why he is working for you, and why I thought I'd ask you if you knew anything more. Just between ourselves?"

Several paces away in either direction, the entirety of Greg and Merritt's conversation fell on unintended ears. The first were Gilbert's. He was lurking away from the crowd in the comfort of a doorway. They had disturbed him waiting for a cup of coffee from a re-opening Grille, and so, innocuously enough, he listened in to the scene.

The other pair tried equally hard to appear unaware. Jon Miller pantomimed his rapt attention upon the small disaster in front of his damaged Mission. He paced around staying close to Greg and Merritt while extending faked attention to his cell phone. Parker, a few steps away, could not hear clearly but felt the friction developing. He deciphered the subtle frowns on his boss's attentive face. Surely this would accelerate Jon's discussions with the Mayor.

"I really don't know if that would be a good thing to do sir. I really don't." The shoe-store owner stood in the doorway to the stockroom.

"Alright, how about five hundred? We're just trying to put an end to these triath-a-lon perverts once and for all. This would make it happen. You'd be doing a service to the community. Just look at all you've been through, and all the trash that we have to clean up in your neighborhood. Just say that the kid had the gun."

The shoe-store owner looked at the man before him, trying not to have a scene develop. "And what did you say your name was again?"

"Al, um Smears. Merritt Smears. I'm a local businessman just like
you, trying to do some good. How about seven-fifty?" Al's cell phone
began to ring. "Hold on, I gotta take this."

The shoe-store owner folded his arms and leaned back against
the door jamb. He was starting to get very annoyed.

Al walked a few steps away to the middle of ladies heels, sizes
9½–10. "Yeah? Hello? Who is there? Hello?"

On the other end of the line, Merritt Smears continued to perspire. It didn't help the connection.

"Can you hear me now? Can you hear me now? Al, it's Merritt.
Greg picked up Lou from the hospital. He's trying to get the story from
me. Mercy Mission is crawling with firemen, utility workers and network
news. We need to get those crates of yours outta the basement."

Al's gaze was riveted on a pair of $12.99 six-inch stacked sandals.
Not pretty. The shoes either. "You make it happen. You're in this too you
know. I'll be at your office in an hour." Al hung up and turned back
toward the store owner. He stared at the empty stockroom doorway.

TWENTY-EIGHT

"Lunch, around 11, we'll re-open at lunch. Sorry, sorry. Thanks. Lunch. Whew," said Luke.

They had nudged their way through the crowd to get back into the Grille.

"Like we need to turn away hungry customers," said Jack. "First of the month again. Time to fire up and start slinging that hash."

"Geez. It smells like an electrical fire in here. Turn on the fans." Luke headed for the bar to start the coffee.

"That'd be the sparks still flying off your butt from last night with Parker," Jack smirked.

"It was this morning, thank you. And you have no room to talk," snapped Luke.

"Me? What do you mean?" Jack ran back and leaned over the bar to confide. "It was more like recreated scenes from Deep Throat, parts six and nine."

"Yeah. I was wondering why you sounded a bit hoarse this morning," Luke added.

"Hoarse?" Jack turned to check his throat in the mirror. " So what are you gonna do about the Black Madonna?"

"How embarrassing is that?" said Luke. "Did I really mud wrestle with that black woman last night or was that just a nightmare? What was I thinking? Liz. I have got to call Liz." He picked up the phone and dialed.

"Gerd Merning. A Betty Fjord Clinic. Magda speaking."

"Liz?" Luke looked baffled.

"Screening my calls hon. Where have you been? I hope you're not calling from the police station. I—"

"LIZ! I'm at the Grille. The street is just swarming here. What a mess. How is Slim?"

"He's okay I guess. Kind of quiet. They're saying he had a gun Luke. Can you imagine? This is serious."

"I heard, I heard. Reverend Pickens filled me in. I told her Slim was with you. How come you didn't call her? And speaking of which, you called Jack before you called me? You got something against mud wrestling, trans-sexual, transvestites or something?"

"No, no—gee, I don't know. I saw the news. I was hysterical and screaming when I talked to Jack. What am I going to do with Slim? I'm not cut out for this mother stuff. I have to get to the salon. Can you pick him up or do I—I don't know what to do!"

"Liz, just keep him there for a couple of hours longer. First I'm going to stop by and have a talk with this shoe-store guy. I'll give back these shoes and see if I can smooth things over. Hopefully he will withdraw his complaint with the police or something. I don't know. We'll just have to see. I'm sure we're going to have to drag Slim down there to apologize face to face, but just keep him out of sight until I see how this goes down. Take a deep breath. One step at a time. I don't expect the police are combing the hair salons right off. Maybe you could take him to work with you. Got it?" said Luke.

"This is worse than a 'Jack in a lame brain' situation."

"Oh yeah, I almost forgot. Jack already deployed a decoy. I hope you're free tomorrow night to come to his—our Dessert Party Benefit for Mercy Mission?"

"You're kidding me, right?"

"Oh, Lamebrain already has Reverend Blanche and Greg Thicke advertising the thing on TV. He thinks it will throw lambs' blood on the trail of the Black Madonna."

Liz giggled. "Just what we need. Mary had a little lamb shank. You better check his menu tonight."

"Right. So maybe you can chat up this Dessert Party with some of your rich babe clients? Jack just may be right about this being good for publicity. Good then. We'll see you tomorrow night? Eight. Just hang in there with Slim, and stay calm. Thanks doll. Bye." Luke paused to watch Jack still preening at the mirror. "Well, that wasn't so bad. What the hell are you doing in the mirror? Admiring Jerry's ass print on your face?"

"How rude. Sex does such wonders for the pallor doesn't it? Even you look healthier this morning. Even if you are a fugitive. So is he a keeper?" asked Jack.

"Parker? Hell yeah, if he'll have me. Hopefully he'll want to have me a lot! I wonder where he went," beamed Luke.

"I last saw him with Jon talking about the insurance claim or something. You aren't the only fire he has to poke these days," Jack jabbed.

"Very funny, ass face. Why don't you go fire up your grill so we can get ready for the lunch dribble."

"Turn on the TV and let's see what the Reverend says about our Dessert Party."

"Dessert Party. What kind of desserts do you have in mind anyway?

"You'll see sugar pot. You think I've been wasting my time staring in mirrors and listening to you? This brain here never stops ticking." Jack turned to leave.

"Just like a perpetual time bomb," Luke thought.

Jerry sat at his desk shuffling the usual shit-load of paperwork. Merritt Smears had arrived shortly after he made it to the office looking damp. Wordlessly, he disappeared into his office. That was only after he delivered a mouthful of cold icy stare with out even as much as the usual "Morning Callahan" bark. Jerry assumed the manhole mess left Merritt with a bad case of distemper, but he couldn't help extrapolate from the tense situation. Add in the showdowns at Town Hall, LIVE! and Hudson Grille on Wednesday, he thanked God it was Friday. He clung to the torrid memories with Jack this morning, and looked forward to the weekend.

He heard the coffee pot rattle in the back room and figured Lou was lumbering around. That was confirmed when the intercom crackled in Lou's back office. Merritt had summoned. Jerry was surprised and silent when he saw Lou's hands padded and wrapped in gauze as he tried to wrestle with the door knob to Merritt's office. He kept telling himself to lie low, mind his own business and keep shuffling papers. Don't even think about picking up that can of air freshener.

While the muffled mumble behind Merritt's door built in volume, Jerry sensed that something somewhere somehow was going to explode. He hummed to himself, hoping he would not be in the range of fire from the unknown.

The sound of the front door grinding its way open against the tight fitting jamb echoed across the room and enveloped him with a strangle-hold of doom. The ripping sound gripped his throat and stopped his heart for a beat. "Jesus Christ, what now," he thought.

Stale cigar smoke and cheap cologne preceded the sight of Al Siegel as he entered the reception area. Like the grim reaper, he sauntered angrily through the opening in the low wall, and crossed behind Jerry's back. He paused in front of Merritt's door, turned the knob—at once throwing open the door, rattling its glass, and slamming it shut all in one seamless indignant effort.

Inside, the volume and garble doubled. The tension in the air became as thick as the smell. Jerry took a slow deep breath and dialed Jack.

"Now let us pray." Reverend Blanche stood in the middle of the stage on the set of Town Hall, LIVE! The red light on camera one was flashing. Behind her sat the Mayor's assistant secretary and a couple of the Mission regulars, their heads hung in sincerity.

"For the members and inhabitants of Mercy Mission, their care and patience in this brief setback, and for our dear sister, Dr. Sue Barrymore, that she too might find salvation and comfort in the arms of our forgivin' Lord. Bless us all sweet Jesus. Bless us all. Amen!" Blanche turned toward her guests for affirmation, hoping no one would notice she had not mentioned Slim's disappearance.

"Amen!" they echoed.

"Nothing against Reverend Blanche," said Jack, "but I kind of miss dishing Dr. Sue's bad hair, bad wardrobe and whoremonger mouth."

"Yeah. I don't see much future in an afternoon of amen's—but she did finally throw in a good plug for the Grille. I hope you can live up to that glowing praise she gave you."

"Calling me spiritually gifted?" Jack pondered. "Even that's a new one for me."

The phone rang. Luke answered, "Hudson Grille, Luke speaking. Hi Jerry. Yes, she is. One second." He passed the phone to Jack. "It's your oral proctologist calling with the swab results."

Jack grabbed the phone with gusto. "Hi handsome. Miss me so soon? EW, no. The three of them in there? Yeah, sounds kinda strange. No we haven't seen Jon or Parker. 'Bout an hour ago when you left. I'll see what we can do. Come straight to the Grille when you get out of there. Yeah. Call if you need me. Can't wait. Bye."

Jack hung up, paused, then spoke at Luke. "Merritt Smears, Al Siegel, and get this—Lou Thicke with hands all bandaged—are holding pow-wow over in Jerry's office. How weird is that? He wants us to get hold of Parker and Jon."

Al stood (and not too tall at that) rattling on at Merritt and Lou, who sat sheepishly at the corner table behind all the golf game clutter.

"I told you to play with a few wires to get the Mission building closed, not blow up half the fucking city! Anyway, a few crates of stuff that don't even have my name on them, in a basement I own, is not a crime. Let's just get that shit out of there tonight anyway. I don't want anyone poking around and figuring out we fucked up and nearly blew out half of Northwest, DC. Second, let's just put this dark fiber crap on hold till this outcry settles down and the telecom market gets healthier. Third. Smears, you think you can get Barrymore a job down there at Sewer & Sanitation? Get her into a pair of them bright orange coveralls. She likes that orange, y'ever notice? Heh! Just kiddin'. I know you're trying to chomp her shrub, and I just love to see you work up a good greasy schvitz. See what you can get lined up with Lou here to move those crates. I'll keep Sue busy on the lines till we can expand shop."

Al stoked his stogie and continued, "I feel like I got my damn hands up everybody's asshole today. Called in that gun tip to the TV station. All but paid off the Pic 'N Pay Store owner to confirm the story. Don't know what we're gonna do about him yet. I ain't worrying though. I told him I was Merritt Smears, heh! Oh shut up you old fart. If I go down, it won't be alone. And, it wouldn't take much to dump something to the networks about you and Barrymore. So while you got it shut, keep it shut Smears. As for you, meat hook, we already have your brother, Greg, sniffing up our butts. So, if you fuck up tonight, we'll just turn the rest of you into ground pork and let them know you tried to blow up the city. Looks like I'm done here. I'll call you tonight to make sure I ain't got any more screws to turn."

Luke and Jack caught the end of Town Hall, LIVE! while serving lunch to a few regulars and some brawny uniforms who were working next door. It hadn't hurt business with all the TV coverage out front of the Mission. It gave some prime exposure to the Grille.

Finally, Parker dropped by with Jon Miller, both of them suffering from over-exposure to pessimistic contractors and dour insurance assessors next door.

"Little early, but you two look like you need a drink," said Luke.

"Doesn't seem long ago we were worried about a little thing like plumbing in the basement," said Parker glumly. "That's small potatoes now. Sure, gimme two large Jack rocks and something new to talk about."

"Well, since you asked," Luke started, "And now that you're sitting, Jerry called from the Development office a half hour ago."

They traded stories of the three stooges conspiring and perspiring in Lou's office, his bandages and Al's rage, and Jon shared something of the earlier cross between Greg and Merritt. All this prompted Jon to check his cell phone again for a message from the Mayor. "Aha," he announced, "he wants a call back with an update, and a meeting tomorrow morning at 11."

"You or both of us?" asked Parker, hopefully.

Jon frowned. "No, I think I can do the meeting alone." He began to excuse himself and, dialing as he went, left without finishing his drink. Parker was disappointed at not being invited along. After all, he had contributed some key intelligence, such as Lou's shifty behavior around the granting of the permit. His boss was being a bit too secretive for his liking.

Jon's departure left Luke and Parker alone at the bar, except for a few late lunchers and Jack fanning the flames of his grille in the back. Parker took a breath and determined to shrug off his funk. He concluded that the cares of the world should be put in a broader context. After all, he had his hot stuff right up front where he needed him now.

Parker reached across the bar with a strong open palm. He wriggled his fingers invitingly.

Luke ensnared a few fingers and leaned up against the edge of the back bar. "Was it earlier this week I was beside myself to meet you?"

"It's been a while since I had my ego stroked. You must have perfect timing." Parker's grin made the hair on Luke's neck stand on end.

"It's Friday night. I probably won't get out of here till midnight," said Luke.

"That'll give us, what, maybe two, three hours of sleep?"

"You'll get plenty of sleep. Don't worry. I'll make sure I get the whole mouthful on the first go."

TWENTY-NINE

"Jack, that looks obscene!" Luke snipped.

"Oh Luke, pipe down. It's just a canoli. Can I help it if I took some artistic liberties?"

"Tell me you're just obsessing over Jerry and not planning this for the dessert party—though like I'm not sure which is worse." Luke paused to inspect Jack's handiwork. "Is he really that thick or are you dreaming?"

"I never lick and tell. Nix on the condom packet garni?" questioned Jack.

"Oh for the love of Christ." Luke rolled his eyes.

"Just step back and admire it for its wholesome goodness."

Luke strained away in fear. "I don't think I can step back that far."

"Nut balls—protein. Creamy filling—protein. That thatch of chocolate chips—TONS of antioxidants."

"Okay, okay, I get it. Very wholesome. But how the heck did you get it to stick out at that angle?" Luke reached in his finger to steal a tip of cream.

"It's not the size of your canoli shell, but what you do with its shape. Humongo here is just the centerpiece." Jack stepped back to admire.

"Well, I can't say it won't create a sensation. Just don't get any ideas with Jerry. You might scare him off."

"He isn't as timid as he looks."

"Alright, enough. I'm heading over to the shoe-store. I'll leave you to your wholesome creations." Luke sounded forlorn at the mission ahead.

"Wait til you see my bundt cakes!" squealed Jack.

"Good-bye, Jack." Luke turned and dragged himself toward the front door.

Luke was nervous walking over to 14th Street, but he was bound and determined. He'd take his lumps, grovel, and even shed a tear to make this all go away. Once inside the store, he bravely opened the plain brown shopping bag and placed the pair of size thirteen sneaks on the orange Formica counter in front of the store owner.

He looked up and smiled at Luke. "Would you like to exchange these or do you want a refund?"

"Return," said Luke. "And the boy didn't have a gun."

It took a moment to register with the store owner, until he looked up and stared Luke in the eye. "I know," he said.

"He took them for this homeless guy we know."

"Don't make it right."

"I know." Luke paused, and then continued. "Will you please take these back and will you please let him come here to apologize?"

"Think I'm gonna let him off that easy?"

"What have you got in mind, and what can we do so you'll withdraw you complaint with the police?" asked Luke.

"That was you dressed up like a black woman last night?"

"Um—yeah," said Luke.

"Black Madonna. You expect me to believe you? You expect me to believe he's a good kid?"

"Um—yeah." Luke hoped he looked sincere.

"It took me two looks, but on the first take, I thought you looked pretty damn good," said the man.

Luke smirked. "Get out of here." He paused then asked, "What did you think on the second look?"

"I may be old, but you think I'm stupid? I did sign up to be a stop on that Triathlon didn't I? My son tried to get me to run last night, but I don't quite have the courage. There sure were some hot bods in that race though. As for that gun business? I gotta tell you. Some short asshole was in here trying to bribe me to confirm that story. I never seen no gun. So I called up my son. He'll take care of all that. M'fucker. Little snot said his name was Merritt Smears. I know Merritt Smears from around town. This guy wasn't Merritt Smears."

"So, Detective Rollins, bring us up to date."

The Mayor sat at his desk facing the casually dressed soft-shoed man on the left and Greg Thicke to his right. They reviewed the surveillance reports from alleyways and doorways prior to Halloween evening. Detective Rollins relayed his revealing tip from the shoe-store owner. Greg recounted his brother's unfortunate accident and his conversation with an evasive Merritt Smears. The Mayor disclosed 'embellished' observations from his sister-in-law, Reverend Pickens. And Jon Miller, whose motives might admittedly be mixed, had bugged him about permit irregularities, in the self-same Bureau of Development.

"Greg, you realize this may cause a rather—excuse my term—explosive situation with the media," said the Mayor, "right before election day?"

"I don't expect any favors, Mayor," said Greg, "but could it wait a day or two?"

The Mayor contemplated over his crossed fingers. "I think it could take that long to get the warrants."

Several blocks north behind the steel locked door in Al's basement, big drama brewed. As Al jangled his keys and aimed to unlock his front gated door, the earth below throbbed and the air before him seemed to ebb and pulse. His alarm was confirmed by the sound of tinkling glass chandelier crystals. He lumbered inside as fast as his stocky, nicotine-riddled frame would allow. Round the bend through the kitchen, down the steps two at a time, he pursued a choked scream and the onrushing swell of humid, coconut-scented air. As he punched the basement lock code, pitched squeals gave way to vicious grunts.

Omph, aiiee, thwack. "Stop pullin' my braid!"

"My God damn ring is stuck in your God damn—ICK! I'm gonna rip this outta your head, you fat-ass can of lard!"

Tanka Rae had tipped over, and Sue Barrymore lay pinned underneath. Kahlua was in free fall, while Chardonay froze in surprise.

"STOP!" Al commanded.

Kahlua landed on her rump with a dull thud.

"—the FUCK'S goin' on here?" he shouted.

Silence hung for an instant till all three began chirping at once like a coop of starving hens.

"She, well she, she think, she ain't, she went, and she can't. She God damn mutha fuckin' asshole bitch!" Whomp, Slap! Then, "You fat, you ho, you slimy fart-ass suckin white skank cunt." Slap. Slap!

"CUT IT!" screamed Al. "Nobody move! Kahlua, what's going on here? SPEAK UP!"

Kahlua cleared her throat and wiggled to sound and look more professional. "Well, it's Ms. Sue. She been hangin' up on customers while she on the phone with Merritt Smear. That cuttin' into our booty fund. S'like money down the can. We don't stand for THAT now. No way. Mr. Al you tell her to pull weight."

"All right, off the floor you two. God damn mother fuckin' cunts. Barrymore, get upstairs. Tanka Rae, go fix that bloody lip. You two, get back on the phones. Don't just look at me like ass wipes. GO!" Al leaned in for emphasis.

They jumped at his command. Tanka Rae spun out the door and padded down the hall to the bathroom. Sue stood and huffed, then exited to plod up the stairs. Kahlua and Chardonay looked at each other then turned to take their seats.

"You two got some quota to make up. Stop gaping and start gabbing!"

Al's little empire started to close in on him as he trudged up the stair. By the time he reached the kitchen, he was shuffling. In the dining room he began to stomp, picking up steam as myriad annoyances nipped at his thoughts. While he held Sue Barrymore with no greater regard than a used condom, his squat fat legs were building up a mounting fury with each and every step.

The concept of that greasy, sniveling, smarmy Merritt Smears catching the eye of Sue Barrymore, the whore who groveled at his feet, made him seethe with decisiveness. Al squeezed his meaty fist around the thin neck of the door knob and twisted.

Inside, Sue stood facing into the corner and turned as she heard the door open. Al stood glaring at her with the oddest little smile on his face.

"Sorry I made you eat shit, Sue," he began, suckering her in.

"Oh, Al, it was awful," she choked, the lump in her throat causing her to tear.

He stood with his hands on his hips, catching his breath, and wiped the corner of his mouth with the back of his hand then said, "Now get your fat white ass the fuck OUTTA HERE! You're FIRED!"

THIRTY

"Oh no. You changed your shirt," said Jack.

"What?" asked Luke.

"That's the second flannel shirt today." Jack chided, "are you try-ing to look like a lesbian? Maybe if you were Parker. But a girl like you? I'm going to deduct points."

"What about you? Who the hell is that on your T-shirt?" asked Luke.

"Hullo? It's Wendell and Cass. Don't you remember the two gay penguins at the Bronx zoo? Now *they* give us a good name. They occu-pied the highest hutch of the flock, and the zoo keepers say their decor was fabulous!"

"Get out," said Luke.

"I'm not going anywhere, I'm busy cooking. How did it go with the shoe guy?" queried Jack.

"This whole town is freaky man," said Luke. "Too small and too much weird crap. Let's see. No gun. No complaint. Slim apologizes, though he'll have to work in the store through Christmas cleaning up and stuff. And get this, the guy's son tried to get him to run the race and he thought I looked HOT!"

"Who the son or the guy?"

"The guy. I don't know who the son is. But I suspect he's either a cop or a gang leader," Luke added. "It sounds like Al Siegel dropped by, trying to bribe the owner to confirm the gun story, but he refused. Sup-posedly the son is dealing with it now. Like I said. Freaky."

"No shit. That little Al Siegel is popping up everywhere, isn't he? Wonder what Jon thinks of all this." Jack was intrigued with the details.

"Jon is meeting with the Mayor tomorrow morning. He should find out more by then. And so, the store owner said he would withdraw his complaint down at the police station after the store closes or first thing in the morning. I hope things work out." Luke wondered.

"So do you think I can get out a little early tonight?" asked Jack.

"What, on a Friday night? And what about all your desserts?" questioned Luke.

"That's what I mean, I have to leave early tonight to go work on desserts." Jack began to sound impatient.

"Is that dessert named Jerry?"

"Well, he said he wanted to help." Jack jiggled up and down to insist.

"Yeh, I bet he will help. Buckle yourself down, here comes Mr. Canoli now."

Jerry walked past the front window, waved happily and came in the front door. Jack was there to wrap him up in arms for a big kiss. Jack wasn't shy when it came to such displays. More accurately, Jack wasn't shy at all.

Luke turned to switch on the TV at the bar, but didn't miss a trick as he caught the rest of Jack's antics in the back bar mirror. "Did he learn that kind of action from Wendell and Cass?" he mused.

"Scotch, soda," asked Jerry. "It's been one of those days." He staggered to the bar stool wiping his mouth on his shirt sleeve. Jack stood back admiring the view, so proud of his handiwork.

While Jack and Jerry continued playing slap and tickle, Luke managed to stifle his gag reflex and call over to Reverend Blanche. Luke assured the fretful pastor that Slim had confessed, had been given absolution, but there'd be some penance to pay to get back on track. Slim was still with Liz but he would be returned very soon, either tonight or, since it was already late, early tomorrow. They agreed that it would be best to stay clear of reporters and hopefully let the story idle for the time being. Reverend Blanche had heard through the Mayor that the entire Mercy Mission/ manhole explosion incident was under investigation. Luke ended on a positive note, inviting her to be guest of honor at the Dessert Benefit, and was rewarded with near canonization. Blanche told him to reinforce the floor boards, because she planned to take a well deserved break from her diet and enjoy herself.

"And now for the news."

"Work continued on multiple manholes today as minor explosions continued around the Dupont Circle area. Intermittent rain interrupted the work, while fire marshals patrolled all manholes in the vicinity to check for further evidence of smoke or flames. There were several incidents of covers blasting off smaller manholes. After fires were extinguished, vented covers were re-installed to allow for escaping gases. Fire Chief Peter Smitten had this to say..."

"I am sorry. All this manhole talk is making my willy itch." Jack pawed at his crotch. "And did they just say Peter Smitten?"

Luke tossed and said, "Here's some ice, honey. Will you take your itch elsewhere? For the love of Christ, poor Jerry must have no idea what he's getting himself into. I don't mean to speak ill of those present, but sometimes..."

"Hey, not so fast!" Jerry spoke up. "I'm new in town, and Jack is definitely a blessing."

"Wait till he ropes you into one of his schemes, like mud-wrestling with a Mack truck," said Luke. "You won't bless him then."

"He's into ropes?" joked Jerry. He took a long swig and gulped with amusement.

"Tomorrow night at Hudson Grille—"

"Oh! Hold on," Luke turned and yelled back for Jack to come up and catch Greg Thicke on TV. Like a little kid, Jack raced up front to the bar.

"—talented chef Jack Betz will present his dessert creations to benefit the re-opening of Mercy Mission."

"Woo-hoo!" yelped Luke.

"Nice, very nice. I may even vote for him now," spoke Jack.

"How cool is that?" said Jerry. "Maybe he isn't such a creep. I wish he'd stop leering at me. I suppose he'll be here tomorrow night?"

"I'll protect you," said Jack. "He makes one wrong move and..."

The news continued with Greg pictured at the polling places being readied for the Tuesday election, followed by a few out-takes of Reverend Blanche from Town Hall, LIVE! Luke's stomach sank when he saw the photo of Slim and LaChuChuWanda from the night before. He could recognize himself of course, although the shot was dark. His profile and statuesque wig were silhouetted in the glow of a street light which blurred out any distinguishing features. He had to admit however, that the photo did have a religious quality that befitted the bold headline "Black Madonna and Child."

Luke was startled out of the horror show looping through his head as Jack spoke. "I guess the media haven't heard you've cut a deal with the shoe-store owner yet."

"Mn, halo'ed trans-racial transvestites must make better copy than mid-term elections," Jerry added. "Too bad you can't enjoy the notoriety."

"Well, if you remember," recalled Luke, "I didn't really want to be in the spotlight—that is until people started whistling at my tight butt. Better that, though, than get known for modeling my boyfriend's pecker out of puff pastry."

"...And finally, police have made some progress in the case of the Black Madonna and Child. The Child, Slim, was lost and believed kidnapped on Halloween."

The three friends were yanked out of their merrymaking to focus on the screen. They watched in horror as they saw the officer guide the head through the door of an unmarked car, lanced by the beacon swirling on the dashboard. "OH MY GOSH!" they harmonized together in a high octave strain, "They took Liz to JAIL!"

THIRTY-ONE

She didn't know which was most demeaning. Getting dethroned by Reverend Blanche, degraded from TV star to phone sex whore, decked by Tanka Rae or dismissed by Al Siegel. Sue Barrymore stared into her glass and poked at the olive with her swizzle stick. It escaped her with each increasingly angry stab. The bartender watched in horror from a safe distance and thought about dialing 911 until he assessed her get-up and realized it was the day after a long Halloween night.

It was considered early, even for a room so dim. Pools of light dotted a path on the dark wood, leading to Sue at the far end of a foggy bar. The long ash from her forgotten butt fed the sheet of smoke that hung above. It did nothing but frame the view of vengeful eyes laden by teary mascara. She glared long and hard at the distance.

"Excuse me, is this seat taken?"

The swizzle snapped, toppling her glass in a tsunami of gin and clanking clatter. She was jerked out of her contemplative bout of self-pity, nearly ejecting the barstool from her ass. Her throat grasped for a suitable verbal lash as she whipped around and braced a hand to the bar.

She burst out with a loud "GOD—" then followed with a be-mused "—damn!" chaser.

He was tall, dark as the room, and looked at her through soft handsome eyes. Though she was only on her second drink, it could have been her fifth, intoxicated as she was at the distraction before her. He stood, shifting around in his soft shoes, thinking back with pleasure to his uptown pedicure and haircut earlier today. After the introductions, he inched closer for the toying banter and sat at the invitation to her disastrous story.

As with the drinks, the two hours seemed like five, but he was the model of attentiveness and patience. Even as she toyed with the snake tattoo on his forearm, he knew the time was an investment, careful not to flinch or laugh at the wrong moment. He let her pour and pour while he nursed his single glass watching ice melt and the whole sordid story of Al Siegel spilled juicily out.

Fortunately the patrons of Hudson Grille that night had all gone home. Jack, Jerry and Luke sat in shock at the news. Everything seemed to veer violently up and down, on their little fringe of U Street.

The phone rang and Luke leapt to pick it up. A frantic barrage hit his ears. When he heard who it was he hit the speakerphone.

"Luke, Luke, omigod this is awful. AWFUL! I am at the District Police Building, can you believe? They are holding me on suspicion of abducting a juvenile! Me! I don't even like fucking kids! I told you I shouldn't have kept Slim and it was long after the two hours you asked me to and I was taking him back to the Reverend and some eagle-eyed over-zealous young cop just swept us up from the sidewalk and I broke a fucking heel on the Manolos. If I ever get out of here, I am going to smack you two so hard, I am never, I mean NEVER going to get myself hooked up in the middle of another one of these lame-brained freaking freak shows of yours, so help me—Christ! You gotta HELP ME!!"

"Easy, easy, Liz, calm, I SAID calm yourself down." Luke tried. "We saw it all on TV. Reverend Pickens knows where he is and she's cool with him coming back tonight or tomorrow. She's certainly not going to press charges. Have the police call her and verify it."

The three men combined to reassure her, and her panic gradually subsided. They even reminded her to look around and see if there were any cute cops checking her out and to get all their phone numbers (and vital statistics) and oh yeah, invite them to the Dessert Party benefit. Jack glowed confidence, consolidating his new friendship with Liz, while Jerry glowed in admiration of the masterful show.

In due course, Jack and Jerry left tactfully, as Parker dropped in for a nightcap after a long day with Jon. He was there to help Luke close up for the night, and then followed Luke home for a second night of discovery.

There was something sexy about his chunk of a man padding around the apartment in his tattered T, unbuttoned jeans and untied sneaks. It seemed as though one more snip would deliver a whole new package of naked goods. Luke lay back on the bed with his hands back to cradle his head. His stomach was giddy with delight.

Parker stood, knees pressed against the soles of Luke's feet, as he looked down at his new found pride. Mischievously, he pushed, threatening to pounce while Luke beckoned with permissive eyes. Slowly with one bended knee after another, Parker crawled over Luke's length. He came to rest blanketing the stir of confined affection, heeding to the arms that wrapped over his back and squeezed.

Luke's feet fluttered, knocking Parker's shoes to the floor. "Gee, nothing like the thud of orthopedic shoes hitting the floor, eh ol' man?"

The wrestle that ensued was filled with glee, an alternation of pinned submission and exaggerated escape. The friction and pressure from each man's pent-up force was enhanced with heavy panting and clenched growling. Relenting to Luke, now king of the hill, Parker was rewarded with a face full of grinning affection.

"Got anything sweet?" said Parker after coming up for air.

Luke sat silent and smiling on Parker's stomach, a calf on each side, with that ridge of pleasure nestled along the crease of his seat and pressing his perineum. He reached and pinched each of Parker's tits through the thin cotton, twisting his squeeze with slow unyielding purpose. Parker's eyes faded shut as his jaw swung open. Luke broke the spell saying, "Don't go anywhere."

Sitting on the living room floor facing each other with crossed legs a few minutes later, they refocused their competitive intensity upon bowls of chocolate ice cream. Flared nostrils blew at curly streams of white cold air, while tongues lashed at giant blobs of dark sweet cream. Their throats swallowed hard, the sharp shots of ecstasy echoing in eyes locked together.

Parker paused and took the back of his spoon to dot Luke's nose with a quick dab of cold chocolate.

"Hey, what was that for?" Luke cried.

Parker paused, taking his amused grin down for a look at the bottom of his bowl. "Thought I might like to see my guy in a black face again..." As Parker peeked back up, Luke's eyes sank in dismay. Parker rolled forward, tilting his head to maneuver a lick at Luke's chocolaty lips.

Luke took a moment to reciprocate, ashamed. "You knew?"

"Yeah, so what. They say you had the best looking butt in the whole race. But I've already confirmed that. You smelled kind of girly last night—that make-up. But I wasn't absolutely sure till I stepped in that pile of wig last night. I'm surprised you didn't hear me yelp!" Parker took Luke's hand.

Luke groaned, "Oh gawd, I am so—embarrassed."

"What the hell for? You won, didn't you? Besides, my commando here is standing at attention trying to salute you with pride. I think he's focused on shooting some missiles into those deep dark hills of yours."

As Parker leaned forward, Luke leaned back looking him straight in the eyes. A disturbing idea had struck. "What did you just say about missiles?"

"I think I just said I want to fuck you brains out, black, blue or otherwise—" began Parker.

"Hold that thought Parker. First we gotta get over to the Mission!"

THIRTY-TWO

"You're crazy. Crazy! Al Siegel wanting to blow up the Mission?" A frustrated Parker jogged behind Luke as they made their way over to U Street.

"Think about it. Everywhere we turn, Al Siegel shows up in the middle. The gun story, the plumbing permit, the health inspectors, Sue Barrymore going off the deep end. You name it, and it has Al written all over it. It all adds up. The crates in the basement. I bet they have explosives in them!"

"Missals, not missiles. Blanche thinks it's Church stuff," retorted Parker hastily. "Al's a dick but he isn't that smart or that stupid." They turned the corner and continued down the street.

"Look, the Mission is closed up tight. Not a creature is stirring. You lose the bet. Let's just end this little excursion and go back to bed."

"Oh come on Parker," panted Luke. "Let's check at the back. They certainly aren't going to do anything out front here in the middle of the street."

"Luke, get a hold of yourself." Parker kept pace behind Luke. "Come on now, bud. Listen, Jon and I are meeting the Mayor in the morning. We'll get the whole story from him then."

"Just humor me, will ya? Just one peek around back. Maybe take a look inside one of those crates."

"I may have to distract you when we get back in that alley." Parker's voice took on an edge.

They made their way past the Mission and up the block to a driveway between two well-worn Federal townhouses. The night was clear and cold, cars passed on the street and sirens wailed in the distance. When they turned into the driveway, things were quieter. It was darker. The two took their time walking down the lane.

"Parker," Luke hushed, "I think I hear something." He jogged forward on the balls of his feet, careful not to make too much noise on the rutty gravel. Luke made it to the end of the driveway and came to a stop, peering out into the back alley that led to the back of the Mission. He looked up then down and pulled hastily back around the corner. Excitedly, he motioned to Parker to be quiet.

"I told you. I told you." Luke pressed his hand at Parker's shoulder to stop him. "Look at this!" he said in a hoarse whisper.

Parker craned out to glance quickly into the alley. His head pulled back with a jerk, meeting eye to eye with Luke as he softly exclaimed, "Holy Shit! They're loading those crates into the back of a Pepco truck!"

Not knowing what else to do or say, they both took another look in the alley to make sure they weren't dreaming. In that instant the beam of a flashlight pierced through the black, highlighting their look of surprise and raising their heartbeats. A man's bark followed, "Hey!" The crunch of his footfall against the gravel and the splosh of a puddle scared them. They froze in place as he barked again and Luke grabbed hard at Parker's thick arm.

"Get out of here." A different voice, low and less threatening, surprised them from behind.

Luke turned his head slowly for fear of a blow. Parker on the other hand whipped right around. Meanwhile the crunch of feet on gravel got closer. Veins were pounding in the back of their necks. Their look of astonishment left them speechless.

"Go on now, do as I say. You'll hear about all this tomorrow," said the man.

Luke grabbed Parker's arm, but didn't have to tug very hard as they sped back down the driveway. Luke nearly choked as he tried to catch his breath and hiss out, "Parker, Parker, that man, that was Gilbert!"

Then they raced all the way home.

"Don't worry? How do you expect me not to worry about it Parker? What the hell does Gilbert know? What the hell was he doing there anyway?" Luke rattled on as Parker lay by his side. They were still recovering after falling in an exhausted heap on the living room floor.

"Look," Parker said calmly, "He said we'd find out tomorrow. We're home safe. I don't normally listen to vagrants, but since I know this one, and it looks like he's not a vagrant after all, I think we should just do as he said. For now. Plenty strange though, I do admit. I just hope the whole block doesn't blow up tonight. I was looking forward to digging in to Jack's desserts tomorrow night."

"Well, you're certainly taking all this seriously, aren't you? Is dessert the only thing that keeps popping into that head of yours?" Luke rolled on his side to face Parker.

"Well, let's just say—let's just say, you roll over and find out!" He poked at Luke's side.

Luke let out a laugh as he was tickled, then placed his order, "Make me!"

THIRTY-THREE

The clock radio sounded off with the well-worn tones of some top 40 post-pubescent bimbo. This served to motivate Luke quickly out of bed most mornings, though today he was left with an emptiness beside him. All that remained of Parker was a faint hint of warmth left trapped between the covers.

The smile returned to Luke's face as the DJ segued into a piece entitled "Manhole Match Game." It hadn't taken long to latch on to the humorous side of a citywide disaster. Nonetheless, Luke switched off the radio to recap his own memories of the previous night's "Nightmare on P & U Streets." His mental fast-forward landed on the sinister alley scene and Gilbert's face. Confused, he went to turn on the TV news in search of an explanation.

Behind reporter number one could be seen another burning manhole. Behind reporter number two, Blanche and her ragged retinue spoke from their temporary encampment in a church social hall. Luke waited impatiently as hot black coffee gurgled into the pot. Anxiously he willed on the presentations of reporters seven and eight, through the commercial breaks. By the time The Today Show arrived, an answer to the alley incident still remained a complete mystery.

Jack lay sprawled in the center of the bed like a large cat, licking the sweet off Jerry's 'jelly donuts' when the phone rang. He growled at the disturbance, crawled up over Jerry and stretched toward the noise. Jerry moaned in regret, then he happily inched down to nest his face between Jack's thighs and return the favor. Jack purred to answer the phone, "Mmmm-is-iz Jack. Morning honey. What's up? Ooh!"

As Luke began to tell him how the sly Fox got the real Black Madonna to stand up, Jack was distracted, stifling cries of ecstasy. After a minute he had to turn over and bite his giggles into a pillow. "NO, of course it's not funny Luke! I totally understand."

This only encouraged Jerry, who rampaged deeper and mercilessly with his lapping as Jack's extremities convulsed. A restrained scream tried to answer Luke, "NO! He didn't!" while the rest of him said, "Oh yes, he will."

"Oh yeah. Yeah, I'm okay," said Jack, as he climbed over to straddle Jerry's thighs. "Yes, he's here. No, we've been up for a while." He winked, releasing Jerry's hard-on to slap at the hairy stomach. He grabbed it again for a bit more reckoning. "You thought WHAT? Bombs?" Jack continued his aggravated assault while listening to Luke's suspicions. He maintained intense eye contact, breathing steadily, phone in one hand, Jerry in the other. He attended to Luke while attending to Jerry, responding enough to mask the signs of his mischievous tryst. Jerry laid witness, trapped between Jack's thighs, straining his hips in a slow and heartfelt quest.

"You went WHERE? You're kidding!" Jack's eyebrow raised as the corner of Jerry's mouth ripped the packet. Instinctively he held his hand firm, planting itself at the base of Jerry's blooming excitement. They held their mutual breaths as Jack leaned forward and Jerry buried his teeth deep into the crook of his bent index finger, trying not to laugh.

"OH my God," gasped Jack, "That's SO incredible. Un-fucking believable," as Luke administered details of his search with Fox in the dark alley. "And then Parker came up behind you?"

Jack held his breath, tensing his glutes, waiting for Luke to deliver the next episode of his tale.

Jerry's nails clawed along the fair fur of Jack's thighs then bit hard into their tense muscled flesh. Jack gulped back the pain that came to his throat. But he could not resist stoking Luke's mounting frenzy. "Go on, go on," urged Jack. "You grabbed his arm?" Jack pointed down with his eyes. Jerry spat in his palm and joined in silent chorus. "OH, that's HOT!" Jack hissed, riding Jerry and coaxing Luke to continue. Luke paused and emphasized every tense moment, exaggerating the dire fear he felt as he gripped at Parker's thick rock hard arm again and again. And again. "By now I bet you were driving Parker NUTS!" Jack nodded and Jerry tugged hard with his other hand.

Jack's chin strained in the air, not sure if he could bear anymore. He paused then asked Luke cautiously, "Do you think the thug loading the boxes was—Lou Thicke?"

Jack held his breath for a response while meeting Jerry with full force half way in the air.

"Of COURSE it was Thicke!!" Luke shouted.

As reality hit, Jack's mind exploded into stars. Luke's revelation echoed violently inside him as Jerry arched again. Then again. Beneath him, Jerry glistened, intent and deliberate as he poked fun at Jack's every squeal, his sweat lubricating the bond between them.

As the story built to its dramatic climax—Gilbert scaring them to death, the close-call escape—Luke milked Jack's surprise for all it was worth. Winding up, Luke drove home the adrenaline rush of racing away on the street in abandon with Parker. They pounded quickly up the stairway to his building, soared up the elevator and jammed the key in to unlock his door. They burst into his apartment dripping wet and gasped together desperate for breath. Finally, when the door slammed hard behind them, they grabbed each other and held on for dear life.

"Omigod, Luke, omigod," Jack panted, as Jerry lost every last inch of his being inside Jack. "GEEZ----US, CHRIST!" yelled Jack. Three huge spurts shot across the air. Jerry ducked out of the way. Jack doubled over, quaking with drenched sobs, giddy and elated. Jerry heaved one sweaty last thrust, and then retreated proud, grinning and spent.

Luke rolled his eyes surprised at Jack's over-the-top reaction. "Jack Betz, are you making fun of me? You sound like a fucking Mary, screaming like that!"

Silence hung as Jack took a moment to catch is breath. Jerry stretched his arms back behind his head, puckered his lips and exhaled a long silent whistle. He tried to look innocent.

"NO, of course not, Luke!" cried Jack in alarm.

Jerry produced the dildo that was behind his pillow.

"I just can't" Jack insisted, "believe you went back there looking for that mangled goon!" Jack's head shook and eyes pleaded as Jerry taunted him. "Are you crazy?" He snatched the toy away. "Wait till Jerry gets a load of THIS one! He'll be screaming louder that I was! Now, let me get it straight. Gilbert's not a vagrant at all? I'll be damned! And you say there is nothing on the news this morning?"

The police were managing to keep the alley incident off the news so the element of surprise would be on their side. This explained the baffled look on the faces of Merritt Smears and Lou Thicke. The two sat at the table in the middle of the dank interview room of the precinct wondering what was going on, being hauled down here so early in the morning.

Detective Rollins had his ducks in a row. With these two low-wattage perps, standard procedure should work. He walked them through what had been observed in the alley, and other places. They seemed genuinely shocked at being caught in the act. Incontrovertible evidence, Rollins called it. Things would go a lot easier for them if they came clean, if they could prove they weren't the masterminds. Merritt and Lou started to squirm uncomfortably. What was in the crates? Where did the bandaged hands come from? Who gave them their instructions? When Merritt started to speak with a stammer, the officer at the other end of the table relaxed and smiled.

In due course Rollins dialed the phone and thrust the receiver toward Merritt with his command, "Now talk nice and slow. Get him to come meet with you."

There was no answer to the call, but the police pressed on unde-terred. As the conversation wound its way without a hitch, their wry smiles grew. For the two future jailbirds, the room began to feel half its size and much more cell-like. Without pausing to celebrate, the cops proceeded immediately to the next task at hand. They hustled Merritt and Lou out of the room and into the car. Vandalism, trespass, injury to utility cables, exploding a destructive device? Al Siegel was in for a breakfast surprise.

And they would also need to talk to Parker Fox.

THIRTY-FOUR

Sometimes, best laid plans can have a mind of their own. After last night's bout of boozing and blabbing, Sue still had no mind of her own. A thunderstorm raged inside her head, pounding her temples like a bass drum. "Holy Christmas," she pondered, trying to roll over while her thoughts flailed at strands of recollection. Her numb legs didn't respond, as her high heels caught themselves in the brake and gas pedals below. She kicked, annoyed, startling herself with inflicted pain. "God damn it, I've been asleep in the fucking car." She winced at the painful frustration of forcing herself upright.

Her eyes darted around collecting realities, snippets of information that belonged to her car, her disheveled state, her whereabouts. She feebly wiped a window of condensation off the windshield.

An empty alley downtown somewhere, she couldn't have driven far. Good thing, in this state. Had she fucked the hot guy in the bar, blown him at least? Didn't taste like it. "God, I'm dying of thirst, let's see if anywhere's open around here." Concentrating her strength into one elbow, Sue forced the car door open.

It wouldn't go far. A flash of sun fell on something in the way, something inert, lumpy and, oh no, familiarly obese. It came back to her in all its glaring horror. There had been that thud as she knocked into something at the curbside after starting up the car last night. She had simply stopped and slumped at the wheel. Now she steeled herself to look at the mass more closely. The vile image swam in and out of focus, causing a riot of emotions to well up in her brain. Prostrate and bleeding from the head, there lay her bloated nemesis, finally cut down to size.

"Oh wow, you are 'ere, I cannot believe eet! ¡Ven, Alberto, mira! ¡La señora está!" A clamor of gleeful voices burst out to greet Liz as she jauntily stepped into the uptown Land of OZ. "You are a free woman, yes? But the TV last night, the police, what 'appened?"

A fireball of energy clicked its heels and shimmied across the shiny tile floor towards her. Two meaty butt cheeks clenched, happily confined within the Saran tight wrap of black racing striped pants. Swinging broad shoulders and outstretched arms of welcome, Enrique kept time to the Latin beat that danced constantly in his head.

To one side, a pair of smock clad maids locked their gaze on the pair of peacocks that swept each other into a warm embrace. The observers watched the pantomime from the safety of the igloos that covered their curler-clad heads.

At the front desk, Alberto stopped absentmindedly toying with his new flock of short white blonde braids. "Meez Osbourn-eh, 'ow are you, we think you are in prison!" His perfectly clipped black eyebrows shot skywards in surprise and delight to see his boss reinstated, for it was pay day to boot.

"Assholes had no case, once the Reverend Pickens told them it was not malicious. Her kid was in good hands after all. Lucky brat, even the shoe-store guy says he will withdraw his complaint. Now all I need is no illegal aliens on my hands, eh Alberto?" Liz was joking until she saw the look of excitement on his naturally tan face fall away like a stone. "Oh no, don't tell me that—" she began, but was interrupted by the arrival of two disarming clients.

"Good Morning Liz," the first visitor smiled warmly. He flashed her a card along with a smile. Jon Miller had decided to take the plunge, and up the ante. "I just finished a grueling morning with my lawyers up the street and thought I would take up your offer. Can you fit me in?"

Liz, for once, was briefly lost for words. Of course, as the owner she didn't often do clients herself any more. But this one? Most definitely. She felt Enrique watching her every move and hoped she wasn't blushing. Her awkward moment was eclipsed (literally) as the next client barreled charismatically through the door. Like being spared the Spanish Inquisition, she was relieved when Enrique's eyes shifted away to lock like magnets on the flowing scarves and hulk of straining gabardine trench coat that filled the reception area.

"Meee-ster Richmon-da, so good to seeee you again!" squealed the prima donna as he wrapped the visitor in his second bear hug.

Alberto jerked back into primetime and realized he should pay attention to the broad oval man beaming over Enrique's shoulder. Liz took Jon's elbow in the gentlest of holds and began to edge him away from the fray. The watching flock of hooded penguins didn't miss these small gestures, and smiled knowingly.

"Phil! How good to see you," said Liz brightly, a few steps away. "You're here for your usual? It looks like Enrique is ready for you!"

Phil unfurled his coat and scarf, finished patting down the welcome party and jovially addressed Enrique, awarding him a booming laugh. "I hope I don't have to pay extra for the full body wrap, eh Enrique? Uh HUH huh huh!"

Phil Richmond was the town's preeminent food critic, and Liz was thrilled to hear him ask for a full morning of body work. With the way this man eats, she thought, it's a wonder he isn't here for a week!

When he had made the appointment, she had jokingly said she could fit him in on a Saturday only if he reviewed the Hudson Grille. It was on his list to review, he assured her. The fact that she was able to bribe him with a roomful of desserts, both sweet and male, played a small part in his final decision. The fact that Enrique was on hand, and effusively welcoming, sealed the deal. She was a veritable Dolly Levi.

Bubbling with confidence at Phil's arrival and the upbeat exchange that ensued, Liz led Jon to the back of the salon. Another deal remained to be sealed. She led him into the supply closet for a kiss that would turn this Bruce Wayne into her Batman.

Luke, Jack and Jerry were at Hudson Grille working feverishly on various components of desserts that had yet to take shape. Luke put on the TV since the three were still anxiously waiting to hear of a clue to the Big Alley Adventure. Luke sat with his legs gripping at his chair. Jack and Jerry, more than happy to stand, busied themselves with the work at hand. They flashed each other knowing smiles while trying to conceal the passion they were replaying in their heads. Their mental bond was palpable.

Luke chuckled to himself and didn't let on. He certainly wasn't deaf or dumb to the manner of creams filling, bananas dipping or fingers licked. *"...death of one the city's most prominent business personalities, media magnate and property owner, Al Siegel. Mr. Siegel was Chairman and CEO of Siegel Studios whose local programming includes the popular midday news and opinion show Town Hall, LIVE! Mr. Siegel was found late last night in the street near his home on 17ᵗʰ Street, critically injured. He died later in hospital. Police are treating his death as suspicious but would give no further details. Over now to Megan Marshall, our reporter on the scene. Megan?"*

"Oh my GOD!" the three viewers chorused, repeatedly.

"To think he was in here with his cronies, just the night before last," said Jerry.

"Maybe he choked on his own cigar, good riddance!" Jack added uncharitably.

"As long as it wasn't food poisoning by Chef Jack," Luke said, then ducking to avoid a flying spatula.

As Luke recalled all the nefarious deeds he suspected Al to be at the heart of, they realized guiltily that with Al's grisly demise their little world might become a whole lot less of a hassle. Then it dawned on Jack: "So Luke, Big Al was part owner of this building. Who do you think owns it now, and our future with it?"

Meanwhile a couple of blocks away, the Courvoisier girls were rounding the corner on their way back to Al's den of sin, and were curious of the bedlam that stormed in the air ahead. A police cordon surrounded the house, and S street resounded with a braying of sirens. As they tried to explain to a fat, implacable DC cop their dubious roles within the building, and the urgency of their mission to attend to the nation's pent-up frustrations, Tanka Rae surprised everyone by yelling out "Fuck!" It had nothing to do with their lurid conversation. Something had struck her on the back of the head.

An increasingly unstable Sue Barrymore was on the warpath. Her emotions were a roiling mix of vindictive delight at Big Al's demise and the stark terror that she might be his killer. Her vengeful rage now displayed itself in the form of a well aimed fourteen-inch missile of Paul Mitchell humidity-resistant hair spray. She advanced armed with two more cans, spraying their contents ahead of her with remarkable if wobbly strength.

Naturally Tanka, Kahlua and Char dove right into the cloud of spray to deliver some more well-deserved punching and clawing toward Sue. The cop, blinded by spray, tried to gather his slow wits to intervene, but—

At that moment, across the street, a seven foot tall column of flaming spew erupted from a tented manhole, sending said tent into a caravan of screeching traffic. Hard hats, dayglo orange overalls and charging black work boots flew in all directions, their owners scurrying for cover and holding hands. The passers-by, the looky-loos and the four wrestling divas weren't far behind, coughing their way through billowing smoke and ash.

Ace reporter Megan Marshall had just been cued in for her report from the scene of the death. "Here live at 17th and S Streets—aaagh," she gasped, as she was thrown back and plastered against the Fox News van. She managed to hold on to her mike while her cameraman caught her saucer white eyes of horror.

Though he was usually calm in a storm, the full course of mounting events was obviously ringing at the mayor's neck. "Gentlemen, I apologize for not getting back to you earlier and for bringing you in on a Saturday," the Mayor began. "Things have been changing by the hour here. Right now I have Reverend Pickens watching TV, calling to tell me Al Siegel is dead." His guests looked at him aghast. "Yeah. Found early this morning not far from his office, pretty beat up. No word on how or maybe who." Holding the phone in his hand, the Mayor sat at his desk facing Jon Miller and Greg Thicke. "I have even more manholes in Northwest continuing to explode. The situation there—well, we can't even keep up with all the calls. And we may have to get up to 17th and S right away. Hold on, Blanche dear, I gotta go. You take care now. Bye. Now Greg, before we leave, I gotta tell you I can't wait any longer to comment publicly on Lou's activities."

"I understand, Mayor, but can you think of any way to spin it, to help my, uh, campaign image?"

"Best I can come up with is to deflect attention from Lou. The whole explosion fiasco I can justifiably pin on Siegel and Smears. Lou just took direction. The crates, the transportation of contraband, that crap I might be able to dump at Al's door, either on him or on Parker Fox."

"Can't hurt him much when he's dead," Greg nodded. But Jon's head was spinning, trying to register all this. He fought back the afterglow of the ministrations at Salon OZ an hour ago to concentrate on the Mayor's startling revelations.

"Contraband? Parker Fox? FOX??"

"Well Jon, you see now why I asked you to come here alone today. Turns out those crates in the Mission cellar were addressed to Parker Fox. Smears and Lou both saw it when they tried to offload them. So they could have been Siegel's but we can't be sure they weren't Fox's."

"Jesus Christ."

"And the cops opened one. No hymn books for the Mission, oh no. Lots of video equipment and a load of contraband cigars, Cuba's best."

"¡Madre de Díos!"

"No, actually, Merritt says they were Montecristos. At least the Big Guy had taste." The Mayor couldn't swear bilingually, but he had a nose for business. He shifted gear. "Now Jon, we all know Al was trying to redevelop that Mission and Grille site. You were the holdout, right?"

"Yes that's true. Just earlier this week, Parker and I tried to persuade him to hold off. The current tenants were coming along just fine."

"Well let me tell you, you were pissing in the wind. Al was maneuvering to buy you out, you know. Using the Studios as collateral for a loan. Cutting Merritt and Lou in for a percent in return for intimidating the tenants to leave. Merritt admitted as much to the cops."

Jon sucked in a breath. So I was right, he thought to himself, they were casing the joint that night at the Grille. And I was fool enough to play nice to them.

"And now I need both of you to help me clean up this fucking mess, flaming manholes and all," the Mayor continued, "so let's get outta here and keep a goddamn lid on it before the media starts to spin this out of control."

THIRTY-FIVE

At the Hudson Grille, they had peeled themselves away from the overwhelming accumulation of Breaking News Firsts to give due attention to finalizing the preparations under way in the kitchen.

"Well Jack," said Luke with a hint of surprise, "I think you are really outdoing yourself this time, and—"

"Voluptuous, aren't they?" said Jack, eyeing one of his creations.

Luke paused, "Well, I was going to say it's—"

"Indecent?" chimed in Parker.

"There is nothing indecent about these cinnamon BUNS! Don't blame ME! Jerry inspired them."

Jerry shrugged, bashfully pleased with himself.

"I bet he did," bargained Parker.

"He may look buttoned down," said Jack, "but he is very creative, and very—"

"Kinky!!" chimed Luke and Parker together.

Jack and Jerry returned a pair of matching smirks then burst out laughing. Jack was on a roll.

"Let's come up with a slew of decadent desserts and have some real fun!" he continued. "Holesome Desserts! Yeah! How about Cranberry Bread Crostini with two scoops of Butternut Marscapone Icing? I could make it pass for a cock ring."

"I think you were up far too late last night taking down Jerry's DICK-tation." Luke goaded.

Jack replied by changing key and going up an octave, "And over here, we have White and Dark Chocolate covered Bananas."

"What's that flourish at the end of the plate?" asked Parker.

Jerry defended, "Just a squirt of lemon coulis, something nice and tart—and this is going to be our Three Mousse Mountain."

"Thick AND creamy," concluded Parker with a cheeky grin. "I could get used to all this."

"Mr. Parker Fox?" A head peeked around the door. It was familiar, but the badge and navy suit that followed it into the kitchen were decidedly not. The four friends gaped in amazement, lost for words. "Yes, this is an official visit. And I should start by re-introducing myself.

Detective Rollins, DC Metropolitan Police. I'm here to talk with Mr. Fox about his relationship with the Mercy Mission."

"What the—?"

"Who the—?"

"What's going on here?" said Luke, pushing the others aside. "Gilbert, what's this badge for Christ's sake? Are you really a cop? And as for Gilbert the tramp that hangs out at the Mission with his tambourine—have you been shitting us all this whole time? And to think of all those frickin' free coffees!!"

"So it WAS you we bumped into in the alley last night!" added Parker, as things dawned on him. "You saw the whole thing! The crates being loaded, we thought they were filled with explosives—did you—?"

"Not exactly," interrupted the newcomer. "We'll get to that. But first, hold on everyone, let me explain a bit."

Detective Gilbert Rollins wiped his brow, perched on a stool and began his revelations. He touched on his cover as the one-eyed soft-shoed vagrant Gilbert. He related the suspicious dealings at the District Development Office and the mounting evidence against Merritt Smears, Lou Thicke and Al Siegel. Even such figures as a TV personality and a political candidate had provided him with material incriminating Big Al. But there was an unexplained piece in the puzzle.

"So Mr. Fox, in the Mercy Mission basement when you worked on the plumbing this week, what else was stored there?"

"You know that, Gilbert, I mean Detective," began Parker, his annoyance showing. "You were there too, for heaven's sake! Six crates, you kicked 'em around. I see why now. One was labeled 'Missals Inc.' so we believed they were for Reverend Pickens."

"Then why were they addressed to you?"

"They were??"

"Sure, to a Mr. P. Fox, care of Mercy Mission."

"Well, I can tell you I didn't sign for them." Parker exchanged a frown with Luke.

"You didn't inspect them? Check what was in them?" the detective continued.

"I really wasn't involved with them. Luke here came up with the idea that Big Al had filled them with explosives, to demolish the Mercy Mission so that he could redevelop the site."

Luke shrugged, with his eyebrows climbing in synchrony.

"How well did you know Al Siegel, Mr. Fox?" Rollins persisted.

"Not at all. He was a business partner of my boss, Jon Miller, but I only met him briefly for the first time the other day when he and his cronies came here for drinks, their foul smoke billowing in my hair."

"Can anyone confirm that?"

"Yes!" the others chorused in close harmony like a barber shop trio.

"OK, well it's like this. I needed to establish whether you might have been Al's accomplice, an old buddy perhaps. You didn't know that the crates contained contraband Cuban cigars, then?"

"Hell, no. I don't have connections in Cuba and I don't smoke. But Al certainly did. Constantly. Christ, he's dead and still screwing everyone. What did kill him anyways?" Parker felt a wave of relief as he spoke. This emotional roller-coaster, which had just sped from the giggles to gut-clenching to gratitude, made his relationship with loopy Luke seem like a walk in the park.

"Well, we don't know the whole story yet. A blow to the head might have been fatal, but how he sustained it isn't clear." Rollins took a breath and picked up one of Jack's banana creations, eyeing it curiously. "We know he went out from his house late last night and by chance ran into the shoe-store owner, who was on his way to the Police Department. The shoe-store owner told us this when he came over to withdraw his complaint about Slim. He said Al had immediately begun raging at him. Al was mad that hadn't been able to coerce him to sabotage the Triathlon, and he was also pretty drunk. They got into a bit of a fight, and though Al was tough, he wasn't very balanced." He let the banana fall on the floor with a splat. The onlookers collectively winced.

"So did he fall, or was he pushed?" asked Parker.

"That's not the main issue," Rollins answered. "My big problem is, my two suspects are no less than Dr. Sue Barrymore and well, get this, my own father. He owns the shoe-store."

The door to the kitchen suddenly swung open and Liz waltzed in, decked to the nines in a sheath of black sparkle. Behind her swishing strawberry blonde pony-tail trailed the adorable Alberto, with blonde braids hoisted up in a black stretch band, his pack of lithe boyhood ripples barely painted with a tank of black mesh. The ring in his navel sparkled above the low slung band of his pewter bell-bottoms.

"LOOK at those yummy desserts!!" Liz clapped, "Shame on you Jack, you're going to upstage my new little black D&G!" As she twirled for effect, her gaze alighted on the surprise visitor. "Gilbert, is that you? My, what a makeover! What's going on here?"

At this, Luke intervened to ask Gilbert to explain his transformation to Liz. That would allow the dessert designer team to get back to work. It was nearly six o'clock and these unforeseen events were jeopardizing their schedule.

Luke drew his lover into the still-empty bar, and pressed him up against the counter. Parker acquiesced but the poor man's mind was still buzzing from the stress of the police interview. "What was that about Gilbert's father then?"

"Yeah, imagine someone that close being a suspect? Like a real hardened criminal?" Luke nudged with his groin. "You had me really wondering about you there for a minute. Can I tell everyone I am dating an almost ex-con?" Parker hung his head somewhere between mock shame and quiet exasperation. Luke reassured him as he nuzzled his face in the crook of Parker's neck. Luke continued, "Look, I don't know who was driving this week's roller-coaster, but it has been quite a pleasure having you along. I just want to let you know you're racking up a lot of my "L" points."

"'L' points? That some kind of Luke-rating system?" Parker hung his head a bit to look into Luke's eyes.

"'L'," said Luke, "Lick, Lay, Lash, um Larceny? No, not that one, but when you're ready, you can trade them in as you please."

Parker paused to hold the moment, then teased back: "How about Lamborghini? That's what I really want."

"Fat chance," Luke laughed.

Parker suggested with a hip grind of his own, "How about we skip Jack's desserts and go lick our own?"

Luke looking over his shoulder spotted the evening's first guest walking in. Once he saw who it was, he sprang apart, whispering urgently to his partner, "Uh-oh, sorry bud, I'm afraid we have to go butter up Phil Richmond first."

THIRTY-SIX

The Dessert Benefit was about to begin. Out front in the Grille, the lights were dimmed low and tables rearranged to make room for the festivities. Candle-lights danced palm frond patterns up the walls and the collection of mirrors reflected a growing animation. The patrons who were invited to stay after dinner, including Phil Richmond who seemed affable enough, mingled with new guests beaming surprise as friends joined together and cordial introductions were made. A cool mix of Claude Challe and a world tour of trip-hop music, volunteered by Parker from his eclectic collection, floated on the air with the buzz that was beginning to build.

Liz darted back into the kitchen. "Jack, Phil Richmond just guzzled down your Lamb Shank à la Jacques! Imagine, Phil Richmond! Eating at the Grille! Aren't you excited?"

Jack exclaimed, "Excited! I nearly had a seizure while I was finishing the reduction! Any more EXCITED and my pastry bag will explode!"

"Clench Jack, clench," warned Jerry taking cover in the sink area. "Let's see what Liz and Alberto" (who was just sidling in) "think of our handiwork. Well you guys...?"

"Ai, yi, yi!" squealed Alberto.

"Oh my," said Liz clutching her cracked ice halter, "Who needs to husband hunt out there? I'll just stay in here and gorge! Those are the cutest pair of—Alberto!! Did you model for these?" She continued to marvel, "I see you guys are trying to appeal to all of Phil's and Enrique's interests. Wait till you get a load of him tonight!"

"Dolled up as usual?" asked Jack.

"Barely," said Liz.

"Well then! Let's all go have a look at the festivities," suggested Jack.

"It's premiere time for Holesome Desserts!" rang Jerry.

Jack, Jerry, Liz and Alberto grabbed a platter each and proceeded through the kitchen doors. The waiting crowd broke into applause, spiked by whistles, cheers and a hearty "Uh HUH huh huh!"

Out front, lipstick and leather lesbians mingled with Levi boys, lycra toys and shiny daddy studs. There were pin stripe movers, tuxed shakers and a flock of mavens with lace.

Jon Miller came up to Parker and Luke as he worked his way through the throng. "You guys really know how to throw a party! And before I get too, uh, involved here, Luke, I have some news for you. I thought you would want to know that the title to these properties is held by the company Al and I formed, Wharton Investments. Now that there's only one director left, I have complete control."

"All-RIGHT!" cried Luke, high-fiving a surprised Jon. Parker grabbed Reverend Pickens as she walked by, so that she too could hear the good news.

"So there's no risk to the tenants in the Grille or the Mission in the short or medium term. Unless you throw too many wild parties, of course! I see Liz was successful in securing Phil Richmond's attendance tonight. Do you think he's here for the desserts or those pants you sprayed on Enrique?"

While Jon's small audience shared a huge sense of relief, in the middle of the room the Latin bombshell and the blonde coiffed über-foodie danced suggestively together. Near the tables stacked with desserts, their energy became the focus of the crowded room. Their behavior raised more party spirit than eyebrows.

"Could those biker shorts be any shorter?" quipped Parker.

"I guess they could, given Enrique, but it is November," said Luke.

"Well at least he has his vaquero's hat, looks kind of butch on him." added Parker.

"Oh yeah, real butch, goes right smart with the FABulous fur vicuña jacket. At least that will keep him a little warmer," tossed Luke.

"And so will Phil Richmond!" concluded Fox.

They scanned the room taking in all the sights. The crowd was in full swing with the music. Parker nudged Luke, "So, do you like my music selections?"

"Yes, perfect," agreed Luke, his own movements confirming his approval. "You get what I like and I know I'm lousy with band names and words. So who's this, Jim Croce?"

"Oh, jeez," Parker feigned exasperation, "Are you trying to rub Veruca Salt into my wounds? Jim Croce? Where do you think we are?

Wichita? This happens to be—wait a minute, now there's a conversation I'd like to hear."

Across the way, Liz stood talking animatedly to a very attentive Jon who was gesturing colorfully, quite unlike his placid, staid old self. She had shed her extravagant eye-glasses for brand new contacts, a vanity gesture that did not escape Luke and Parker. Jon's eyes seemed riveted to her shimmering body and beaming face. At one point, she flung her arms around his shoulders, nearly spilling her Appletini on his sharp striped shirt. Neither noticed, but Luke and Parker caught it all for a later inquiry.

Parker continued to read the crowd, then drew their attention to the other side of the room. "Uh-oh, there's trouble." He put his arm around Luke's waist to wheel him into position.

Jerry stood, back pinned up a smidge too close to one of the potted palms. He seemed to be locked in conversation with Greg Thicke. Greg Thicke was adding urgent comments to the mix as he patted his hand on Jerry's shoulder.

"Interesting," assured Luke, "It looks like Greg is—well, I sure hope Jack isn't around. Boy, are we going to have a LOT of catching up to do tomorrow."

The party continued to build momentum, and the line still waited for second and third desserts. Enrique squealed out from the gently jostling conga which in itself was like a long layered confection. In front of him was Phil Richmond of course. Behind him was sweet Alberto and one of the old Mercy Mission regulars who had made it across town from her temporary home. Also in the line were a jubilant Reverend Blanche, wielding a sporty cane a bit too wildly, and an embarrassed-looking Gilbert Rollins still in his business suit.

Then there was Slim, carrying his friend's tambourine just as faithfully as he previously did for the undercover Gilbert down on his luck. How cool was that? He actually knew a real life undercover agent! Even better, after a painfully stern talk about shop-lifting, he had vouched and helped to get his mom released early. She surprised Slim by showing up tonight at the party where she now happily danced in line behind him. Behind her followed a train of Levis, leathers, khakis and lace. And so, it continued, cruising past mirrors, smiling through potted palms, clinking glasses and smacking lips.

"Come up front with me," said Luke to Parker, "I'm going to need some help."

They squeezed their way past hugs and handshakes, ending up at the bar. Parker steadied the barstool and helped Luke climb up to see over the layer of heads, which all turned, shushing quiet to watch his ascent. Forks tuned themselves on the edges of glass and hushed silence for Luke to begin.

"Thank you, thank you, one and all for joining us in this benefit for Mercy Mission, next door. I want you all to turn and give a big round of applause to my best friend and business partner, originator of all the wackiest ideas including this one. I hope you all had your fill of his, um, interesting desserts. Mr. JACK BETZ!"

"I simply WORSHIPED the banana!" boomed Phil. The quick statement took everyone by surprise but was engulfed with an "Ai, yi, yi" and a wave of clapping and cheers. Jack nudged Jerry to share in the success.

"I would say more than a few of us have been through quite a storm in the past couple of days," continued Luke. "Let's all hope that's behind us and that we stand alongside each other to help re-build Mercy Mission! Now, let's all eat more SWEETS!"

"Hear, hear," started the cry. It echoed then faded into a chorus of reverie and grew into a new rhythm for dance. Wedgies and Weejuns, sneakers and sling backs, the high heeled and well heeled—all kept prancing on into the night. Liz and Jon danced slower than most, and more closely together. Reverend Blanche drew a reluctant Greg Thicke onto the floor, where he proceeded to display an utter lack of coordination, but his sportsmanship probably won him a couple of extra votes the following week.

The party caught its second wind and allowed Luke and Parker to escape for some fresh air. They walked hand in hand, in search of some more "L's" and into the cocoon of moonlight. Luke stood in front of Parker wrapped in his arms. He shifted his weight and leaned back with a sigh. "Yup. I'm sure glad THAT week's behind us." Parker smiled in agreement, his eyes lighting up as he invited naughtily, "Now, how in the world are we going to top that?"

"Now, how in the world are we going to top that?" asked Jerry, back in the kitchen with Jack, surrounded by mangled remains of confectionery.

The two guys looked at each other and Jack raised a brow.

"No, I'm serious," insisted Jerry, "how are we going to top the premiere of Holesome Desserts?"

Jack lined up two eclairs. "Ever my diligent PR man. You had just better be glad Greg Thicke was trying to pump you for information about Al Siegel rather than something else, or I'd really be giving you a topping to remember." He braced his stance, wiggled his butt, then aimed to cream his delicious confections. "Just Say..."

"Oh PLEASE don't," begged Jerry.

"SQUEEZE!" piped Jack, to a hearty chuckle and a loud round of groans.

EPILOG

Betty (the band) was still harmonizing when the doorbell rang. We were expecting Jon Miller, of course, and Liz jumped up to greet him enthusiastically. "Merry Christmas, handsome. And what have you been working on today of all days?"

"I'll tell you in a minute," he began, but as Reverend Pickens followed him inside, the two were engulfed in a chorus of surprised greetings. Blanche hugged Parker and me in turn, then somehow managed to keep her red feather concoction of a hat in place while Jerry and Jack enveloped her in a three-way embrace. The boys hoped that the joint arrival of Jon and Blanche was the good sign they were looking for.

"Yes, I have agreed to your proposal," she announced with a smile, "and my landlord Mr. Miller here has approved it too. From now on, If you can secure the necessary permits, your company Holesome Desserts can use the Mission basement to begin production. Though where the market is for those kinds of pastries, the Lord help me, I truly cannot imagine."

"Yo mama!"

"Yippee!" Jack and Jerry jumped up and down with delight, taking their Blanche sandwich with them.

"But just one thing, boys." She pulled herself free, wagging her finger. "When anyone here is around the good people of the Mission and refers to that doggone company, I don't want to hear that crazy name. I want you to refer to it as HOLY Desserts. Is that clear?" We all groaned. But somehow we could see the fit. If the Mission basement was to be a den for devils food cakes and cookies, God's logo would be a bonus.

"You mean H-O-L-E-Y Desserts?" joked Jack, at which we giggled and groaned again. To illustrate his point, he picked up the Double Cock Ring cookie we had been toying with, and waved it around. Blanche blanched. Parker whooped with glee, suggesting it was a nickname we should publicize, giving t-shirts to any Mission member who might help with the baking.

Hilarity prevailed for a while, until Jon waved his arms and pointed to the stereo. "Luke, would you mind switching off the music and put on WAMU? Blanche and I were listening on the way over here, and NPR was prepping a piece on my ex-partner's death. Murder, whatever." We all sobered up a bit and sat back to listen. In the two months that had passed since the turbulent turmoil of our Halloween Week, we had heard nothing of the investigation into Big Al's death and misdeeds.

"Arraignment proceedings have taken place in the case of the homicide of Al Siegel, the famous property and media baron in the city, who died on November first. The police made an arrest and the suspect appeared in court yesterday. In a dramatic development, Dr. Sue Barrymore, the well-known TV show host and personality, was charged with Gross Vehicular Manslaughter while Intoxicated, and was later released on bail of two million dollars."

"Wow."

"No shit."

"Over on the steps of the Courthouse on Indiana Avenue, our reporter was able to obtain a brief statement from the accused as she left the building. Dr. Barrymore said, quote, I want all my viewers to know that I am not guilty. I am not guilty of any freakin' manslaughter. Mr. Siegel got into a fight with a business acquaintance Mr. Russell Rollins, fell and unfortunately cracked his head. That's all I have to say. Unquote."

"Russell ROLLINS? You mean, as in Gilbert Rollins?" asked Liz, incredulously.

"Gilbert aka Detective Rollins. He told us, you remember, that one suspect was his own father. That must be it. His father was the shoe-store owner, the guy who tangled with Slim." Parker voiced my own thoughts but beat me to it.

"And maybe tangled fatally with Al."

"Quiet, guys, just listen," Jon scolded.

"...blow to the head, apparently from the curb, knocked Mr. Siegel un-conscious, but it was not fatal, so charges against Mr. Russell Rollins will likely be dropped. His internal injuries were the cause of death, and were consistent with an impact by a car. Evidence at the scene implicated Dr. Barrymore's car, although she herself had left the scene by the time police arrived. She failed a breath test administered at 7 a.m. And that seems to be the summary of the prosecution's case.

Meanwhile, newly elected city councilman, Greg Thicke had this to say..."

"No shit!" repeated Jack, louder, as though we hadn't heard it the first time. "Dr. Doom meets her doom."

"Hallelujah! Best Christmas present yet," chimed in Jerry.

"Well actually," Jon continued conspiratorially, "it isn't. When we walked in, Liz asked what I had to work on today." He twisted Liz's fingers in his own and they exchanged a sparkling look, then turned together to address their small audience gathered around.

"What I was working on, while you dissolutes all sat here feasting on erotic desserts, was a new agreement with the management of another company I now own. You know it as Siegel Studios, though the name will be changing. To Miller Osbourne Studios."

Liz beamed with pride, while the rest of us looked on agape. What on earth would Liz be doing with a TV studio? "Perhaps this is coming on a bit quick," Jon continued, "but two months ago when I made Liz's acquaintance, I was impressed with her grasp on the pulse of the town and how well connected she is to the urban affairs grapevine. I guess you really can't help it with a salon like OZ. So after I saw her wrap the inimitable Phil Richmond around her finger, which is no small feat, and the intoxicating morning I spent in her care watching her work a floor full of tough old broads and queens—you have to admit she will be a capable resource in helping me fine tune our programming. Liz won't be giving up her own business at Salon OZ, however. I just hope you guys will stand by her when she has to spend a lot more time with me after hours."

Jack interrupted Jon's soliloquy with the quietest little "Liz has a boyfriend, Liz has a boyfriend…" At which everyone laughed and started clapping. The boys were really glad Liz had found her Santa.

"But wait, there's more. You all know Liz has her ear to the ground. Well she heard from Jack about a certain well recommended PR guy. And so, Miller Osbourne Studios will be inviting to join them, if he is willing, as their new director of PR, none other than—Jerry Callahan! Would you be interested, Jerry?"

Jon was enjoying being the center of attention as well as the bringer of glad tidings. Jerry meanwhile was simply flabbergasted. He couldn't believe the turn in his luck. Holesome/Holey Desserts had a new home, Dr. Sue had her come-uppance, and now he had FUCK YOU value with his miserable job in the Bureau of Development office. After Merritt Smears had been forced to resign a month ago amid all the scandal, Jerry had been doing the work of both of them. All that and he no longer felt shy or self-conscious around his very own cracker Jack. That was probably the best gift of all.

At that moment, while we were all digesting Jon's exciting announcements and congratulating Liz and Jerry, Blanche caught our attention by brandishing her copy of the *Washington Post*. She pointed to the New Year's Eve Dining supplement for all to see. "Hip Hip Hudson for New Year's" was the headline above the Phil Richmond column. We could not have been more thrilled to see it.

"See, he even likes the music!" gloated Parker as he read the lower part of the page. Jack and I grabbed the newspaper in a tug of war of urgent anticipation.

"'Mouth-watering Lamb Shank à la Jacques—unique, erotically inspired desserts—designer tapas of manchego and mache—cool edgy city vibe—cosmopolitan gay-and-straight-friendly crowd...'" Jack read aloud in extracts, turning Richmond's lavish and expansive prose into a Zagat-style summary. "'Highly creative, nothing rebarbative.' What the fuck does that mean?"

Well as long as we scored 29/30, I didn't care. As Jack continued to read to us from the review (was he skipping the critical bits?), I allowed myself to luxuriate in the plaudits that Jerry, Liz, Parker and the others began heaping upon us, sitting around the fire that Christmas Day. I finally found myself able to relax and count my blessings. (That too was Parker's influence.) It had been a hard year, especially around Halloween. But it sure helped to have a lover whose wealthy boss was your landlord. With that kind of backing, I could begin to fantasize about a Hudson Grille chain. Would we call the next one Just Desserts, perhaps? Or Just Say Cheese?

Strange but true,
the start of *Just Say Cheese*

I love a cheesy gay romp... Once upon a time (though not all at once) there really was a trans-racial transvestite named LaChuChu-Wanda, this ad for Bible-robics, news chock full of exploding manholes, ranting talk show hosts, Halloween hi-heel drag races, a designing life in the food/restaurant biz, writing obtuse epistles to my best friend Liz, channeling alter egos and most of all, a hammer-happy husband like Parker, who had the nerve to take three, count 'em three laptops to the beach for "fun" work... So there it was—lemons to lemonade—I came armed with a head full 18 characters and a book outline to keep me amused. I also got to use one of the laptops.

After three such summer vacations and mid-year diversions, I was a little cheesed out until the real Liz passed the manuscript on to her husband who polished my construction. To Anthony Bladon, my editor, wizard of Oz, trusty Henry Higgins if there ever was one, my thanks. Not many would just say "Gouda!" and run with it for a good time. Brilliant!

Left: LaChuChuWanda, sans wig after a hard night's run

Front cover: LaChuChuWanda with Parker and Luke

Cover illustrations by: Mark Ksiazewski